Highland Fling

EMILY HARVALE

Emily Harvale lives in East Sussex, in the UK.
She can be contacted via her website, twitter or facebook.

Author contacts :

www.emilyharvale.com

www.twitter.com/emilyharvale

www.facebook.com/emilyharvale

www.facebook.com/emilyharvalewriter

www.emilyharvale.com/blog

Also by this author:

Lizzie Marshall's Wedding

Acknowledgements:

Thanks to my wonderful friends for their support and friendship, particularly Julie Bateman, James Campbell and Sherry Thomas.

To Karina for the gorgeous cover – and for knowing exactly what I wanted. – www.missnyss.com

Special thanks to David of DC Creation, not just for building me my website but also for designing my newsletter and all the other clever things he does; for always being at the end of a phone or email when technology gets the better of me and particularly for never getting annoyed when I say 'What's this button for?' for the thousandth time. – www.dccreation.com

Thanks also to Heather at Aviemore Library for answering my rather foolish questions.

To my twitter followers and friends, facebook friends and fans of my facebook author page; it's great to chat with you.

And to you, whoever you are and wherever you may be, for buying this book – Thank You.

Best wishes,

Emily x

ISBN 978-1480079229

Print edition published worldwide 2012
E-edition published worldwide 2012

Cover design by missnyss

This book is dedicated to Margaret and James Millgate,
with all my love.

Chapter One

'It's too early Max.' Lizzie Marshall tucked a long strand of wavy, brunette hair behind one ear and tried to keep calm.

'Please honey.'

'But it doesn't give me enough time –'

'Sweetheart,' Max turned on the charm, 'they'll pay handsomely and it is only four days. They'll be no trouble, I promise.'

Max had promised things before and Lizzie felt an urge to remind him how they'd turned out, but this wasn't the time. Having yet another argument over the phone with him, wasn't on her list of "things I must do today".

'You don't understand Max. March is only three weeks away and there's a lot to do. The roof needs repairing and–'

'That's why I thought you'd be pleased. You said money was tight and as you won't take any from me, I figured I could help you in this small way. The place they'd booked has had a fire or something, so they're pretty desperate, and cost is no object. I'd be really grateful. One of them works with me and ... I sort of said I was sure you'd do it. You will, won't you sweetheart?'

'That's just typical of you Max! You've got to stop assuming that you can just snap your fingers and I'll do your bidding. Those days are gone.'

'Darling,' he purred, 'don't be like that. You know how much I love you. I thought we'd settled all this over Christmas – and you seemed very happy to do my bidding then, as I recall. God just thinking about those two weeks gets me horny. Hey. It's Valentine's next week, why don't I whisk you away to Venice? We can stay at the Danielli, just like on our honeymoon. Remember? Then we can talk properly about getting you moved back in here. It would be great to wake up with you beside me again every morning instead of just a few snatched moments every few weeks ... Lizzie? Are you still there Lizzie?'

Lizzie had opened her mouth to interrupt him several times but with each word he spoke she was more astonished and now, she was struggling for what to say.

She could picture him, leaning back in his chair, his feet up on the desk, his long, lithe sun-tanned body dressed in pristine Armani; looking like he'd just stepped out of an advert for the gold Rolex he wore. He would be gazing out of the window of his executive corner office at Brockleman Brothers Bank, confident he was closing another deal.

'I'm still here,' she said, trying to control the anger bubbling up inside her, 'and it's where I'm staying.'

'But Lizzie –'

'No! I thought I'd made it clear that Christmas and New Year were ...,' were what? Yet again, she'd fallen into his arms, temporarily forgetting the pain he'd caused her and for twelve blissful days, they'd been like they used to be – until she'd seen the email and realised, it was from *that woman*, '... were based on a lie.'

For a moment, Max didn't respond and, struggling to keep her emotions in check, Lizzie stuck the phone under her chin, yanked open the oven door, took out a tray of meringues and banged it down on top of the Aga.

'Darling.' His voice was as enticing as a chocolate soufflé. 'It wasn't a lie. It's over. I swear. It was over that night you ... saw us together. I'm not interested in her and anyway, I told you, she's been going out with some guy for the past two years and is engaged to be married.'

'So? You *are* married and that didn't stop you! And you did lie. You said you'd sacked her.'

'I said she no longer worked for me and that's the truth. She works for Martin in legal.'

'She sent you that email about a meeting.'

'A client meeting. I've explained all this. Legal were involved and she was emailing a reminder to everyone. Sweetheart, how many times do I have to tell you, it was a mistake; she was a mistake ... and I've been paying for it ever since.'

'You've been paying for it! Max of all the .... Oh forget it. I'll do the bloody stag party. But not as a favour to you – just because I need the money. And get one thing straight, Max. I am never going to sleep with you again and this time, I mean it. It's over!'

Lizzie slammed the phone down, furious at Max for assuming he could twist her around his little finger; furious at herself for letting him, once again. Unable to calm down, she called Alastair, her Labrador, who'd been curled up in his basket beside the Aga and stormed out of the house. In a blind rage, she drove the three miles to her friend Jane's, to tell her about Max's call – and the early booking.

Jane Munroe's refurbished croft had been left to her by a maiden aunt. She had originally intended to use it as a holiday home, staying there for a few weeks and renting it out for the rest of the time. It held many happy childhood memories, so selling the place was not an option as far as she was concerned.

It didn't take long though, for her to realise that the croft and Kirkedenbright Falls was where she wanted to be on a permanent basis, so she sold her flat in London, gave in her notice at work and headed for Scotland.

Earning a living wasn't an issue; as an illustrator, she could work from home and when Lizzie bought Laurellei Farm and started running it as a bed and breakfast, Jane also became Lizzie's part time employee. She helped out with anything and everything during the tourist season.

'So what are you panicking for?' Jane was totally unfazed when Lizzie told her about Max's call. 'We can get the place ready in time.' She switched on the kettle and leant against the worktop to wait for it to boil.

'I suppose so. It's just Max. Why do I always let him do this to me?' Lizzie slumped on to a chair at the kitchen table.

'You don't really want me to answer that do you?'

'No. I don't want to go over all that again, thanks very

much, but frankly, the thought of six guys on a stag do doesn't fill me with joy.'

'It'll be fine.' Jane made the coffee and handed a mug to Lizzie then sat on a chair across the table from her. 'It's just like the booking you had last August bank holiday and that went okay.'

Lizzie's light blue eyes opened wide in astonishment. 'That went okay! If you call a broken leg, a sprained back, three black eyes and a broken jaw okay, not to mention the damage they did to the hen house and the pig pen, then you're madder than I am.' She shook her brunette waves and sipped her coffee.

Jane giggled at the memory. 'Oh come on Lizzie. It was funny you must admit. They had a great time and they paid for the damage – rather well if I remember correctly. It wasn't your fault they got drunk on the local brew and ended up trying to ride Peter and Penelope.'

'No. If I remember correctly – it was yours. And why they were trying to ride the pigs I'll never understand. The farm is for rest and relaxation, to experience life on a small holding, to get away from the stresses of city life –'

'Oh God. Spare me the sales pitch. I helped write it. You can't lay down the law about how people spend their time. You provide bed, breakfast and access to miles of open country and outdoor pursuits, but you can't stop people doing their own thing and with city guys that's getting drunk, chasing chickens and riding pigs. That's it. It goes with the territory. You know that, you were married to one for four years.'

'I still *am* married to one,' Lizzie reminded her. 'Got any biscuits? I need chocolate.'

Jane strolled over to the dresser and grabbed the biscuit barrel. She pulled off the lid and offered the barrel to Lizzie. 'Well, the good thing is, knowing what they're like means you can charge them more.'

Lizzie took two homemade chocolate chip cookies and dunked one in her coffee. 'Yeah, I know. It's just ... I've got a really bad feeling about this booking and I just know there's going to be some sort of major disaster. I just know it.' She bit into the soggy biscuit.

'Beware the Ides of March!' Jane cackled, taking two biscuits for herself and sitting back down. 'Look Lizzie, you're a thirty-two year old business woman. Portents of doom and all that crap have no place in your life. Now, drink your coffee and I'll come back with you and get started on the spring cleaning, oh, and we'd better make sure there's plenty of food for Peter and Penelope; we need to fatten them up in case the guys try to ride them.'

Lizzie groaned. The first week of March was when she'd usually start to get the house ready for the tourist season which ran from Easter until September, so taking this booking meant bringing forward her maintenance and spring cleaning schedule and three weeks was not a lot of time to do that, even with Jane's help. 'D'you really think we can be ready in time?'

'It'll be a push but of course we can.' Jane finished her coffee and glanced towards the kitchen window. It had started raining. 'They say we may have snow in March.'

Lizzie dropped her head into her hands, 'Oh God. That's all we need. Why can't I ever just say no to Max?'

'Have you seen the weather?'

'And a good morning to you too Jane.' Lizzie held the phone to her ear as she stretched beneath the duvet, 'I'm still in bed. Why?'

'It's just started snowing.'

Lizzie leapt out of the Elizabethan four-poster, slid her size four feet into grey, fluffy, cat character slippers and dashed to the window with the phone still pressed against her ear.

Opening the heavy, midnight blue damask curtains, she stared mournfully at the mountainous snow clouds, gathering like a huge flock of over sized black sheep, and watched the first tentative flakes drift down towards

Laurellei Farm.

'Why today? What the hell am I going to do with six loud mouthed, alcohol guzzling, womanising, arrogant city bankers if we all get snowed in? Bugger, bugger, bugger!'

'I thought you'd be pleased,' Jane said drily. 'I'll be over in about twenty minutes.'

Lizzie hung up then hurried to the shower.

Fifteen minutes later, she was dressed in jeans and a hand knitted blue jumper. She tied her brunette waves into a pony tail and peered at her reflection in the dressing table mirror. Was that a grey hair? She tugged at it but it held firm and she decided she had better things to worry about than one stray sign of her age. With the life she'd led over the past few years, she was surprised she wasn't totally grey.

Her fluctuating weight was now firmly under control and she looked almost the same as when she had married Max six years ago. After she discovered his affair, Lizzie lost almost two stone, which was a lot as she had never deviated much from the recommended weight for her five feet two inch frame. Later, when she had settled in at Laurellei Farm, she regained the two and put on a third – even she couldn't resist her own homemade shortbread and cakes – and it had been quite a battle for her to regain her figure.

Now, she didn't bother weighing herself. If her jeans felt tight, she cut down – and looking after the house and the animals kept her pretty active, as well as catering for her bed and breakfast guests during the season.

She'd been dreading this weekend though. Why hadn't she just said no? She shook her head. Thinking about Max again wasn't going to help. It was a miracle that she and Jane had been able to get everything done in time, although, now it was snowing, she wondered whether the quick repair to the roof would hold out.

She heard the rumble of an engine and headed towards the back stairs which led directly from the additional living space in the barn conversion into the original kitchen of the main farmhouse. She jumped down them two at a time and reached the kitchen as Jane was pulling up in front of the house in her battered Land Rover. Lizzie yanked open the kitchen door letting a swirl of snow fall on to the doormat.

'I told you this booking was a mistake,' she yelled as Jane hurried towards the warmth of the kitchen. 'Are the roads okay?'

'At the moment they're fine. The gritters have been out and it's not settling yet but it looks like it may be bad.' Jane closed the door behind her and dashed over to the Aga to warm her hands, bending down to stroke Alastair, who was curled up in his basket next to it, as usual.

Lizzie made coffee and handed Jane a mug. 'The one time I open early and it snows. I wonder if they'll cancel.' She pulled out a chair and sat down, resting her elbows on the large antique pine table.

Jane shook her head and sipped her coffee. 'Didn't you say they were coming up on the overnight train from Euston?'

'That's what the email said.'

'Well, according to the weather report it's not snowing down south and it's only just started up here so they must be on their way. They would have called otherwise.' Now warmed up, she sat on a chair opposite Lizzie.

Lizzie sighed. 'I was sort of hoping they would. I'm really not looking forward to this weekend and now with the weather –'

'Sometimes I despair of you Lizzie Marshall! Why must you look on the black side of life these days?'

Lizzie pulled a face. 'Because I've turned it around and it's black on both sides.'

'C'mon. It'll be fine. You used to be bright and cheery and ready to take on the world. What's got into you lately? Since when have you let a few drops of frozen water get you down?'

'Since I discovered the roof leaks.' Lizzie leant back in the chair and sighed.

'It'll hold out, and think of all the lovely money you're going to make. Six city bankers on a stag party, that's a licence to print your own notes! And if they get snowed in here for the entire four days, you can charge them extra as they'll have to have all their meals here, not just breakfast.'

'God, I hope they don't get snowed in.'

Jane helped herself to a pecan and maple syrup plait from the cake tin, which was in front of her on the table, and held one out to Lizzie. 'Excuse fingers.'

Lizzie smiled and took the proffered treat.

'It's going to be great, you'll see.' Jane picked out pieces of pecan nut and popped them in to her mouth. 'I could live on these,' she said. 'I hope at least one of the guys is good-looking. If we're going to be snowed in with six of them, I want to have a bit of fun, don't you?'

'I just want to get through it with no broken bones.'

The phone rang and Jane answered it as she was nearest. 'Oh hi Joe ... Yeah fine thanks, you? ... Yeah ... Oh dear ... Really? ... Good ... Yeah ... Thanks ... Bye.'

Lizzie raised her eyebrows and sipped her coffee as she watched Jane over the rim of her mug. 'It's good to know the art of conversation isn't dead,' she said when Jane hung up.

Jane stuck out her tongue and swished her copper-coloured waist length hair, like a model in a shampoo ad. 'Well, Miss misery guts. As you may have gathered, that was Joe from the station. The train's running on time despite the weather, and the party of six – assuming they were sober enough last night to get on the right train – will be arriving at Kirkedenbright Falls in approximately half an hour.'

Jack Drake slept soundly, despite the train occasionally lurching, and was unaware that his friend, and best man to be, Ross Briarstone studied him through weary eyes.

Ross refilled his glass with champagne and emptied it in one swallow. They'd all been drinking since before they boarded the train at eight twenty last night and Ross had lost count of how many bottles they'd gone through. He didn't care though. Alcohol numbs the pain, people say, and Ross's pain would need a lot of numbing.

He watched Jack sleep and a pang of jealousy flickered in his brain. They didn't call him lucky Jack for nothing, Ross thought. He certainly had the Midas touch. Everything turned to gold for Jack Drake – and not just in a financial sense.

Ross let out a deep sigh. He wished he could rest his muddled head on a fluffy pillow and stop it spinning but when he leant back and closed his eyes, Kim Mentor's voluptuous breasts appeared in his mind. He smiled as memories flooded his brain but the smile soon vanished. Only two weeks to go and they'd be lost to him forever. Kim's breasts, along with the rest of Kim, would soon be married – to his best friend, Jack.

'What you dreaming about mate?' Pete Towner nudged Ross back from his thoughts.

Ross's pale green eyes were shot with little red lines and he couldn't see clearly through the haze of inebriation, so he merely grunted in reply, a fleeting twinge of guilt creeping over him before he closed his eyes again and began to snore.

Pete turned his attention to Jack, the bridegroom to be, who was slumped across the seat, his feet curled beneath him, empty champagne bottle in one hand, the inflatable doll his mates had given him – dressed up to look like Kim – in the other.

'Jack. Your best man's really out of it mate. Good thing we're sober eh or we might go right past Kirkede ... Kirkeden ... the place we're going to. You awake Jack?' Pete poked him with his finger.

Jack sat bolt upright, still clutching the doll but the bottle slid to the floor with a resounding thud, making him wince. His head felt like a cement mixer as he tried to focus his usually clear sapphire blue eyes. The voice he knew but he

9

couldn't quite make out the features and he opened his eyes as wide as he could hoping that might help. It didn't. 'Yeah,' he said, 'We there yet?'

'Nah. But someone said we'll be stopping at Aviemore in five minutes and I think it's the one after that.' Pete turned his head slowly to peer through the window. ''Ere Jack. Someone's got really bad dandruff. It's all over the window sill, look!'

Jack stared at the window. He scratched his head and licked his lips. 'That's not dandruff. That's snow.'

Pete's eyes opened wide in amazement. 'No mate. Can't be snow. It's March! 'Ere lads, wake up. Jack's so drunk he thinks it's snowing.'

Ross was the last to come to and he shook his head several times before he could manage to speak. 'It is snow,' he said and they all stared out of the window in stunned silence.

'Good thing Kim's not 'ere,' Pete said after a few minutes, 'couldn't walk in 'er stilettos, eh mate?' He nudged Ross's arm and winked.

'Kim's brill,' Ross said, 'you leave her alone.'

'Oooh! Anyone would think it was you marrying 'er mate, not Jack. Something you want to tell us?'

Ross screwed up his brows. 'No,' he said rather too loudly. 'I just think she's brill that's all and Jack's a lucky man. Eh Jack? You're a very lucky man. Here's to Lucky Jack.' He raised his empty glass. 'Hey! Where's all the booze gone?'

They all laughed except Jack, who turned his attention to the fields and hills beyond, now covered in a fine white dusting of snow. The Cairngorms rose up in the distance and he admired their rugged beauty. The peaks and high plateaus were pure white but patches of their craggy black, grey and green faces were visible, although slowly disappearing behind a curtain of heavy flakes, falling faster and thicker by the minute. Jack watched the flakes land against the glass pane and slide down, joining the ever increasing pile on the sill.

He breathed against the pane and started doodling; he'd doodled ever since he was old enough to hold a crayon or something else to draw with, and it had become almost second nature to him; he often did it without even realising.

A very lucky man, Ross had called him. Funny, he didn't feel like a lucky man. In two weeks time he'd be a married man and that was something he wasn't absolutely certain he wanted to be.

Was it just pre-wedding nerves? he wondered. Since he'd got back from his last business trip just over two weeks ago, he'd made a real effort to be romantic – but that was the problem, it had been an effort, and surely it shouldn't be? Kim had seemed different too.

He couldn't put his finger on it but he couldn't help feeling that something was missing and, since he'd been back, neither of them had seemed that interested in sex. They'd only made love once in just over two weeks. Not that that mattered. Sex wasn't everything right? He let out a long sigh and admitted to himself that even that had been an effort.

He closed his eyes and leant his head back against the headrest. Was he making a mistake marrying Kim? He'd asked himself this question a dozen times since their engagement but he'd never found a satisfactory answer. It had all happened so fast; spiralled out of control. He should've told her he wasn't ready for marriage; should've stopped the whole carnival before it'd set off on its route, but he hadn't. Perhaps he did want to marry her after all. If only he could be sure.

'We're 'ere mate!' Pete leapt up from his seat then wished he hadn't. His head swam and he had to lean against the window to steady himself until the dizziness passed. 'C'mon lads,' he said after a while, 'it's time to 'ave some fun.'

He grabbed his bag, marched to the door, opened it and threw the bag out on to the snow-covered platform, sending a cloud of white powder into the air around it.

'Wow! Look at that snow,' Pete said, half turning to Jeff who was standing behind him. 'I've only got these shoes with me an' all.' He lifted his right leg in the air so Jeff could see his designer slip-ons and toppled backwards as he did so, knocking Jeff into Steve, who was rubbing his eyes in an effort to come to.

'Be careful mate! Steve said. 'You nearly had my eye out.'

'Shit it's bright out there,' Ross said, fiddling in his bag for his Ray-bans whilst Jeff, Steve, Phil and Pete stepped out on to the platform and Jeff slid over, landing on his bum.

'You're no Torvil or Dean,' Pete said, laughing as Jeff struggled to get to his feet. He noticed the others were staring at him strangely. 'What?' he said, realising why, 'my mum likes them! What can I tell you?'

Ross shook his head, Ray-bans now firmly in place as a shield against the brilliant white of the snow. 'Sometimes I worry about you mate,' he said, then glancing back at Jack. 'You coming Jack?'

Jack was leaning against the wall, bag in one hand, inflatable doll in the other, looking at his doodle on the window pane. It was a snowman wrapped in chains. Shaking his head and sighing deeply, he leapt off the train, falling flat on his face in a pile of snow.

It was unfortunate that this was the first sight Lizzie and Jane got of their weekend guests, as they waited on the platform to greet them.

Chapter Two

'It's worse than I'd expected,' Lizzie said waving at Joe and forcing a cheery smile she certainly didn't feel.

'Oh I don't know,' Jane said, 'the one lying flat on his face looks quite promising. I wonder if either of us can get him in that position sometime over the weekend.'

Lizzie grinned despite herself. 'Oh God. Trapped for the weekend with six drunken louts and a sex-mad woman. Can life get any better?'

'I know. It's going to be hell for me but I'll get through it somehow.'

Lizzie's mouth fell open. 'I meant you.'

Jane winked at her. 'I know,' she said and sauntered towards their guests. 'Good morning gentlemen. Having problems with the snow? This is Lizzie and I'm Jane. We're your hostesses for the next four days.'

Lizzie saw the look on four of the men's faces, watched another trying to struggle to his feet whilst the sixth lie flat on his back in the snow. Yep, she thought, this is going to be one hell of a weekend.

Jack stared up at the sky and blinked away the snowflakes as they landed on his eyelashes. The cool wet particles made his face tingle. He closed his eyes and licked his lips, tasting icy water. He could feel the cold, fresh air hitting his lungs and he sucked in a mouthful.

'We do have rooms, sir. You don't have to sleep on the platform.'

He opened his eyes and blinked several times. Smiling down at him as if he were a naughty child, was a beautiful brunette. He thought for a moment he was dreaming but he could hear his friends laughing and, as he realised where he was, he sat bolt upright.

'Oh shit!' he said, suddenly feeling sober, 'I fell in the snow.'

13

'So I see. I'm Lizzie,' the beautiful brunette said 'and ... is this your fiancée?'

He blinked again. She was staring at something beside him. He looked down and saw, to his horror, the inflatable doll, still clasped tightly in his grip. Without thinking, he let it go just as a gust of wind caught it and blew it down the platform.

'We'd better get that before it reaches the village,' Lizzie said. 'It'll cause a riot.' She chased the doll but every time she got near it, another gust whipped it away.

Jack staggered after her, slipping and sliding in the snow, in his black leather brogues, arms flailing in his slate grey suit.

'Jack! You shouldn't be chasing women,' Phil yelled, 'especially inflatable ones!'

'Jesus. I ain't seen anything so funny in years.' Pete roared with laughter holding his stomach as if it hurt.

Lizzie reached for the doll and managed to grab its leg just as another gust was about to take it. The doll hung in the air with Lizzie trying to maintain her balance on the slippery surface when Jack careered into her, knocking them all to the ground where they ended in a heap, Jack on top of Lizzie, Lizzie on top of the doll.

Hoots of laughter rang out from the others.

'Not in a public place!' Pete shouted, accompanied by loud cheers.

It took Lizzie and Jack a few seconds to realise what had happened and regain their breath.

'Are you okay?' Jack asked, genuinely concerned.

'I'd be better if you weren't lying on me.'

'Oh! Sorry.' He placed his hands either side of her body to push himself up but as he did so the doll burst with a loud bang making Lizzie scream.

Instinctively, he threw his arms around her, pulling her away and rolling her over so they ended up as they had been but without the doll. Lizzie on the ground, Jack on top of her, staring into each other's eyes, so close that their lips

14

were almost touching.

Jack felt an overwhelming urge to kiss her. He parted his lips, all thoughts except one gone from him, then the whoops of laughter, further up the platform brought him back to reality and he quickly rolled himself to a sitting position next to her.

The doll deflated with loud fart-like noises and Lizzie burst out laughing, breaking the tension of an awkward moment.

Jack scrambled to his feet and held out his hand to help her up, avoiding eye contact. Once they both got their footings he brushed clumps of snow from his suit.

'Not exactly dressed for this weather,' he said, a faint smile hovering on his perfectly shaped mouth as he bent down to pick up the deflated doll.

'I've got a puncture repair kit at the house,' Lizzie said unable to stop herself, 'we may be able to save her.'

Jack's eyes shot to her face and he saw the laughter there. 'Thanks', he said, 'we're very close. I couldn't bear to lose her.'

'I felt that way about my husband at first,' Lizzie said, but she had no idea why.

'I can't believe the weather,' Jack said in a feeble attempt to make conversation once they were in the Land Rovers on the way to Laurellei Farm. Ross, Phil and Jack were with Lizzie leaving Pete, Jeff and Steve with Jane.

'I'm sorry, what did you say?' Lizzie was thinking about what had happened at the station. She had an uneasy feeling that the man now sitting beside her, with chestnut brown hair and the deepest sapphire blue eyes she'd ever seen, had almost kissed her – and an even worse feeling, that she'd have let him.

'The weather. I can't believe it.'

'Nor can I.' Lizzie kept her eyes firmly on the road. 'It's been threatening all week but I didn't think it would come, especially as it's been so warm until a few days ago. I just hope we don't get snowed in.'

'Is there a chance we might?' Jack's eyes lit up at the thought of it.

'It's possible if we get as much as the weather report is saying we will. Last year we were snowed in for three days over Christmas and ...' she remembered last year and how Max had arrived unexpectedly, just before the snow and how – no, she mustn't go there.

'And ...' Jack prompted.

'Nothing,' she said, glancing at him from the corners of her eyes.

He resembled her husband in a way but Max had blond straight hair, always combed back from his model-smooth face, whilst Jack's thick chestnut brown hair was cut short around his ears with just a hint of an unruly fringe to one side. They were both undeniably handsome but Jack had more of a rugged outdoors look, and Max's eyes were green whereas Jack's were a very definite deep blue.

They were about the same height, somewhere in the region of six feet and a similar build, although from what little she'd seen of Jack, he was slightly broader across the shoulders than Max. They both clearly liked expensive, quality clothing; Lizzie recognised bespoke tailoring when she saw it. And watches. The understated Omega Jack wore didn't come much cheaper than Max's rather flashy Rolex.

'Any chance we could stop at an off-licence and get some booze in?' Ross was asking from the back seat. 'Don't want to be snowed in without a few bottles of fizz and some beers, if that's okay with you?

'No need,' Lizzie said, praying the pigs would survive, 'there's plenty in the house and I charge the same as you'd pay in the shop, plus, my neighbour makes a home brew and he brought over a few bottles the other day.'

'No disrespect but I can't stand home brew. Tastes like gnat's piss. Ow! What d'ya thump me for?'

'There's a lady present,' Phil said.

'Oh, yeah. Sorry.'

'Don't worry about it. I've heard far worse and even said it. I used to work in the City.'

Jack turned to face her. 'London you mean?'

'Yes. Why are you so surprised?'

'Um. Well. It just seems a long way from here, that's all. What did you do?'

'Not far enough sometimes,' Lizzie said. 'I was a solicitor.'

'Yeah?' Jack found himself wishing he'd met her then. 'When? Why did you leave?'

'Oh, sometimes it seems like a lifetime, but I only moved here just over two years ago. I ... I needed a complete change and Jane had moved up here the year before so it seemed like as good a place as any. It was supposed to be a ... a sort of sabbatical but Laurellei Farm came up for sale and, well, I just knew I had to buy it. Sounds silly I know but –'

'No. It doesn't sound silly at all. I'm a firm believer that things happen for a reason. And your husband. Is he a farmer or something?'

Lizzie's laugh sounded almost maniacal. 'Or something,' she said. 'He wouldn't know a sheep if one jumped up and bit him on the nose – and believe me – I have often wished one would. He's in London. He works in the City.'

'When do you see him then? Does he come all this way for the weekends?' Jack sounded incredulous.

Lizzie was surprised. She rarely discussed her private life with anyone, let alone a complete – and very handsome – stranger. 'I don't, usually. We're separated.'

'But not divorced?' Jack knew he shouldn't pry but for some reason, he really wanted to know. He saw her hands tighten on the steering wheel and spotted the wedding band and a massive diamond solitaire sparkling up at him from her left hand. He wondered why he hadn't noticed them before and the disappointment he felt took him completely by surprise.

'No,' she said after a while, 'we're not divorced.'

'Sorry. I should mind my own business.'

'Yeah Jack. Stop interrogating the lady,' Ross said, still wondering what they were going to do about the alcohol situation. If he was going to get through this weekend he would need copious amounts of the stuff.

'There's the house,' Lizzie said changing the subject.

Jack peered out of the window but kept glancing towards Lizzie. He'd seen how sad she'd looked when she'd talked about her husband and how her face had brightened when she'd pointed out the farmhouse.

What was her story, he wondered, and why did he care? He was getting married in two weeks to a girl he'd spent the last two years with. So, why had he held his breath waiting for a total stranger to tell him whether or not she was divorced and why had it irritated him so when he'd seen the rings, which had answered the question before she had?

And yet, she'd said they were separated and they lived hundreds of miles apart. He'd have to find out exactly what was going on between this woman and her far off husband before this weekend was over – even if he had no idea why it should affect him in the least.

The farmhouse was much larger than it looked from the road and was about a mile down a narrow lane which was bordered on one side by a row of trees, and surrounded by fields. There was a front lawn dissected by a gravel drive and a yard-come-parking area to the left, all of which were now covered with a layer of snow.

The house was built from local pink granite and had large double casement windows on the ground floor, two each side of an ancient oak door. Above, were four slightly smaller double casement windows and to the right of the house was an ancient barn, about half the size of the main house, which had obviously been converted into more living space.

'It's a really handsome house,' Jack said as Lizzie pulled up outside the oak door.

She beamed at him and sighed deeply like a proud parent. She loved the place and was pleased that he'd called it handsome. It seemed appropriate.

Jack watched her as her eyes swept lovingly over the facade whilst his friends grabbed their bags from the back of the Land Rovers and Jane led them into the stone, lime washed hall.

'Yes it is,' Lizzie said. 'It hadn't been lived in for almost twenty years and needed a lot of work so it wasn't quite as grand as it is now – and the barn was almost derelict, but I fell in love with it the moment I saw it and I knew I had to have it, no matter what the cost.'

Lizzie's eyes met his briefly and he knew exactly how she had felt.

He grabbed his bag and watched her walk towards the house. She stopped in the doorway and smiled back at him.

'Christ Jack,' he said, his voice no more than a whisper, 'pull yourself together, you're engaged.'

Inside the house, the large hall had several doors on either side. Towards the back was a wide, wooden staircase leading up to the eight bedrooms with en suite bathrooms, four at the front, four at the back all opening from a long, solid oak-floored hallway.

The rooms were all the same size and similarly furnished, the only real difference being in the colour and the decoration and whether they were front or rear facing. None of the guys seemed bothered about this, so rooms were chosen as they walked along. Ross and Pete had the first two front rooms, Steve and Jeff the first two rear rooms then Phil had the next front and Jack, who had noticed the view was slightly better to the front, took the end front.

Each room was furnished with antiques; a double bed, an armchair and small table, dressing table and chair, wardrobe, a chest of drawers and two bedside cabinets.

Each had a window-seat and matching curtains and bedding. One was pale blue, another was pale green, one had a toile de jouy theme, another a light coloured tartan, one had birds of paradise, another tiny spring flowers, one was a pale yellow and the last one, the one Jack had chosen, was a crewel work pattern in a deep, dark red and green on an ecru background.

Jack took a shower, which seemed to revive him, and then he unpacked. The drawers and wardrobes had the faintest smell of sandalwood and Jack assumed it must be from the wax used to polish them. It was a pleasant, soothing scent, used for centuries for its calming properties. Jack smiled wryly, perhaps it would work on him, he'd felt anything but calm since the moment he arrived at Kirkedenbright Falls station.

He dressed in black casual trousers, a black T-shirt and a light grey cashmere v-neck sweater. He pulled on a pair of black socks and checked that his shoes had dried out from the snow. He'd wear his boots when they ventured out later.

He took out his camera and strolled over to the window. Sitting down on the window-seat, he stared out at the acres of snow-covered fields and the copse beyond. It was like something from a Christmas card scene and he half expected to hear church bells ringing and carol singers to turn up at the door, even though it was March. The snow was easing now and the outline of the Cairngorm mountain range was visible in the distance. He could imagine the view from here on a bright, clear day and hoped he'd get a chance to see it.

He leant his head against the window frame and breathed on the pane, then with one finger, he doodled, his mind miles away until he heard Phil's voice.

'Jack. Oh! ... um ... we're going downstairs. Jane says there are coffee and homemade biscuits in the sitting room.'

Jack wondered why Phil was looking at him oddly. 'Okay, I'll come down. Are you all right? You look like something's up.'

Phil's brows shot up. 'I'm fine mate,' he said, nodding towards the window then heading towards the stairs, 'it's you who's got a problem.'

Jack glanced back at the window and jumped to his feet as if he'd been bitten by a poisonous snake. He'd drawn a huge, elaborate heart with a large and unmistakable 'L' inside it.

He wiped the glass with the sleeve of his jumper and watched the droplets of water trickling down the pane, his head spinning. What was happening to him? The last time he'd doodled a love heart to his recollection was when he was twelve and had a crush on his French teacher. Perhaps he was still drunk; they had a lot of champagne on the way up and quite a bit before they got on the train.

He rubbed his forehead with the back of his hand. Shit. Phil had seen it. Would he tell the others? Would he make a joke of it in front of *her?* He raced from the room jumping the stairs three at a time and burst into the sitting room. The others were all there and they stared up at him in surprise.

'You okay mate?' Pete said.

'Fine. Why?' His eyes found Phil's.

Pete grinned. 'You ran in 'ere like the devil 'imself was after you. Seen a ghost?'

Phil shook his head in answer to Jack's unspoken question and Jack relaxed slightly.

''Ave some of these biscuits Jack,' Pete was saying offering him a plate of homemade shortbreads and chocolate chip cookies and Jack took two. 'They're top banana.'

'This is some place eh?' Steve said, his eyes taking in his surroundings.

Heavy crewel work curtains hung at the casement windows, beneath which, was a window-seat strewn with several plump cushions. Two overstuffed, oversized, sofas, one green leather, the other red and green tartan chenille, formed an L-shape on one side of the ornate stone fireplace. Three leather wing chairs and one club chair were on the other side.

The massive hearth with its black, wrought iron fire basket and shining, black fire-irons held a roaring log and coal fire and either side of this were a wrought iron coal scuttle and a large wicker woven log basket, containing what was once a tree, chopped into fire-size logs. Set back from the fire and centred between the sofas and chairs was a long, low, oak coffee table.

On the other side of the room from the fire were a large antique oak sideboard, a writing desk and chair, an ornate drinks cabinet and the door into the main hall. Opposite the front window, at the other end of the room were several bookcases full of books and on the same wall as the fireplace, a door connecting into another smaller sitting room which housed the television, DVD player, two comfy sofas, four chairs and a smaller fireplace, which backed on to the main one.

'Do you think that's a real fire or one of those gas effect things?' Jeff asked staring into the flames.

'It's real, thickhead,' Steve said munching on two biscuits at a time. 'They don't make gas fires that big. I'll tell you something, if she cooks this good and owns this place I might just make her one of my girls.'

Jack choked on a biscuit.

'I don't think you will,' Phil said, 'she's already spoken for.' His eyes met Jack's.

'Yeah?' How do you know that?' Steve asked.

Phil sipped his coffee and Jack held his breath. 'She's married. She said so on the way here.'

'So, what's going on then?'

Jane dropped on to the rocking chair she'd pulled in front of Alastair's basket and stroked Alastair's ears whilst Lizzie frenetically stirred the contents of the cast iron pot on one of the Aga hotplates.

'What do you mean?'

'Well, for one thing you're going to wear a hole in that

22

pot.'

Lizzie stopped stirring. 'It's nothing.'

'Yeah, yeah. I've known you for years Elizabeth Marshall and I've never seen you quite this edgy.'

'I'm just anxious about this weekend that's all.' Lizzie resumed stirring.

'Why? The guys seem a nice bunch – especially Jack – aha! Do I detect a flicker of interest?'

'What? Are you mad? It may have escaped your attention madam but I do believe he's the bridegroom!'

'Intended bridegroom. He's not married yet Lizzie.'

'What are you going on about? Sometimes I really do think you've lost your mind. Hand me the pepper please.'

'Oh come on. Don't give me that high and mighty, holier than thou crap and don't look at me like that either.' Jane got up and got the pepper from the herb cupboard. She passed it to Lizzie. 'I saw the two of you on the station platform.'

Lizzie glanced at her. 'Yes. We were chasing an inflatable doll – if you remember.' She added pepper to the soup she was making, then tasted a teaspoon full.

'But look what happened when you caught it.'

'Nothing happened.'

'Okay, okay. If that's the way you want to play it fine but I saw the look on your face when you got to your feet. You were blushing from head to toe and you only do that when you really fancy someone.'

Jane tapped Lizzie on the hip and Lizzie moved slightly so that Jane could get the rolls out of the oven.

'You are mad! It's official. I wasn't blushing. My face was red from the cold.'

'Yeah right. I've seen you cold and I've seen you when you fancy someone and I can tell the difference. In fact, you had the exact same look when you met Max.'

'What? I did not! Anyway, look where that got me. Do you really think I want to go through it all again with someone else? No thank you.'

23

Jane sighed, removing the rolls from their oven tray and placing them on a cooling tray on the kitchen table. 'Okay, you weren't blushing and you're not crazy about him and –'

'Crazy about him! I don't even know him.'

'You don't have to know someone to be crazy about them Lizzie – and I saw the way he looked at you.'

Lizzie put the lid on the soup pot and turned the hob to simmer. She tried to sound casual when she said, 'Looked at me?'

'There you see, I knew you were interested.'

Lizzie threw a tea towel at Jane but it missed and landed on Alastair making him jump from his basket, barking loudly.

'Sorry boy,' Lizzie said, scowling at Jane.

'There, there boy.' Jane stroked him and he settled back down but kept one eye on Lizzie and one ear up as if unsure whether another missile might come his way.

'Look Lizzie, I'm just saying that you're interested in him and I'm pretty certain he's interested in you. No, don't argue. When you said they'd have to split into threes to go in the Land Rovers, he instantly said he'd go with you then quickly added Ross and Phil to his group. You can't deny that. And the look he gave you on the station platform. Phew! It could have melted glaciers.'

Lizzie tutted and shook her head. 'Okay but so what? He's getting married Jane.'

'So you admit it?'

'I admit nothing. I will merely say that it's been a long time since I've met such a good-looking man.'

'And had one on top of you. Don't throw it! You'll hit Alastair.'

Lizzie put down the wooden spoon she'd aimed at Jane.

Jane pulled out a chair and sat at the kitchen table. 'Look Lizzie, you could do with a bit of fun and let's face it, that's what a stag party is all about isn't it? Fun. So, if you fancy him and he fancies you what harm is there in a quick fling?'

'A quick ...! Jane. That's almost exactly what Max said

when I found him in our bed with *that woman!*'

Jane frowned. 'Sorry. But that was different. He *was* married. This guy isn't.'

'He's engaged and that's almost as good as far as I'm concerned. I'm sorry Jane but I don't think infidelity is something to encourage. And besides, I'm thirty-two years old – as you are so fond of reminding me, I've got a house that constantly needs repairs and costs a fortune to run. Animals, that eat me out of house and home. A husband who thinks we can still make a go of our marriage despite the fact that we live over six hundred miles apart, rarely see one another and I've told him repeatedly it's over, and a mad friend who thinks having a fling with a man just weeks before his wedding is perfectly acceptable. Don't you think I've got enough to worry about without having to deal with a broken heart too?'

Jane poured herself and Lizzie mugs of coffee from the coffee pot. 'I'm not suggesting you fall in love with the guy. I'm only saying you need to have some fun. And it might help get Max out of your system once and for all. He's not going to believe it's over if you fall into bed with him every time he turns up here and turns on the charm and let's face it, if he found out you could play at that game too, he might stop taking you for granted. Besides, if Jack keeps looking at you the way he has been – I'd say it's pretty much a done deal.'

Jack knocked on the kitchen door moments later and peered around it. 'Everything okay?' he said, seeing Lizzie's flushed cheeks and Jane picking up a broken mug and a wooden spoon from the floor. 'We heard something smash and I thought you might ... um ... need a hand.'

Jane smiled at him, although his eyes were fixed on Lizzie. 'No we're fine thanks. Just dropped a mug, that's all.'

'Oh ... okay.' He turned to leave then stopped. 'Those biscuits were delicious. Did you make them?' His eyes rested on Lizzie's bent head.

'Yes,' she said without looking up.

'Just one of her many talents,' Jane said beaming at him. 'Do you like the mugs? Lizzie makes those too. Sells them as souvenirs. Perhaps you'd like one to take back with you – as a reminder of Lizzie – and the weekend.'

Both Lizzie and Jack's eyes shot to Jane's face but she ignored them and stroked Alastair who had come to see if what she was picking up, was edible.

'Yes. Yes. I probably will.'

'Unless something else takes your fancy,' Jane purred, thoroughly enjoying herself despite everything Lizzie had just said. 'Lizzie is good at lots of things as I'm sure you'll discover – but I must get on. Things to do, animals to feed, and all that stuff. Come on Alastair.' She stood up, threw the broken mug in the bin, grabbed her coat and was gone, leaving a confused Jack and a furious Lizzie staring after her.

Chapter Three

'Coast clear?' Jane asked poking her head round the kitchen door twenty minutes later, with Alastair doing the same.

Lizzie sighed and shook her head wearily. 'Give it a rest Jane, please.'

'You're no fun. Where are they? Still in the sitting room?'

'As far as I know. I said I'd call them when lunch is ready.'

'Oh good, more money for you.'

'When I start charging for soup and rolls, things really will be desperate.'

'Things are desperate. The roof leaks, remember?'

'Yes but it's only soup for heaven's sake. Make yourself useful and go and tell them it's ready will you?'

Jane was about to open the door when Jack knocked and walked in. 'Anything I can do? Lay the table or something?'

'Or something,' Jane said, an innocent smile on her lips.

'You can tell the others it's ready,' Lizzie said, glowering at Jane.

'Proper little helper isn't he?' Jane said when he'd gone. 'Comes running when the china breaks. Comes running to help with lunch. You should ask him if he's any good at mending roofs. Save yourself a fortune. And if he is, if I were you, I'd keep him.'

Lizzie sucked in her breath. 'You're not going to let this drop are you?'

'Nope! Shall I take the bowls through – or shall we see if Jack comes back?'

'God give me strength.'

During lunch the snow stopped and the afternoon sun broke through the clouds, its rays making the crisp, virgin snow look like alternating stripes of white and golden caster sugar.

'Hey!' the sun's come out,' Ross said.

'Wow! Looks like a little winter wonderland out there. What d'ya say we go for a stroll after lunch and get our bearings?' Phil said. 'Can we reach the village by foot?'

Lizzie looked up from her soup. All through lunch she'd tried to avoid eye contact with Jack who'd been staring at her almost non-stop for fifteen minutes, a small furrow forming between his intense blue eyes. Jane was watching her and grinning like a Cheshire cat and for some reason, Phil kept giving her strange looks too, so she was glad of the possibility of a peaceful afternoon.

'Yes but it'll take a lot longer in this,' she said, nodding towards the snow-covered fields, 'and you won't be able to see the path, although it's marked on signposts and is only a couple of miles. We can drive you if you'd rather.'

'Nah. You're all right. Can I 'ave some more of these?' Pete said, grabbing another bread roll from the plate filled with a selection of them, ranging from white to wholemeal and seeded. 'Did you make these too?'

Lizzie sniggered. He was behaving as if he hadn't eaten for a week. 'Jane made them.'

'Wow! They're bloody lovely!'

'Thank you,' Jane said, bowing her head towards him, 'we aim to please.'

'I bet you do,' Pete said, winking at her.

'Is there a pub in the village?' Steve asked. 'What?' he saw the look Jack gave him. 'It's after twelve and I could murder a pint.'

Lizzie grinned. 'Yes there is. It's the first building you come to when you reach the village. There's also a shop that carries an amazing variety of stock and has a small post office and an off licence in it.' She knew that would please Ross.

'You could take Alastair,' Jane said. 'He knows the way to the village so you wouldn't get lost and he's allowed in the pub. He drinks bitter.'

28

'Who's Alastair?' Ross asked.

Jack was grinning. 'A Labrador. He's in the kitchen.'

'Yeah?' Pete yelled. 'I love dogs. Does 'e really drink bitter?'

'He does,' Lizzie confirmed, 'although he's only allowed a small bowl. There's one with his name on behind the bar.'

'Nah? You're kidding?'

'I'm not. They really do have a bowl especially for him. It's for water but he does like bitter and we let him have it as a treat. Oh that's the telephone. Excuse me.' Lizzie strode into the hall to answer it.

'Well, that's it then,' Pete was saying as she came back in, 'we're off to the pub.'

Lizzie started to collect the plates.

'Let me help,' Jack said, jumping to his feet.

'No. We're fine thanks. You go off and enjoy yourselves.'

Jack felt like a child being sent out to play. He was getting the distinct impression that she was trying to keep him at arm's length.

'That was my neighbour Iain Hamilton on the phone,' Lizzie was saying. 'He owns Heatherdown, the large farm that borders this place. It seems he's decided to have a ceilidh tomorrow night. Everyone's invited.'

'Including us lot?' Phil asked.

Lizzie nodded. 'He'll send his son Fraser for us at seven. He's got a sort of open wagon they use in the summer to take tourists around the farm so we'll all fit in.'

'Great!' Pete said. 'What's a cei ... .whatever?'

'A sort of party with drink and music and dancing.'

'The 'ighland fling, you mean?'

'Well, maybe, if you're lucky. They do have traditional Scottish dancing and they're always great fun. They're pretty regular events up here and oddly enough, the worse the weather, the more the Scots like to party. Most, if not all of the village will go. We'd better make some savouries and cakes to take with us Jane.'

'Sure. You guys will need to save some energy for that tomorrow. Ceilidhs get pretty lively let me tell you and it'll be a late night – with plenty to drink.'

'I was hoping to do some climbing over the weekend,' Jack said 'but with this weather that doesn't look like it'll happen so I guess it'll just be walking and photography anyway. Nothing too exhausting.'

Lizzie was surprised. Clearly Jack was a man of varied interests. The only thing Max was really interested in was money – and women, she reminded herself. But why did she keep comparing Jack to Max? This must stop.

'So you're an outdoors man then Jack?' Jane said, glancing at Lizzie and raising her eyebrows in a meaningful gesture.

'Well, I wouldn't say that exactly. I can be just as happy indoors as out.'

'I bet.' Jane cast another glance in Lizzie's direction. 'Climbing and photography though. What got you into those?'

Jack didn't notice the pointed remark. 'I used to climb with my dad but mum spent the whole time worrying so now we just do walking weekends every so often. It was dad who got me into photography too. Although since he's moved house, every time I go to visit we end up doing repairs to the place. It's a bit of a wreck.'

'Well, well, Jack,' Jane said, 'you are full of surprises.' And the look she gave Lizzie said it all.

'What about the rest of you?' Lizzie asked, trying to get Jane off the subject of Jack, 'what do you like to do?'

'Make money,' Steve said.

'And spend it,' Jeff added.

Pete just shrugged. 'Be with my mates.'

'Drink,' said Ross, 'talking of which, we'd better get a move on.'

'Are you sure you trust us with your dog?' Phil asked.

Lizzie smiled. 'Don't worry. If Alastair's not happy,

he'll leave you and come home. Don't give him more than a small bowl of bitter though. I'd like one sober male in the house tonight.'

Phil grinned. 'Scout's honour.'

'Would you like dinner here or will you be eating at the pub?' Jane asked.

The guys glanced at one another. 'Here, if that's okay with you?' Jack said.

'Yeah. What time? We'll fit in with you.'

Again the guys exchanged looks. 'Seven-ish?' Phil said. They all nodded.

'Seven-ish, it is,' said Lizzie, thinking that meant more like eight. 'We can come and pick you up as you'll never find your way in the dark, even with Alastair. When it gets dark in the country, it gets really dark. There aren't any street lights in the fields, although if it's a full moon you might just about manage with torches.'

'Didn't think about that,' Ross said, looking concerned. 'Tell you what guys, why don't we head back earlier then, about five-ish? I could do with a lie down later anyway. Not sure I'm fully recovered from last night and the journey up here.'

Jack's eyes met Lizzie's for a second before she turned away. 'I know exactly what you mean, mate,' he said.

'Right then, pub, kip, dinner at seven?' Phil said. 'Ready?'

They all got up together and headed to the door.

'There are some spare wellies and boots in the hall cupboard,' Lizzie said, 'if any of you didn't bring them. I think we've got most sizes.' She had noticed that Pete still had his designer label footwear on, as did most of the others.

'I've got boots upstairs,' Phil said.

'Me too,' said Jack.

Pete grinned. 'I'm definitely an indoors man, if you know what I mean?' He winked at Lizzie.

She grinned back. 'I know exactly what you mean. There

are some jackets in the cupboard too. Help yourselves. I'll get Alastair.'

'We'll be home by five,' Jack said as they left fifteen minutes later, then realised he'd used the word home, 'er ... back ... I mean.' His brow furrowed and he looked flustered. 'Um see you later.' And with that he strode off with Alastair at his heels.

'Well,' Jane said as she and Lizzie watched them head towards the village, 'Jack just gets better and better, doesn't he? I told you if he mends roofs you should keep him.'

Lizzie watched until Jack was out of sight. She found herself hoping he would turn back and wave but he didn't and she rebuked herself for being such a fool. When he'd said "home" something inside her reacted and a warm, cosy feeling had swept over her. God she was stupid where men were concerned she told herself. Max could twist her around his little finger and Jack just said the word "home" and she instantly saw a version of Little House on the Prairie.

'He's not mine to keep,' she said, unable to subdue the rising disappointment she felt.

Jack had wanted a chance to have a word with Phil and at last he'd got it. Phil was throwing sticks for Alastair to fetch and the others were racing Alastair to see who could get to them first. Alastair was winning, paws down.

'About the window Phil,' Jack began, not really sure what he was going to say.

Phil picked up a stick and tapped Jack on the arm with it. 'Forget it mate. Didn't see a thing.' He tossed the stick high in the air and Alastair raced after it showering them with snow.

Jack was relieved. 'Don't know what's the matter with me; must be the drink. Still half pissed or something.'

'Pre-wedding nerves, mate, that's what it is. She's pretty tasty too, if you like that fresh faced, unmade up, natural beauty type. Never fancied brunettes myself. I'm more a blonde bombshell kind of guy but even I had to look twice at Lizzie. Mind you, Jane's pretty stunning too. Must be something in the water up here.'

Jack studied his friend's face. He'd known Phil since he was a kid, along with Ross, but since Jack had been dating Kim, none of them seemed so close anymore. 'Yeah well, it's just madness anyway I'm engaged and, as you said, she's married.'

Phil smirked. 'That was just to put Steve off. You know what he's like. She's separated, and in my book, that's as good as single. What harm is there in a final fling anyway? That's what stag do's are for. It's not as if we're talking anything serious here are we Jack? I mean, she's about as opposite to Kim as opposites can get.'

Jack caught the look in Phil's eyes but wasn't sure what it meant and now wasn't the time to ask. Conflicting emotions were whirling around in his head and he didn't want to start a conversation that might lead him somewhere he wasn't ready to go.

A snowball hit him square on the chest taking him by surprise, quickly followed by several more. Phil was hit too.

'You want war?' Phil yelled, grabbing a handful of snow and laughing; he threw it directly at Pete's head.

The battle raged until they reached the village and six men – looking more like yetis than city bankers, stood outside The Drovers Rest, the village pub, with Alastair, who now resembled a polar bear cub.

The Drovers Rest was an old wayside inn dating from the sixteenth century. Inside it had a small dining room to the left, containing six tables with four chairs at each, and a large open fire. To the right was the bar, filled with battered leather armchairs, wooden chairs and stools and several ancient rickety tables of varying shapes and sizes.

There was another larger open fire and when the guys entered the bar, Dougall Fairbright was tossing three massive logs in to the flames.

'Ah, so you'll be Lizzie's men then and wanting a wee dram no doubt.' Dougall said smiling broadly. 'Come in, come in and seat yourselves by the fire. And Alastair, my lad. You'll be wanting your usual.'

Alastair barked in confirmation, his tail wagging like a windscreen wiper, before settling himself in front of the roaring fire, eagerly awaiting his drink.

Three hours later, the same men were staggering back towards Laurellei Farm having bought drinks for several of the locals and learnt a few Scottish ballads – and Rugby songs – which they were now singing as Alastair, the only sober one, led them home.

Lizzie and Jane spent the afternoon in the kitchen, baking various cakes and savoury delights to take to the ceilidh and it was almost five when Lizzie heard the guy's raucous laughter and looked at the clock.

'Look at the time. I can't believe the guys are back already.' She glanced through the window and saw they were building snowmen – or trying to. A couple of them looked as if they were having trouble just standing up.

'They'll be freezing,' she said as Alastair raced into the kitchen shaking off layers of snow in the doorway. After greeting both Lizzie and Jane enthusiastically, he headed for his basket beside the Aga.

'You could offer to warm one of them up,' Jane said, grinning.

'Don't start Jane. But thinking about it, I'd better put extra towels in their rooms 'cos they'll be soaked and they'll all want baths or showers.' She finished her cup of tea and headed for the utility room.

'Oh, you're no fun,' Jane teased.

Neither of them heard Jack come in and make his way upstairs.

Jack stepped into the shower and luxuriated under the heat of the water. He had tried to watch his alcohol intake at the pub. He was already confused enough without adding, "being out of his head with drink", to it.

On his way back to the house, whilst the others were singing, he thought about what Phil had said earlier. He was right. Lizzie was the total opposite of Kim. Lizzie had brunette hair that fell in soft waves to just below her shoulders and bounced when she walked – although it'd been in a ponytail when he'd first seen her that morning on the platform. Kim's was long, straight and dyed blonde.

They were both stunning but in different ways. Lizzie was petite and had a natural fresh faced beauty as Phil said, whereas Kim was five feet nine, looked like a model and wouldn't dream of going out without full make-up on.

Lizzie was slim, although not as slim as Kim and she was in proportion, almost perfect proportion, whereas Kim's ample breasts always made her seem a little top-heavy. Nothing stood out about Lizzie and yet, Jack had a feeling that if he walked into a room and saw them both for the first time, it would be Lizzie he'd notice.

So he was attracted to her. So what? It didn't mean anything. He'd been with Kim for two years and it worked. Hell, they would be married in two weeks and spend the rest of their lives together. Phil was right. It was pre-wedding nerves – and too much alcohol.

Fidelity was important to Jack and he'd never cheated on anyone he'd dated. But he remembered how he'd felt during that moment on the platform when Lizzie lie beneath him. The urge to kiss her had been almost overwhelming. Where was his fidelity then? He'd never felt like that before.

His mind raced. He could just kiss her. That wouldn't be a problem would it? The trouble was, he'd like to do more than just kiss her – and that would be. He felt a sensation of arousal trickling through his body. It had been a long time since he'd felt like this.

A final fling, Phil had said. What harm would it really do? Perhaps it was exactly what he needed. It might even do him good. Prove to him that Kim really was the one. Get rid of his doubts and get this craziness he'd been feeling since he'd set eyes on Lizzie, out of his system. They were both adults and they'd never have to see one another again. If she were willing ...

He closed his eyes and let the warm water wash over him. He wondered what she'd feel like and began picturing her with him – in the shower. Visions of their naked bodies, clinging to one another under the cascade of water crept into his mind. As he washed himself he imagined touching her, his hands exploring and caressing and his mouth covering hers in long, slow, wet kisses.

Oh God, what was he thinking? He was engaged.

But a final fling wasn't really that serious was it? And he did need to be sure. Marriage was for life – or at least – it was as far as he was concerned. Yes, he had to be sure.

He could make it clear that it was just a fling and if Lizzie was okay with that, what harm could it possibly do? Kim would never know and in a way, it was for her benefit too. She wouldn't want to marry someone who had doubts about whether she was really "the one". Not Kim. She wasn't the type to play second fiddle to anyone.

And Lizzie? Was she the type who'd be happy to sleep with another woman's fiancé? Jack shook his head. Somehow, he doubted it. What was the matter with him? He must get a grip before he did something stupid. He turned the temperature of the water down a notch but it didn't wash away his thoughts – and his thoughts were all about Lizzie.

'Would you tell the guys what time it is in case they want to lie down for a while before dinner,' Lizzie said her arms full of fluffy white towels.

'Sure. Then can I rummage through your wardrobe for something to wear tonight? Something sexy and alluring.'

'Yeah, help yourself. But if it's sexy and alluring you want you're out of luck. That doesn't describe anything in my wardrobe.'

Lizzie headed through the hall in the main house, to the bedrooms the guys were occupying.

She knocked on the first door, even though she knew they were still outside as she could hear them singing something that sounded like a rather bawdy version of a Scottish ballad. She grinned, as a mother would with a mischievous child, and entered the room. She placed the towels on the bed then went to the next room and did the same.

Opening the door to the final room, a cloud of heat hit her and she could see the windows were steamed up. She strode towards the radiator and cursed quietly. It was red hot. The boiler must be playing up again. She'd have to ask Iain Hamilton to have a look at it sometime over the weekend. He was good at that sort of thing.

She heard Jane shrieking with laughter and peered through the window. Jane was having a snowball fight with the guys and although it was five to one, she appeared to be winning.

Five to one? Where was the sixth? Lizzie raised her hand to wipe the condensation from the window so that she could see more clearly but her hand froze in mid air and her breath caught in her throat. There, doodled on the pane was a huge, half wiped out, love heart with a still visible letter 'L' in the middle of it.

The en suite bathroom door opened and a stark naked Jack walked in – a toothbrush stuck in his mouth – quietly humming to himself. He was rubbing his hair with a towel and droplets of water ran down his broad, and relatively hair free, chest.

Lizzie's mouth fell open and her fingers rested against the window pane. She couldn't move, she couldn't speak and try as she might, she couldn't stop her eyes from taking in every inch of him.

She felt the colour rush to her cheeks and her heart thumping in her chest, and she wondered if it were possible to die from embarrassment.

Jack too, seemed frozen to the spot. He saw her fingers pressed against the window pane and the half wiped out heart – which seemed even clearer now than when he'd first doodled it – and all he could think of was that she'd seen it. His mind raced trying to think of something to say.

He saw her eyes travel the length of his body and come to rest below his waist and, as her mouth fell open, he realised he was naked. Hastily, he tried to cover himself with the small towel he'd been using on his hair.

Lizzie's eyes shot to his face and he gave her a weak, apologetic smile but before he had a chance to say anything, she fled from the room, slamming the door closed behind her.

Lizzie raced along the hall in the main house to the door that led to the barn conversion and her private rooms. All she could think of was getting to her bedroom and shutting the door. She struggled with the doorknob and Jack's naked body flashed before her eyes. Oh God! Why had she stared at him? He'd seen where her eyes went and she cringed at the memory. How would she ever be able to look him in the eye again? It was bad enough before but after this!

She reached her bedroom and dashed inside pushing the door shut behind her. In her haste she didn't see Jane searching her wardrobes.

'God you made me jump!' Jane said.

Lizzie shrieked. 'I made you jump! Bloody hell. You nearly gave me a heart attack.'

Jane saw the look on her face. 'What's up? You look like you've seen the devil.'

Lizzie shook her head. 'Worse than that,' she said, 'don't ask. I can't tell you.'

'Oh come on. You can't dash in here and say things like that and expect me to keep quiet. What's happened? Oh my God! Did he make a pass at you?' Jane tossed the selection of clothes she'd had draped over her arm, on to the back of the chair.

Lizzie shook her head. 'Worse than that.'

'Worse? Personally I'd have thought that was quite good but okay, what?'

'Before I tell you, you must swear never to mention it again.'

'Now I'm really interested. Okay, okay. Don't look at me like that. I swear.'

'I ... oh God. I've just seen him naked!' She dropped on to the bed.

Jane's eyes grew wide and her mouth fell open, then she burst out laughing. 'You can't be serious. When? How? Did he see you?'

'Just now. He must have come in earlier whilst the others were still outside. He's got the room at the end and I'd –'

'Yes. Yes. Get to the naked bit.'

'I am! The room was hot and full of condensation so I went to the radiator and ... oh my God ... the heart!'

'Radiator? ... heart? Lizzie what are you babbling about? I'll get you a drink. I brought a bottle of red up to help us get ready.' She poured Lizzie a glass and Lizzie gulped it straight down. Jane poured her another. 'Slowly now,' she said handing it to her and pouring one for herself.

Lizzie gulped at the second glass then took a deep breath. 'There was a doodled love heart on the window pane Jane, with my initial in it. It had been half wiped away but was still visible. He'd drawn a love heart on the window! Can you believe that?'

Jane shook her head. 'That is worrying,' she said, 'I thought there must be something wrong with him. No one's that perfect and there it is – he's got the mental age of a ten year old.'

'What?'

Jane was laughing. 'Oh come on Lizzie. What grown man would draw a love heart on a window? He'd have to be really besotted. It was probably one of the other guys who saw exactly what I'd seen on the platform and was ribbing him about it in the same way I've been ribbing you. Or, there is a chance I suppose, that his fiancée's name begins with the letter L.'

'Oh. I hadn't thought of that,' Lizzie said, taking another gulp of wine and handing Jane the glass for a refill.

'Well.' Jane handed her back a full glass. 'We can easily find that out but get on with it. How did you get to see him naked and ... more importantly, what mark would you give him out of ten?'

Lizzie almost choked on her wine. 'Oh God! I can't bear to think about it. It was awful.'

'Really? What, deformed you mean?'

'What? No!' Lizzie tutted. 'I meant the whole episode. It was so embarrassing and the worst thing was that I just stood there, mouth wide open, ogling him.'

Jane sniggered. 'What? You mean you stared at his dick?'

'I couldn't take my eyes off it.' Lizzie hung her head in shame.

Jane fell back on the bed roaring with laughter. 'Oh God! I wish I'd been there. Why do I always miss the best bits? What did he say?'

'Nothing. He just stood there.'

'Oh how hysterical. What did you say?'

'Nothing. I was too busy staring at his dick, remember. Eventually he covered himself with a towel but we both knew I'd got an eyeful. Oh hell. I'll never be able to face him tonight. What am I going to do? Jane! Stop laughing. It's not funny.'

'Oh it is. Believe me it is.' Jane sat up, 'So, did you just run from the room?'

'Yes. What else could I do?'

'Well ... I could have thought of something if it had been me. Never one to waste an opportunity but there it is. I'm just surprised you remembered what it was and didn't try to hang a towel on it.'

Lizzie tutted again. 'It hasn't been that long since I've

seen a naked man. Max was here at Christmas and New Year, remember?'

'How could I forget? Anyway, you haven't said. Marks out of ten?'

Lizzie licked the rim of her wine glass with her tongue and took a deep breath. 'Fifteen,' she sighed.

'Wow!' Jane emptied her glass in one gulp.

Chapter Four

An hour later Jane and Lizzie had showered and changed and were in the kitchen making dinner. Stilton and pear tartlets to start, followed by twenty-one day matured Angus beef and red wine casserole, dumplings and hasselback potatoes with a fine grating of stilton on top, then chocolate crunch pudding and custard for dessert.

Despite Jane's earlier comment, she had chosen a plain but elegant fitted skirt – which was shorter on her than on Lizzie as she was a few inches taller, at five feet six – and an emerald green cashmere sweater that exactly matched the colour of her eyes.

Lizzie had chosen navy blue fitted trousers and a navy blue v-neck blouse with a soft ruffle fringe. Her hair hung loose about her face and she wore little make-up, just mascara and a hint of lipstick.

At seven precisely, they heard the guys making their way down to the dining room.

'Shall I go and see what alcohol they want to drink?' Jane asked. 'I mean, they haven't had any for two hours, they must be gasping.'

Lizzie smiled in spite of the fact that she was shaking. The thought of facing Jack again after the fiasco in his room did not appeal and if she could have shut herself in the kitchen and left it all to Jane, she would have.

She knew that wasn't an option. Jack must be feeling embarrassed too, not just about the nakedness but also about the doodled heart and the sooner they faced one another, the better.

'Yeah but will you pour me a large glass of wine first, please. I think I need it.'

Jane smiled and poured the wine. 'You're getting as bad as them. It'll be fine.'

'You always say that and it never is.' Lizzie took a big gulp of wine. 'That's better. Tell them dinner will be ready

in the moonlight and she saw something in them that both frightened and thrilled her. She had the oddest feeling that this was going to be a life changing event.

'God Lizzie,' he murmured, wrapping her in his arms, 'what the hell have you done to me?'

'Nothing –,' she began but his mouth came down on hers stifling any further reply.

So this is how heroines in the movies feel when they're being kissed by a superhero, she thought, during the first few seconds of his kiss. She was sure she was floating. She couldn't feel the ground beneath her feet. She was definitely spinning, she must be. She could feel his mouth on hers, gentle yet demanding, and even if she'd wanted to resist, she wouldn't have been able to, but she didn't want to.

She was travelling at light speed and her entire body was tingling from the inside, out. The kiss grew deeper, more passionate and Lizzie wrapped her arms around him, clinging to him as if she would fall to her death if she let him go, kissing him back with the same intensity, as he slid one hand through her hair and pulled her even closer.

'Lizzie! Telephone.'

Jane's voice broke in on them like cold water on a fire and Lizzie felt her feet return to the ground with a thud, although in reality, they'd never left it.

'Lizzie,' Jane called again. She couldn't see her friend but she knew she wouldn't have gone far.

Alastair barked in reply.

Jack still held Lizzie in his arms, their eyes locked as if they were caught in a magnetic beam and were being pulled together, both breathing heavily in the cold night air.

'Lizzie. It's Max,' Jane called out.

'Oh God,' Lizzie said.

'Who's Max?' Jack asked, his voice not quite his own.

'My ... my husband.'

Jack let go of her so suddenly, she almost stumbled.

47

'What the hell do you want, Max?'

'And a good evening to you too sweetheart,' Max said after a startled pause. 'I was just calling to check that everything is going okay. Is there a problem? Do you need me to come up?'

'No!' Lizzie almost screamed down the phone. 'Sorry Max. It ... it's been a strange day. Everything's ... fine.'

'Are you sure? You sound ... different somehow. They're not giving you a hard time are they?'

Lizzie almost choked. She considered telling him what Jack had been giving her when he'd called, but she knew she wouldn't.

'No. You were right; they're a great bunch of guys. No trouble at all. I'm just tired. Long day. In fact ... I was just thinking about bed when you called.' Max wouldn't know how true that was and a trickle of guilt ran through her as she remembered the feel of Jack pressed against her.

'Lizzie? Did you hear me?'

'Sorry Max, miles away. What did you say?'

'I said, don't let me keep you up then. I'll call tomorrow. Goodnight sweetheart – and pleasant dreams. Maybe you'll dream about me. I'll certainly be dreaming about you.'

'Goodnight Max.' Lizzie hung up. Max, she realised with a little surprise, would definitely not be in her dreams tonight.

'I'll love you and leave you, if that's okay?' Jane was standing by the door to the kitchen.

'What? Oh yes of course. You're welcome to stay though, you know that.'

'I know. But I need to sort out something to wear tomorrow night and I've got a few things to do. I think the guys might be making it an all-nighter so I don't suppose they'll want breakfast too early. See you about ten-ish. Call me if you need me to come over earlier. Lizzie? Are you okay?'

'Yeah I'm fine. Just tired, sorry. Come later if you want. I can manage breakfast. Is Jack ... I mean, are they all in the sitting room?'

Jane's brows knit together. 'You sure you're okay? You look ... a bit flustered.'

'I'm fine, honestly.' Lizzie wasn't ready to tell Jane about the kiss. She wasn't sure what was happening to her and she needed time to get her head around it.

'Okay, if you say so. Phil went up shortly after you went out and Jack's just gone up – he said to say goodnight, by the way. He seemed in a bit of a mood to be honest. The others are still in there. I'd leave them to it.'

'Oh.' So Jack had gone to bed. What did that mean? Was he angry because Max had called? Did he even care? Was it just a brief kiss? The result of a long day and twenty-four hours of drinking. Maybe tomorrow he'd have forgotten he'd even kissed her.

'I said, Goodnight Lizzie. Are you really okay? I can stay if you'd rather.'

'No.' Lizzie pulled herself together. 'I was just wondering what they would do tomorrow. You go. I'm off to bed. Goodnight.'

Lizzie walked with Jane to the main front door and hugged her goodnight then stood by the door and watched until she was out of sight. She went back into the kitchen to check Alastair was curled up in his basket – he was – then she ambled towards the sitting room.

'I'll say goodnight, if you don't mind guys. Breakfast can be anytime you want it. I'll be in the kitchen after I've fed the animals, from about seven thirty.'

'Goodnight,' the guys all said at once.

'Don't mind if we stay up for a bit do you?' Jeff asked.

'No. See you in the morning. Everything's locked that needs to be, so just switch off the lights when you go up would you?'

'Yeah. Night,' Pete said, and they went back to their game of poker.

49

Jack needed to think. Things were spiralling out of control and he had to sort them through in his mind. When he'd decided earlier that a fling with Lizzie wouldn't hurt, in fact, would be a good way to put his doubts to rest, he'd assumed that what he'd been feeling were just pre-wedding jitters and one night with Lizzie would put them in perspective. Now, he wasn't so sure.

What he hadn't thought about – hadn't given a moment's consideration to – was, what if he wanted more? What if he actually had feelings for Lizzie? Why would he have felt such a pang of jealousy when he'd discovered her husband was calling her if he'd just wanted a one night stand?

This was crazy. In real life, you didn't fall in love at first sight and change your whole future for a total stranger. It just didn't happen. Did it? But Lizzie didn't feel like a total stranger. When he looked into her eyes it was as if ... as if what?

As if he'd found something he didn't even know he was looking for. God, now he really was being ridiculous.

It was the *forever* bit that was making him feel like this. Once he was married there'd be no other women in his bed. From then on it would only be Kim and somehow, that didn't feel as good as it should have.

He didn't understand. It wasn't as if the thought of being with just one woman forever bothered him. He liked the idea. His mum and dad had been happily married for forty years and they were still as much in love now as when they'd married. More so, his father had once told him. So, what was the problem?

'Snap out of it, Jack,' he said out loud as he opened the door to his room – and the realisation hit him as if he'd left the window open. A sudden blast of the cold, hard truth.

Kim was the problem. He loved her but not enough. Not nearly enough. If he had, he knew that thinking about making love to someone else wouldn't even cross his mind. And when he'd kissed Lizzie just now, all he wanted to do was make love to her.

But she was still married and despite what she'd said, she still went running to the phone when her husband called. Still wore the wedding and engagement rings on her left hand.

He remembered what it had felt like to kiss her – and he remembered something else – she had kissed him back, one hundred and ten percent, she'd kissed him back and with a longing and a passion he was sure had equalled his own.

What the hell was going on? Was she playing a game with him? Did she think they could have a quick fling and then she'd wave him goodbye? Was she using her wedding ring as a shield against getting emotionally involved with other men or was she using other men to get revenge on her husband for something he'd done?

'Shit!' he said. He wouldn't be able to sleep. Not with all this going on in his head. What he needed was a drink.

Lizzie tossed and turned all night. She hadn't felt like this since she'd discovered Max's affair with *that woman* and she couldn't make sense of it. She hadn't even known Jack for twenty-four hours and yet – she felt as if she'd known him all her life. A cliché – but it was true.

This was Max's fault. He'd persuaded her to take the booking. She wouldn't have met Jack if she'd said no. Why couldn't she ever say no to Max? But she could, and she had – once.

Two years ago when she'd found him in their bed with *that woman* and she'd packed a bag and fled to Jane's. Two years ago, when she'd walked into Laurellei Farm and knew she had to buy it. Two years ago. God had it really been that long? Max had asked her to stay. Pleaded with her in fact – and she'd said no.

What had happened since then? She'd bought the farm, set up a bed and breakfast with Jane's help. Settled into a completely different life. Started to rebuild a future. A future without Max.

No, Max was still very much a part of her life. He was

still her husband. He still came to see her. He still ... oh God, only eight weeks ago he'd been in this bed. She could remember the feel of him, the smell of him.

What was she doing? She still loved Max despite his betrayal. Still went weak at the knees when he touched her. Still saw him as a part of her future. Or she had until today. So what had changed?

She had never considered being with anyone else, sleeping with anyone else. Until Jack. When she was in Jack's arms tonight all she wanted was him. Max hadn't entered her head for even a nano-second. How could that be? Could she really have fallen into bed with Jack and not given Max a second thought?

Like the ghost at a party Max haunted her mind. She loved him but could she love someone else as much? Until today she would have said no – but now? She had to decide, once and for all. Could she really face a future without Max?

Lizzie hadn't slept well. She'd finally drifted off in the early hours of the morning only to have the strangest dreams of Max and *that woman* and Jack and herself and they all seemed to be dancing in some sort of never ending circle. She couldn't remember the details but she'd awoken feeling their lives were all entwined in some horrible, farcical way.

The snow had held off and the morning promised to be bright and clear, if rather cold. She'd take Alastair for a walk then do some baking and go over things in her mind. Baking always helped her think clearly and it also produced bread and scones and cakes and rolls, true comfort food – so it was dual purpose.

Lizzie forced a smile. She'd thought her life had been complicated before – but now... Wow. What a difference a day makes. She showered and dressed in jeans and an Arran jumper Jane had knitted her for Christmas and with her hair loose, she headed down towards the kitchen. Instead of taking the back stairs leading from the barn conversion into the kitchen, she used the main hall.

All the doors to the guy's rooms were shut and she felt a mixture of relief and disappointment. Part of her was hoping Jack might be up so that she could see what he'd do; whether or not he'd remember the kiss. Part of her was dreading it and hoped he'd sleep until Jane arrived so that she would have some moral support.

She started humming to herself to try to lift her spirits. Whatever happened, she'd put on a brave face. Jack was here for three more days and it was Iain's ceilidh tonight. Another drunken evening no doubt.

Jack might try and kiss her again and she had to be ready for it, had to see this for what it probably was as far as Jack was concerned. A final fling. By the time she reached the kitchen, she'd stopped humming.

Alastair's ears pricked up when he heard her footsteps and he was ready and waiting by the door when she walked in.

'Good morning gorgeous. How are you?'

Alastair barked softly; as if he knew there were hangovers in the making upstairs.

'Come on then,' Lizzie said opening the kitchen door and letting a freezing gust of wind in. 'Oh! That's cold boy. I think I might leave you to it until I've had a cup of coffee.'

Alastair glanced up at her then sped off towards the snowy fields. Lizzie pushed the door to and put the kettle on. She made coffee and toast as she started sorting out the breakfast plates and bowls. Twenty minutes later, she had set the table in the dining room for breakfast.

She marched into the hall and put on her thick coat, a wool hat, scarf and gloves and decisively headed out into the cold to join Alastair. He wouldn't have gone far, and he would be fine on his own but the cold air might help clear her head and she had to feed the chickens and the pigs.

As she walked, she suddenly remembered Max's phone

call when he'd asked her to take the booking. "One of them works with me," he'd said. But none of them had mentioned they knew her husband. Why was that?

It couldn't be Jack. He'd asked who Max was when Max had called last night, so who was it and did he know about *that woman*? Was that why he hadn't acknowledged the connection? A sudden thought flashed across her mind. Had Max asked him to "keep an eye on her"?

No. Why would he? It wouldn't even occur to Max that Lizzie might be interested in someone other than him. Max had made it abundantly clear he was certain Lizzie would go back to him – it was just a matter of time. And Max seemed happy to give her time.

She wondered, as she fed the animals, if Max was seeing other women and she almost laughed out loud. She could be such a fool sometimes. Of course he was seeing other women. This was Max. Why hadn't she let herself think about this before?

Alastair came bounding towards her from behind a hedge. She had just left the small barn, where the chickens were deciding whether or not to venture out into the snow, and he nearly knocked her over as he raced up to be stroked.

She bent down and tickled him behind his ear and he barked appreciatively.

'Good morning,' a voice said from behind her, making her jump and she turned so abruptly that she lost her balance and tumbled from her bending position on to her side.

Jack was next to her in an instant and was helping her to her feet.

'Are you okay?'

'Why must you keep making me jump?'

'Ah. Um. Sorry. Should I cough loudly in future or whistle or something so you'll know I'm approaching?'

'That might help.' Lizzie brushed the icy snow from her coat. 'I'm fine thanks. You can let go of me now.' That sounded far sharper than she'd intended it to.

Jack hadn't realised he was still holding her arm and quickly dropped his hand from her. 'Sorry,' he said.

Silence hung between them and Lizzie wrapped her scarf tighter, just so that she was doing something.

Alastair leapt up at Jack in a friendly greeting. 'Good morning boy,' Jack said. 'Are you always this lively in the morning? I wish I had your energy today.' He rubbed Alastair's fur playfully and Alastair wriggled contentedly.

'He wasn't drinking nearly all day yesterday,' Lizzie said trying to sound light-hearted.

'Um. Yeah. About yesterday ... '

Lizzie held her breath and waited.

'Did I ... well, I had a hell of a lot to drink and it's all a bit hazy. I ... I hope I didn't do anything I shouldn't have.'

Lizzie was taken by surprise. So, that was how this was going to go. Either he really couldn't remember or he was going to pretend he couldn't. None of it. Not the being naked and her ogling him, not all the meaningful looks. Not that kiss. Fine.

'Like what?' Lizzie gave him her most innocent look.

Jack's cheeks reddened – but that could have been from cold, she reasoned.

'Um ... like ... like ... just anything.'

She smiled at him but he was trying to avoid eye contact.

'Not as far as I'm aware but perhaps you'd better check with Jane. I'd better get back and start breakfast. Are the others up?' She started walking towards the house. She had to get away from him; tears were pricking at her eyes. So that was the end of that, she thought, irritated that she cared so much.

Jack fell in step beside her. 'Lizzie I –'

'Alastair! Come on boy. Sorry Jack. I must dash. I've just remembered my husband said he'd call again this morning.'

She quickened her step but she needn't have bothered. Jack had stopped in his tracks.

55

Chapter Five

'Morning!' Jane danced into the kitchen.

'Well. You're certainly in a good mood. What's brought this on?'

Lizzie was baking again. She started as soon as she got back after talking to Jack. She needed to take her mind off that particular subject and baking helped. It always had. Whenever she'd been miserable or worried in the past, she'd baked. Why on earth she'd followed her father into his Law firm and not her mother into her restaurant, was still a mystery to her.

'It's a lovely day! Have you been out?' Jane dropped her overnight bag on the floor and took her coat off, hanging it on the rack beside the kitchen door.

'Yes and it's freezing.'

'Certainly is, but I love days like this. Cold and clear and sunny. Feels like spring's coming. Oh. I saw Jack on my way over. He seems to be going for a rather long walk. He had almost reached my place. Hope he doesn't get lost.' Jane strolled over to Alastair who was in his basket as usual, and tickled him behind his ear.

'I rather hope he does.' Lizzie banged the tray of cheese straws she was making for the ceilidh, on to the table.

'Oh dear. What's happened? Wait. Let me make coffee first. I've got a feeling we're both going to need it.'

'Perhaps he really doesn't remember,' Jane said fifteen minutes later when Lizzie had told her about last night and this morning. 'He must have had loads to drink yesterday. Pete told me they started drinking as soon as they left the office then drank virtually all the way up here, with hardly any sleep. Then they spent a couple of hours in the pub and they were pretty hammered after that, believe me. They had wine with dinner and then liqueurs. It was a wonder Jack could stand up let alone kiss you!'

Lizzie frowned. 'He didn't seem that drunk. He wasn't slurring or anything.' She sieved flour into a large ceramic mixing bowl then added a slab of butter, some baking powder and a pinch of salt. Lizzie rarely weighed her ingredients; she was an instinctive cook and judged everything by eye, by taste or from memory.

'Some people don't. You think they're stone cold sober but they can't remember a thing!' Jane said, passing her the jar of sultanas.

'That's true I suppose. Oh, I don't know. It's just this morning, when he asked if he'd done anything. I just got a feeling that he knew exactly what had happened and wanted to pretend it hadn't!' She began rubbing the butter and sugar together with her fingertips until it had formed a breadcrumb-like consistency then she added the sultanas. 'Pass me the sugar too would you, please.'

'You should have told him,' Jane said, handing her the jar of sugar.

'Yeah right! And how would that have gone. Actually Jack I saw you naked and ogled your body then later you kissed me and the Earth moved – for me at least. Oh sorry, you don't remember?' She tossed some sugar into the mixture and stirred it.

'Well you wouldn't have said it like that, obviously but you could have said something. You could have said he kissed you at least. Then you would have known if he was pretending by the way he reacted to that.'

Lizzie shook her head. 'Too late now. Better to act as if it didn't happen anyway. I was so confused by it all. Couldn't think straight. It would have been so awkward for the next few days. Especially if he did know what he'd done and regretted it. He's engaged after all!' She added a few dribbles of milk, mixed it all up then passed the bowl to Jane.

'I guess so.' Jane dusted her side of the table with some flour and turned the mixture out on to it. She began lightly kneading the dough. 'Oh well. We've got the ceilidh to look forward to tonight. What are the plans for today?'

'No idea. Jack's the only one up so far and as you know, he's gone walkabout.'

Lizzie prepared a baking tray for the small rounds Jane was cutting from the dough. She placed them on the tray, brushed them with a little milk and egg and popped the tray in the oven.

'I thought we'd do some more food for this evening and depending on what the guys have planned, we'll either have a late lunch as a main meal and skip dinner 'cos there'll be food at the ceilidh or have an early lunch and light supper. They might go somewhere for the day I suppose, so we'll have to wait and see.' Lizzie started preparing another batch of scones, this time without the sultanas.

As if on cue, there was a tap on the door and Pete poked his head in. 'Morning,' he said rather sheepishly. 'Don't suppose you've got any 'eadache tablets?'

Lizzie smiled and Jane went to the cupboard to get some. She handed him two with a glass of water.

'Cheers,' he said. 'Anyone else up?'

'Me,' Phil said from behind him. 'How're you feeling mate?'

'Like death warmed over.' Pete swallowed the tablets with a sip of water.

'Jack about? He's usually an early riser.'

Pete shrugged.

'He's gone for a long walk,' Jane said as both Pete and Phil came in and sat by window on the window-seat. 'Not sure when he'll be back. Apparently, he's suffering from mild amnesia this morning.'

Lizzie threw her a 'don't you dare' look.

'I bet!' Pete said. 'Jack doesn't usually drink much and 'e was really putting it away last night. In a right mood 'e was. Couldn't sleep or something so 'e came back down and played poker. We went up about two but Ross and Jack looked like they were staying up all night. Think we've probably emptied your booze cabinet. Phil'll settle up today.' Pete rubbed his aching forehead.

Phil nodded. 'Glad I went to bed early,' he said, watching Pete.

Lizzie's eyebrows shot up and she realised her mouth was open. 'Jack came back down?'

Pete threw her an odd look. 'Yeah, not long after 'e went to bed. Couldn't sleep.'

Lizzie and Jane exchanged brief glances.

'No wonder he's got memory problems,' Jane said.

'Breakfast anyone?' Lizzie suddenly felt decidedly more cheerful.

'I think I can hear the others,' Phil said, 'and look, there's Jack.'

Jack's memory was starting to return but it wasn't making anything clearer. He thought he remembered Lizzie as being friendly, very friendly but she seemed rather distant today. Something she had said though, about her husband calling had triggered something in his mind – he just wasn't sure what it was.

Last night he'd dreamt he was outside in the snow, kissing her and that she was kissing him back and when he woke up, he thought it had really happened but it must have just been a dream.

He also thought he remembered something to do with him being naked and Lizzie staring at him but maybe that was part of the dream too. If only he had gone to bed at a reasonable time last night instead of staying up with the guys to play poker and drink until the early hours of the morning with Ross.

It hit him like a snowball in the face. He had gone to bed! He remembered! He'd gone upstairs but gone back down again. Why? He racked his brains. He hadn't dreamt about being naked with Lizzie in his room. That had happened.

So why hadn't she mentioned it? Perhaps she was trying to save him the embarrassment. He could see that.

And he had kissed her last night – and she'd kissed him back. That's what had triggered his memory. Her husband had called last night when they were kissing!

Oh Shit! No wonder she'd been off hand with him this morning. Not very complimentary to say you can't remember kissing someone. And she would hardly remind him of something like that. Especially as he was engaged and on his stag do.

She must think he was an absolute prat. He'd have to sort things out with her – and he'd have to sort things out with Kim too. That's one thing he remembered quite clearly. Somehow, he'd have to call off the wedding.

He could see Phil waving at him from the kitchen window and as he got closer, the smell of bacon hit his nostrils. Nothing like a cooked breakfast to make everything seem right with the world. It would all work out. He was sure of it.

'So what d'you want to do today?' Phil asked, sticking another sausage on his plate.

'It's too icy for climbing,' Jack said 'and to be honest, I think my blood alcohol level would make me a danger anyway. I'd quite like to take some photos. Some of the scenery around here is breathtaking.' He didn't mean his eyes to settle on Lizzie but somehow they did.

Phil shook his head benignly. 'I think I get the picture. Are these sausages from your own pigs Lizzie?'

'Oh no! I'm a hypocrite I'm afraid. Can't kill anything but I still eat meat. My pigs are pets. They're very intelligent – and better behaved than some men I know.'

Jack choked on his bacon.

'You all right mate?' Pete said, slapping him on the back and causing Jack to lurch forward with such force his chest landed on his plate and egg yolk covered his beige sweater.

'I am now thanks mate,' he said, casting Pete a sardonic look.

'Take that off and I'll wash it,' Lizzie said.

'Now Lizzie!' Pete joked, 'you 'ad your chance to get Jack's clobber off last night and you passed. Don't start this morning!' He had no idea why Lizzie, Jack and Jane all stared at him as if he'd conjured up the devil. 'What? You didn't want to play strip-poker!'

The relief was almost audible and as Jack caught the expression on Lizzie's face, they both knew what had gone through their own minds. His eyes held hers until she looked away.

'Seriously Jack,' Jane said, 'you'd better take it off before it stains.

'Jack stood up and pulled the sweater over his head. Underneath he wore a plain navy blue T-shirt. I'll go and get another one. Thanks for this.' He handed the sweater to Lizzie who had risen from her chair to take it.

Jack followed Lizzie into the hall but instead of going upstairs to get another sweater he went into the kitchen behind her.

'I think we need to talk,' he said.

Lizzie was flustered. This was an unexpected development.

'Oh. What about?' She tried to sound calm but her heart was pounding in her chest as she turned to face him.

Jack raised his eyebrows and slowly a devilish grin spread across his face. 'You suffering from memory loss now?'

Lizzie's eyes shot to his. Why did he have to be so damned handsome? And that grin ...!

'I ... I don't know what you mean,' she lied.

Jack sighed deeply. 'Okay. Fair enough but that walk helped my memory and I realised that what I thought I'd dreamt, actually happened.'

Lizzie blinked several times. 'Oh.'

His brows knit together above confused sapphire eyes but his voice was gentle when he spoke. 'Is that it? Oh.'

'Well what do you want me to say?'

'That you didn't mind me kissing you, for a start.' Jack

took a step closer.

Lizzie dashed into the utility room and put the sweater in the sink keeping her back to him so that her eyes wouldn't betray her emotions. Jack followed her and stood in the doorway. With his height and broad shoulders he dominated the space and Lizzie felt her temperature rising and the colour rushing to her cheeks.

'Well? Did you?'

'Jack,' Lizzie half turned to face him, 'I really don't think ... no! Stay there Jack!'

Jack was closing the gap between them.

'Jack. Don't!' Lizzie hadn't meant to snap but she couldn't handle him kissing her again, not this morning, even though, somewhere inside her, she desperately wanted him to.

Jack stopped just inches from her. 'So you did mind?' His features formed granite angles and the longing cleared from his eyes. 'Well. Please accept my sincere apology. It won't happen again and I'm sorry if I've caused you any offence.' He turned on his heels and left before Lizzie had time to gather her wits.

She leant back against the wall and let out a huge sigh. This just stumbles from one little drama to another, she thought.

'We're off,' Phil said, sticking his head round the kitchen door a few minutes later.

Lizzie stayed in the kitchen; she couldn't face Jack again just yet. 'Okay, don't forget the ceilidh tonight. Fraser's picking us up at seven. Are you eating out or do you want something here?'

'I think the plan is to have lunch at the pub. Jane said there'll be food at the ceilidh tonight, so she suggested we come back and have afternoon tea here about four-ish. Is that okay?'

Lizzie glanced up from the cake mixture she was stirring. 'Yeah. That's perfect.'

'See you later then.'

Lizzie went to the window and waited. One by one the guys went out of the front door and strolled towards the snowmen they'd built yesterday; now showing signs of slowly melting in the March sunshine, despite the cold in the air.

She heard a cough from the direction of the kitchen door and spun round to see Jack standing there. He had put on a pale blue sweater over his T-shirt and had his jacket thrown over one arm. Her heart skipped a beat. The pale blue only emphasised his incredibly blue eyes.

'Tried not to make you jump this time,' he said sheepishly.

'Thanks.' Lizzie tried to control the emotion in her voice. She pretended she had been plumping up the cushions on the window-seat, not staring out for a sight of Jack.

'Look. I don't want to go out without clearing something up.' He took a step forward.

'Jack really there's –' Lizzie took a step back.

'Lizzie please. Just let me say this okay?'

She swallowed the lump forming in her throat and fiddled with a cushion, staring at it as if in a trance.

Jack hesitated. He knew what he wanted to say but didn't know how to say it. He'd been thinking – he seemed to be doing a lot of that lately – when he went to get another sweater and something had occurred to him.

'I'm not very good at this stuff so I'm just going to say it and if it comes out wrong then I'm sorry. I was drunk yesterday but not so drunk that I didn't know what I was doing. The thing is, what I was doing was totally out of character for me and I wanted you to know that.' He sighed loudly as if he had got something off his chest.

'O ... kay,' Lizzie said hesitantly, cushion still in hand.

'I haven't finished. When I kissed you last night it was because I wanted to, not because I was drunk ... although I was very confused and I didn't really know why I wanted to kiss you...' He dragged a hand through his hair.

'Thanks!'

'Oh ... I didn't mean it like that. I meant, I'm engaged and I wouldn't usually go around kissing other women –'

'That's good to know.'

'Please let me finish. This is difficult.'

'Sorry. I thought you had.'

Another deep sigh. 'I'm trying to get it out right but I'm not sure I am. Look, the thing is, yes I was drunk, yes I'm engaged but I kissed you because I really wanted to, even if I didn't know why, I knew I wanted to. And it was partly because ... I was having doubts about getting married.'

'Oh ... And now?' Lizzie found a loose thread and nervously twisted it around her finger.

Jack looked relieved and a huge smile spread across his full, firm mouth. 'Now I don't.'

Lizzie felt as if she'd been slapped across the face. 'Glad to have been of use. I'm happy for you.' She tossed the cushion on to the window seat.

'You don't look happy.'

'Well I am. I'm sure you'll both have a wonderful future together.' She strode to the kitchen table and picked up the flour jar. She needed to bake.

'Jack! You coming mate?' Ross yelled from outside.

Jack's brows furrowed. 'Yeah,' he yelled back. 'You don't understand.' His eyes were firmly fixed on Lizzie's downturned face. He took a few steps towards her. 'We're not going to have a future together. I'm going to call it off.'

Lizzie could feel her mouth fall open and knew she must look as dumbstruck as she felt. She raised startled blue eyes to his. 'W ... Why?' The large kitchen table was between them.

'Because, if I'm not sure of anything else, I am sure of one thing. I just don't love her enough to spend the rest of my life with her. If I did, I wouldn't have kissed you last night even if I was drunk and I certainly wouldn't have tried again today – when I was sober.'

'Oh.' Lizzie couldn't think of anything else to say but she could feel a smile forming on her lips.

Jack's eyes held hers. 'Now that's cleared up, there's something I'd like to know. I don't know what's going on between you and your husband and I don't suppose it's any of my business but last night ... you kissed me back and I know I didn't imagine it. You definitely did! Did you regret it this morning?'

Lizzie stared into his eyes. She wasn't really sure what was going on but her whole spirit felt lighter. 'No.'

'Jack.' Ross's voice grew closer.

Jack smiled briefly at Lizzie then turned to go. He stopped and looked back, his expression serious, his hand holding the kitchen door open. 'Why did you stop me kissing you this morning then?'

Lizzie sucked in her breath and shook her head. 'I'm just so confused. You're engaged, I'm still married and we only met twenty-four hours ago. I don't know what's happening – and it's all happening so fast.'

Jack nodded. 'That's what I thought. Perhaps we should talk about it some more, or something. Can we? Later?'

Lizzie simply nodded.

Again he turned then looked back, the devilish grin brightening his entire face, making him look even more handsome. 'If I tried to kiss you when we come back, would you let me?'

His sapphire eyes twinkled and Lizzie had to stop herself from running to him and throwing herself in his arms. She returned his grin. 'I would say there's a very good chance I might.'

Jack's grin broadened into a huge smile and his dark eyes smouldered. 'I'll hold you to that.'

He hadn't seen that Ross had come to get him and had been listening for the last few minutes.

'Jack,' Ross said, pretending he had just come in.

'Yeah, coming.' Jack winked at Lizzie. 'See you later,' he said to her. Then he was gone.

Lizzie dropped on to a kitchen chair. Had Jack really just said he was calling off the wedding? She was replaying the conversation in her head when Jane came in, loaded with plates from breakfast.

'Day dreaming?'

Lizzie looked up, a bewildered expression on her face.

'What's the matter now?' Jane asked, depositing the pile of plates on the worktop.

Lizzie shook her head. 'This weekend is getting more like a French farce by the minute.'

Jane pulled out a kitchen chair and sat down. 'Tell me.'

Lizzie told her how Jack had followed her and tried to kiss her and how he'd stormed off when she'd stopped him, then about what he'd just said.

'Bloody Hell! Well. I suppose he must have wondered why you'd been more than happy to kiss him last night when he was drunk but wouldn't this morning when he was sober. That's reasonable I guess. Then maybe he thought it was because you might have been a little tipsy last night too and sober this morning and not prepared to kiss an engaged guy.'

'Maybe.'

'God! This is giving me a headache just thinking about it. I need coffee.'

'Me too.'

Jane put coffee and water in the machine and switched it on. 'Well, then he must have thought it through and as he said, he realised he wouldn't be kissing you if he really loved his fiancée. God! The man's nothing short of a saint.'

Lizzie frowned. 'That's the really weird bit. Why did he tell me that?'

'Lizzie, from where I'm standing, it's all bloody weird.' Jane began loading the dishwasher.

'Do ... do you think he's lying?' Lizzie got up and grabbed two mugs.

'Lying! Why?'

'Well ... he wanted to kiss me and I stopped him. Maybe

he thinks if he tells me he's going to call off the engagement I'll fall into his arms and he can have his cake and eat it. Then when it's time to go back he can say he'd made a mistake and he does still love her etc. etc.'

'My God! Where did that come from?' Jane pushed the start button and the machine whirred into action. 'Your trouble is you've spent too much time with Max. Not everyone tells lies to get someone into bed.'

Lizzie looked hurt. She put the mugs on the table and grabbed the coffee pot from the machine.

'Sorry Lizzie,' Jane said, getting a jug of milk from the fridge. 'But c'mon. There are some decent men in this world you know.'

'Not in the City there aren't.' She poured the coffee.

'Oh that's a bit cynical. They don't all sell their souls the minute they get inside the City boundaries. Give the guy a break. Perhaps he's a thoroughly decent man who's realised he's with the wrong woman. It happens and it's a good thing it's happened now and not after he's said "I do".' Jane poured milk in both mugs then put the jug back in the fridge.

'Yeah. I guess so.'

'Actually, I think this smacks of the pot calling the kettle black.' Jane said, putting her mug of coffee to her lips.

'What does that mean?'

She nodded towards Lizzie's left hand. 'You're the married one in this little charade madam.'

Lizzie's eyebrows shot up and her eyes darted to her hand. 'He knows I'm separated.'

'Right. And nothing says separated quite like a wedding and engagement ring on the third finger of a woman's left hand does it?'

Lizzie put her mug down on the table and studied the rings. She twisted them between the thumb and forefinger of her right hand. 'Are you suggesting I should take them off?' She sounded as if she'd been asked to cut off her arm.

'That's entirely up to you. All I'm saying is, if the roles

67

were reversed, would you trust a man who tells you he's separated and still wears his wedding ring. I know I wouldn't. But hey. That's just me.'

'I'm not sure I'm ready for that.'

'Then I would say that's something you need to think about. You've told Max it's over. If you really mean it this time, then at least moving the rings to your right hand would be a start. And whilst Jack didn't say he's calling off the engagement because of you, it sounds to me like he's saying he'd like something to happen between you two and whether that's just a fling or something more isn't just up to him you know. It takes two to tango and if you're going to dance, you'd better decide which partner you want to dance with. Wow! That was almost profound. I need more coffee.'

'I need chocolate. Throw me a brownie from the red cake tin would you?'

Jane got up and got the red cake tin from a stack of differently coloured cake tins, took a brownie out for each of them and put them on plates. She put the cake tin back on the shelf she'd got it from.

'Oh! Let me show you what I'm wearing tonight,' she said enthusiastically and put the plates on the table. She dashed over to her bag where she'd dropped it earlier and pulled out a short, pale blue, tight fitting crepe dress with a very low neckline. 'Must leave something to the imagination – but not too much,' she winked. 'I'm wearing my over the knee sexy boots; shoes just don't do this dress justice.'

Lizzie shook her head. 'Jane, there's still about four inches of snow out there and we're not going to a disco you know.'

'I know. That's another reason why I'm going to wear my boots. Anyway, you remember the last one of these Iain had for Valentine's night. We wore trousers and boring blouses and all the other women had made an effort and dressed up. I felt really under dressed.'

'That's how you ended up! I still have nightmares about seeing you and Iain in the barn that night.' Lizzie shivered mockingly.

'So I had a fling with Iain Hamilton. So what?' Jane stuffed the dress back into her bag.

Lizzie was surprised by Jane's tone. She thought it had just been a drunken fling and she and Jane had even laughed about it after, but she'd noticed Jane's attitude changed whenever Iain's name was mentioned, and now she was starting to wonder if her friend had real feelings for him.

'D ... d'you really like him?' Lizzie took a bite of the brownie.

'Don't look so surprised. He's nice.'

'I know he is but ... '

'But what?' Jane stomped back to the table and dropped on to the chair she'd been sitting on earlier.

'Well ... he's quite a lot older than you and ...' Lizzie trailed off. Her friend was looking a little annoyed.

'And what? He's only thirteen years older and forty-five isn't old.'

'No ... but –'

'Oh for heaven's sake Lizzie. Just say it.'

'Well, I just think that, if you really like him, having sex with him may not have been your wisest move.'

Jane's brows shot up? 'What's that supposed to mean? And when did you become such an expert?' She began pulling her chocolate brownie into little pieces.

'I'm not. This weekend is proving that. All I'm saying is ... just don't throw yourself at him tonight. Make him chase you.'

'Meow! What's brought this on?' She threw a piece of brownie into her mouth.

Lizzie reached out towards Jane and squeezed her hand. 'I just ... I don't want you to get hurt, that's all. Why didn't you tell me how much he meant to you? I ... I thought it was just a drunken fling.'

'I didn't really know until that night. Well, that's not entirely true. I knew I really liked him but I didn't know how much. Not until ... after – for all the good that did me.'

'Has ... has he asked you round for a drink since then?'

Jane frowned. 'No. But it was only two weeks ago and he's got the farm to run and now Fraser's back he hasn't exactly got the place to himself has he?'

'There's your place. Has he called?'

'Noooooo.'

'Perhaps you should have played hard to get.'

'Don't know how that game goes.' She snatched her hand away from Lizzie's fingers. 'Okay, so I make a fool of myself sometimes. I'm thirty-two and I'm still single!'

'I wish I was. Marriage isn't all it's cracked up to be. I'm proof of that.' Lizzie leant back against her chair but kept her eyes on her friend.

'I think that depends on whom you marry.'

'Touché!' Lizzie sat back up and reached out for Jane again. 'Look, I'm just saying. Iain's old school, the type who likes to chase the woman he wants not have her throw herself at him.'

Jane ignored the offered hand. 'What's got into you?' she snapped. 'You're not usually a bitch! Feeling guilty 'cos you're thinking of cheating on Max? Oh God. I'm sorry. Now I'm being a bitch.' She took Lizzie's hand.

'No. It's me. I'm sorry. I shouldn't have said those things about you and Iain. Let's face it, I'm no Vestal Virgin. One look from Max and I'm falling into bed with him – and a total stranger kisses me and I'm almost doing the same with him. And you're right. I do feel as though I'm cheating on Max, although god knows why. We're separated and he's the one who cheated, remember?'

'How could I forget? Sorry. Doing it again.'

'Okay,' Lizzie poured them both more coffee from the pot, 'let's call a truce. We're both a bit frazzled over our love lives.'

'I haven't got a love life,' Jane said sipping her coffee

and sighing. 'At least Max calls you regularly and comes to see you occasionally.'

'And that's a good thing because ... ?'

'Well, he cares about you and wants you back and that counts for something. I still think he's a shit and you could do better but at least he cares. Iain couldn't care less about me and you're right of course. If he'd wanted to see me he could have. He just didn't want to.'

'Max only cares about himself Jane, believe me. And he only comes up here to remind me of what I'm missing – and because I'm so bloody gullible, that always ends up involving sex. It's like he thinks he owns me and I couldn't possibly not want to be his wife. So he turns on the charm and like the idiot I am, I fall for it then, wham! It all comes back. Oh Hell. Let's change the subject. I'm sick of trying to understand men.'

'Me too.'

Chapter Six

Jack hummed as they walked along the lane. It was a beautiful morning and now that his head had cleared he felt better than he had for a long time. He stopped every so often to take a photo. The scenery was stunning. Everything was still covered in snow although it had melted a little in yesterday afternoon's sunshine.

Last night the temperature had dropped and this morning little icicles hung from the trees like glass Christmas decorations. The sun was slowly melting them and tiny drips of water ran down them, dropping to the ground like mini water bombs, creating small craters in the snow where they landed.

The Cairngorm mountain range was clearly visible in the distance, rising up from the snow-covered landscape and Jack wondered whether anyone would be skiing. The last snow had been at Christmas and since then, there'd been unusually mild weather. The resorts had snow machines, he knew but he remembered hearing that conditions weren't good and many resorts had closed to skiers already. Perhaps yesterday's fall had been enough to improve things.

Jack focused his camera on Phil, Pete, Steve and Jeff. They were taking pictures of one another in silly poses; balancing on walls, playing snow angels, throwing snowballs – and Jack felt as if things were like they used to be.

Ross was walking beside him in silence and Jack suddenly realised Ross seemed to be dragging his feet like a sulky child.

'You okay mate?' he asked. 'Still feeling rough from last night?'

Ross glared at him from hooded eyes. 'No. I'm fine.'

'You sure? You're a bit quiet this morning.'

'Just thinking about things, that's all.'

Jack nodded. 'Yeah, me too.'

Ross stopped walking. 'Anything you want to talk about?'

Jack stopped and turned back to his friend. 'Yeah. But I'm not sure now's the time.'

'Now's as good a time as any,' Ross pushed.

Jack's eyes formed tiny slits. Ross was acting very strangely. 'Perhaps. But I'm not sure I'm ready to talk about it yet. Still need to sort a few things out in my head. Once it's said, it's said and there'll be no going back.'

'Ooh! That sounds very dramatic,' Phil said. He'd seen Jack and Ross stop and wondered what was going on. They both looked so serious. 'Once what's said?

Jack glanced at Phil.

'Jack's got some big secret, he's not ready to share,' Ross said rather loudly, not bothering to disguise the sarcasm.

Phil's eyes darted from Jack to Ross as Pete, Jeff and Steve joined them.

'There's no secret,' Steve said. He had heard Ross's remark. 'Jack's got the hots for Lizzie, any fool can see that and he's planning how he can screw her. Good on yer mate! Thought about it myself.'

Phil saw the look in Jack's eyes and grabbed him by the arm shaking his head lightly. He knew Jack wouldn't hit Steve, Jack wasn't the violent type, but he might say something he'd later regret.

'As usual, Steve's judging others by his own standards, aren't you mate?' Phil said. His eyes lightened and rested on Steve.

Steve looked puzzled then shrugged his shoulders. 'Whatever. It's a stag do and that's what it's all about. I hope there's some talent at this thing tonight 'cos I certainly plan to do some screwing.'

Pete smiled. 'I want to 'ave a go at the 'ighland fling. Need to get pissed first though, if I'm gonna make a prat of myself.'

Jeff nudged him. 'You don't need to get pissed to make a prat of yourself, mate. Comes naturally. Hey. Let's ask at the pub if there's anywhere we can get some kilts from for tonight. That would be a right laugh.'

'If you think I'm wearing a skirt and no knickers,' Pete said, 'you can think again mate.'

The tense moment was past.

'What? Trying to pretend you're not that sort of girl,' Jeff put his arm around Pete's shoulders and laughed.

'At least I've got the legs to wear a skirt,' Pete said, playfully pushing Jeff away.

'I wouldn't boast about that in the pub,' Steve said, 'people might get the wrong idea.'

'I'm not sure the locals would approve of us ridiculing their national dress,' Phil said. He started walking again and the others all fell into step.

'We wouldn't be ridiculing it,' Steve said, 'we'd be trying to blend in.'

'Yeah well. I'm not so sure they'd see it like that,' Phil said.

'Why would they sell them then, if they didn't want people to wear them? I'm going to ask in the pub. Come on. Stop dawdling. We're wasting good drinking time,' Jeff said, quickening his step.

Neither Ross nor Jack spoke until they reached the pub.

'I hope they haven't spent all day in the pub,' Lizzie said, 'the thought of trying to keep six drunken men under control doesn't appeal to me.'

Jane smiled; she was back to her usual cheerful self. 'It appeals to me. Well, the thought of six men, that is.'

Lizzie giggled. 'Yeah right. Neither of us can cope with one let alone six.'

'Actually, you've got two. Max and Jack – and that's the real reason you're worried. You want Jack to be sober so he'll kiss you as he promised to.'

Lizzie blushed. 'I think it was more of a threat from

where I was standing.'

'Ooh! Getting all of a flutter are we?'

Lizzie put the finishing touches to a lemon drizzle cake she was making for afternoon tea, sighing as she did so. 'He's a really good kisser, if yesterday was anything to go by, so yes, I am getting a bit flustered just thinking about it to be honest.'

'Wow! If that's the effect the guy has on you when he's miles away in a pub I don't know how you managed to say no this morning when he tried to kiss you.'

'Fear. Pure, unadulterated fear.' Lizzie inspected the lines she'd made in the lemon icing on the top of the cake and was satisfied.

'Of what?'

Lizzie took a deep breath and shook her head. 'Of not being able to stop.'

Jane grinned and nodded. 'Yeah, but now you know he's not engaged anymore things are different.' Jane piled the scones they'd made that morning on to cake plates.

'He's still engaged Jane. Unless he's told her over the phone and that would be a really shitty thing to do. So it would still be cheating – technically and even though we're separated, I would still somehow feel I was cheating on Max – but we're not getting into all that again. What's the time? They should be back soon.'

Jane thought she could hear singing and she strolled over to the window. 'As if on cue,' she said, 'and it looks like you were right to worry. Ross and Jack look as though they're holding each other up and the rest of them don't exactly look sober.'

Lizzie closed her eyes but didn't say a word.

'Honey, we're home,' Steve yelled from the hall, nudging Jack.

'Sssshh!' Pete hissed so loudly it made his head hurt.

Jane and Lizzie went into the hall.

'Any chance of coffee?' Phil asked, surprisingly sober.

'Yes, of course,' Lizzie said. 'Can you get them into the

sitting room? We'll bring it in there.'

'Come on guys,' Phil said, grabbing Ross by the arm and steering him and Jack forward.

Pete, Jeff and Steve all grabbed one another and Pete grabbed Ross's jacket so that they formed a sort of wavy line, all following Phil to the comfort of the luxuriously plump armchairs and sofas.

Lizzie noticed Phil was carrying four large shopping bags bearing Flora MacDonald's logo and wondered what they'd bought.

Flora and her family ran a small woollen mill a mile or so the other side of the village, selling traditional clothing and souvenirs from the local area, as well as further afield. Her mill was always popular with tourists, especially because of her name. She was no relation to the Flora MacDonald whom legend says helped Bonnie Prince Charlie but she didn't stop the tourists from thinking she was.

Arran jumpers were always a popular choice, Lizzie thought, even though they were very expensive, not that price would have deterred any of these guys, she realised.

When Phil had asked how much they owed her for the drink they'd consumed yesterday, he didn't bat an eyelid when she told him. In fact he asked her if she was sure that really covered it all and when she said yes, he pulled out a massive bundle containing several thousand pounds of fifty pound notes. He paid up and gave her extra despite her protestations – just in case she'd missed anything, he'd said.

Lizzie went back into the kitchen and made coffee. Alastair, who'd been in his basket beside the Aga for most of the afternoon, apart from when Lizzie had taken him for a long walk, got up and stretched, then followed Lizzie and Jane into the sitting room. He trotted up to each of the guys in turn, then over to the fireplace where he curled up on the rug in front of the hearth. He was a male with limited interests.

Lizzie poured coffee whilst Jane offered cakes and scones, trying to avoid the several pairs of hands reaching out for her. Steve in particular seemed determined to get Jane to sit on his lap and there was no way she was doing that.

Lizzie couldn't help but notice that Jack was making a real effort to pretend she wasn't there and when she handed him a cup of coffee, he thanked her without even looking up.

He's had second thoughts already, she thought, feeling a little irritated.

'Did you have a good day?' she asked, directing her question to Jack.

He nodded but still avoided her eyes. 'Yep!' he said and hiccoughed.

'Took lots of photos,' Ross said slowly tipping sideways in his chair.

Phil grabbed him and sat him upright. 'Bit of a session, I'm afraid. Think they'd all better lie down for an hour or so before we go out tonight.'

'Will they be okay?' Jane asked doubtfully.

Phil nodded. 'Yeah. They're used to this. Be fine after a kip and a shower.'

Lizzie made a mental note to give extra towels to Phil before they went upstairs.

'So how come you're sober and they aren't?' Jane asked.

'One of us had to be. We'd never have found our way back otherwise.'

'Survival strategy,' Jane said and smiled. 'Can you manage to get them all upstairs?'

'Yeah, they're like sheep.'

Alastair lifted his head and barked.

'He's offering his services,' Jane said, 'he thinks he's a sheepdog.' She stroked Alastair's head and avoiding Steve's hands.

Phil grinned. 'Might just leave them here.'

Jack, Ross, Pete and Jeff were all struggling to keep their

eyes open.

'There's a pile of tartan throws in the window-seat. I'll get them,' Lizzie said. She lifted the seat and took out six, handing a couple to Jane. Lizzie covered Ross then laid one gently on Jack. She gasped in surprise when he opened his penetratingly blue eyes and grinned up at her, then closed them again. Five seconds later, he was sound asleep. 'Men,' she said under her breath.

Jane gave a throw to Phil. 'That's for octopus hands,' she said.

Phil tossed it to Steve. 'Go to sleep, mate, and leave the lady alone.'

Steve sniggered, then huddled down and closed his eyes.

'Would you like one,' Lizzie asked Phil, 'or are you going upstairs?'

'Best stay here and keep an eye on them. But I'm fine thanks. I'll get them upstairs later.'

'Well, there are two Thermos jugs of coffee and help yourself to cakes and anything else you want. We'll be in the kitchen if you want fresh coffee or tea.'

It was idiotic and she knew it but Lizzie couldn't stop herself from feeling just a little disappointed that Jack had been back for almost two hours and was sound asleep in an armchair in the sitting room.

At least he'd smiled at her. That was something she supposed but when Phil came in and asked if they could have some fresh coffee because most of them were awake and had emptied the two Thermos jugs, she found herself hoping that Jack would pop his head round the door and say "hi", if nothing else. God, she thought, for an intelligent woman, she was being really stupid.

She handed two pots of fresh coffee to Phil who had waited in the kitchen for them – robbing her of an excuse to go in to the sitting room – and then she decided to take Alastair out for a quick walk before going upstairs to get ready for the evening. Jane offered to take him but Lizzie felt she needed the fresh air.

Outside, the temperature had dropped again and there was now an icy crust forming on the remaining snow. The snowmen had turned into misshapen blobs but they held their ground even if they were half the men they were yesterday.

Lizzie checked on the pigs, Peter and Penelope. The guys had only been to look at them once and had been very well behaved – although Steve did say that he thought they'd be better on his plate. At least none of the guys had tried to ride them so she should be grateful for that. And so far, the chickens had also been left alone. It was only day two though, so there were still two days to go.

The thought of that made Lizzie stop in her tracks. Jack would only be here for two more days and then what? So much seemed to have happened in the last two days and yet really, nothing had changed, except perhaps, the way she felt.

'It's me. I know I said I wouldn't call you but I had to.'

Lizzie heard the voice and recognised it as Ross's but she couldn't see him. She was standing outside the feed barn at the back of the converted barn so he must be in there. He wasn't outside and he was definitely close by.

Lizzie realised he must be talking to someone on the phone and was about to move on when his next words stopped her.

'It's about Jack.'

The person on the other end of the line must have said something because after a few seconds Ross said, 'No. I told you I wouldn't. You know what Jack's like.'

At that moment Alastair came bounding up barking so Lizzie had no choice but to quickly walk away. She took a few steps in the opposite direction, then turned and pretended she was just walking towards the small barn.

Ross poked his head out, looked slightly startled, then forced a smile and pointed towards the phone.

Lizzie smiled, nodded and headed away from the barn

back towards the house. She would have given anything to know who Ross was calling and what he was going to tell them about Jack, and for one tiny moment she wondered whether Ross was the one who worked with Max and whether it was Max he was now talking to. If only Alastair hadn't barked, she thought.

But she was being ridiculous. What did she think was going on? That Ross was playing private detective and keeping an eye on her, reporting anything untoward back to Max. That was just plain silly. But one of them did work with her husband and hadn't mentioned it – and she couldn't help but wonder why. She shook herself mentally; what was wrong with her? Why didn't she just ask them? And having realised that it really was that simple, she dismissed it – but she still couldn't help wondering who Ross was talking to – and what he was telling them about Jack.

Ross waited until Lizzie was out of earshot. 'Sorry, someone walked by. So, how are you?'

'How do you think I am? I'm going bloody mental!'

Ross didn't seem surprised. 'You're not the only one. How the hell do you think I feel?'

'Well then do something!'

'Like what? Do you really want me to tell my best mate on his stag do that I slept with his fiancée when he was in Hong Kong for three weeks?'

'Yes! Or let me tell him.'

'Kim. I told you. I can't. Jack would be devastated. It would be bad enough if he knew you'd slept with someone else but to find out it was me! He'd never forgive either of us. He's been my best friend since we were five. I can't do it.'

'You should have thought of that before you slept with me. And it didn't stop you coming back for more did it?'

'Christ Kim! We've been over this. It should never have happened. I still don't know how it did. And yeah, it should only have been that one time but shit, I just couldn't keep

80

away and believe me, I tried.'

'We should have told him as soon as he got back. It wouldn't have been so bad then.'

'Really? Don't you think I wanted to? But he seemed so happy to be home and looking forward to the wedding and ... God I just couldn't.'

'So you dumped me instead.'

'I ... I thought what happened between us was just one of those crazy things and that you and Jack would go back to the way you were and I'd ... get over it.'

'And how's that working out for you?'

'Kim. Please. I'm trying to do the right thing. What we had was great but it was only three weeks. You've been with Jack for two years and the wedding's all set. If it had happened before ... it might have been different.'

'Well. When Jack got back two weeks ago and you dumped me you said you'd never call me and unless my maths are totally wrong you've called me at least ten times since then and that's not counting today! Are you planning to do this when Jack and I are married? Not sure how that's gonna work.'

'Oh shit! I just can't stop thinking about you. About us. If you knew how this is eating me up you'd have a bit of pity on me.'

'Well then let's tell him! Let me tell him if you can't.'

'But I couldn't go out with you if you broke up with him. That would be just as bad. I told you. I explained all this.'

'You and your bloody stupid standards. I meant what I said Ross. I'm not going back to being on my own. I love you more than I love Jack now but I will marry him, if you won't be with me. Believe me, I will, unless you've got the balls to stand up to him like a man.'

'For God's sake Kim! This isn't about standing up to him. I'm not scared of him thumping me. In fact, it would make me feel a hell of a lot better if he did. This is about me not wanting to break the heart of a guy I really care

81

about. A guy I've known nearly all my life. Why can't you see that?'

'All I see is someone who's happy to sleep with his best friend's fiancée behind his back but not man enough to own up to it! I actually thought you might tell him this weekend do you know that? How bloody stupid am I? I actually believed you when you said you loved me. Well, you can sod off and don't call me again unless it's to say you've told Jack about us.'

'Kim. Wait! Don't hang up. That ... that was sort of why I called.'

Kim hesitated. She'd been about to slam the phone down. 'Why? Are you thinking of telling him? Do you mean that?'

'I may not have to, exactly.'

'D ... d'you mean he knows?'

'No! No. I don't think he's got any idea. But ... look I'm not sure how to say this but ... I think he may be having second thoughts about marrying you.'

Kim gasped. 'What? What do you mean? What's he said?' Kim didn't like the thought of Jack dumping her, even if it would solve her problems. Kim didn't like any man dumping her but it had happened more than once. She was beginning to think she chose men badly.

'Nothing exactly but there's this woman –'

'What woman?'

'The woman who owns this place. I think Jack's fallen for her ... Kim? Are you still there Kim?'

'Yes. I'm still here.' Her voice had mellowed as if she'd had the stuffing knocked out of her.

'Well! That's a good thing isn't it?'

'Is it? Why exactly?'

'Well, you know what Jack's like. Fidelity's important to him so if he's thinking of sleeping with Lizzie –'

'Lizzie! Her name's Lizzie? Lizzie what?'

Ross was surprised. 'No idea. Why? What does it matter what her name is? The thing is, if he's considering sleeping with her then he must be thinking about breaking up with you.'

'Is he considering sleeping with her?'

'I would say so, yes. He told me last night that he'd kissed her and even that surprised me but I thought he was just drunk and that's why he'd done it. Then today I heard them talking and he was stone cold sober.'

'What were they talking about?'

'He was asking her if he could kiss her again and would she let him or something.'

'And would she?'

'Well I think she said yes. I couldn't really hear her but when he walked away he was smiling like the cat that'd got the cream.'

'Really?'

'Kim? You don't sound as pleased as I thought you would.'

'You expect me to be pleased to hear my fiancé wants to sleep with another woman?'

'Well. Yes. Don't you see? If Jack finishes with you – and I'm pretty certain he will if he sleeps with Lizzie – then, after a small amount of time we can pretend that I was comforting you and we fell for each other. That way he'll never know we cheated behind his back and we can stay friends.'

'You and Jack can stay friends you mean.'

'Well, yes.'

'So let me get this straight. You can't date me if you tell him or if I dump him but if he dumps me that's okay and you'll start dating me as if those three weeks never happened?'

'Yes. Don't you see? If he dumps you then he won't be the one getting hurt and he'll be pleased that you and I have hooked up. I do love you Kim. I meant it. If Jack finishes with you, we can be together.'

Kim let out a long sigh. 'I really don't understand any of this and I still think if you really loved me you'd tell him but – and I never thought I'd hear myself say this – let's just hope my fiancé cheats on me.'

Chapter Seven

'You look absolutely fantastic Jane,' Lizzie said, as she and Jane stood in the kitchen getting things ready to take with them to the ceilidh.

Jane was wearing the short, low cut, pale blue dress and was now pushing and pulling her breasts to get them just right. 'Are you sure it's really okay? Shouldn't I wear a long skirt and high neck blouse as Iain's so old fashioned?' She shot Lizzie a mocking glance.

Lizzie grinned. 'I didn't say he wouldn't like the outfit. Any man would. I'm just not ... No. I'm not starting that again. There are six guys in this house whom I'm sure we can safely say, know how to have a good time and at least one of whom, knows my husband, as Max arranged this weekend. Let's give them something to talk about and show Iain Hamilton exactly what he's missing at the same time. Is the punch ready? If so, let's have some.'

Jane poured them both large glasses of the warm punch they'd made earlier. 'I think you might get to see Mr Jack Drake naked for a second time, looking like that,' she said. 'Playing hard to get's gone out of the window then?'

Lizzie grinned. 'Yep. Okay, I think that's them coming down stairs now. Let's go through shall we? I'll take the punch if you can bring the glasses. The wine and the canapés are already in there.'

It was Jack's turn to stare open mouthed whilst his eyes travelled the length of Lizzie's body. She may not have been naked but the black cashmere dress fitted her like a second skin and the curved, sweeping neckline which exposed not just her shoulders but also gave a hint of cleavage showed off her figure to perfection.

The dress was short but not too short, revealing just a few inches of her legs above her over the knee boots, which were almost identical to Jane's, and the sleeves were long but began off the shoulders due to the curve of the neckline.

'Bloody hell!' Phil said, a cheese straw hovering in front of his mouth.

The others all whistled except for Jack, whose eyes were like lasers burning into Lizzie's flesh.

She saw the small furrow between his brows and wondered exactly what was going on in that undeniably gorgeous head of his. Then she saw what he was wearing. What they were all wearing – kilts!

Lizzie and Jane exchanged startled glances, then Jane burst out laughing and Lizzie joined in.

'We don't look that bad,' Pete said, a slightly hurt expression forming on his elfin features.

Lizzie shook her head. 'No. You don't. It's just a surprise that's all. In fact – you've got better legs than me!'

'Not from where I'm standing,' Steve said, appreciatively looking Lizzie up and down.

'Well. Thanks. Did you get them from Flora today?'

'Yeah,' Pete said. 'She's a really nice lady. Phil was worried they'd think we were taking the pi ... making fun of the locals but we asked in the pub if anyone would mind and they all said it was okay. Flora did too. Not sure about this 'andbag thing though,' he said, waving the sporran up and down.

'Don't do that mate,' Ross said, 'looks like you're making obscene suggestions.'

Pete grinned. 'You should be so lucky.'

'Well, I think you all look fabulous,' Jane said. 'Let me take a photo.'

'Yeah!' Pete yelled. 'Jack. You've got the best camera and it's got one of those timer things so we can all be in it.'

Jack didn't say a word but went upstairs and came back with his camera. He set it up so that it was facing one of the large sofas. Pete started organising everyone into position and when Steve made a grab for Jane, Pete slapped his arm.

'No! You stand back there with Jeff; Phil you sit on the sofa in front of Jeff; Jane, you sit on Phil's lap; Ross you sit on the other end; Jack you sit in the middle; Lizzie you sit

86

on Ross's lap and I'll stand back 'ere next to Steve.'

'Shouldn't Lizzie sit on Jack's lap?' Ross said.

Seven pairs of eyes shot to his face.

'Why?' Jack said rather sharply.

'Because it's your stag party! Wouldn't look right if you didn't have a woman on your lap.'

'That's true.' Pete agreed.

Jack looked flustered and muttered something inaudible but Pete was already pulling him and Lizzie to the sofa and pushing them into position.

'Why not have two women on his lap?' Jeff said. 'One on each knee. Here, sit down Jack, Jane you sit there and Lizzie, there.' He arranged them so that Jack was leaning back against the cushions and Jane and Lizzie were perched on one knee each. Jack's long legs were spread to accommodate them and his kilt fell between his thighs preserving his modesty.

'Good thing we didn't go commando,' Pete said, grinning broadly. 'Jack. Put your arms round them mate!'

Jack's arms had been stretched across the top of the sofa and he seemed reluctant to move them but Pete took control and put them around Jane and Lizzie so Jack's hands were on the women's hips.

Lizzie could feel Jack's fingers and even though they were only resting lightly on her, it was if she were being branded by a hot iron. She kept her eyes forward and tried not to think about the fact that there was very little between her body and his, just a few pieces of fabric.

'Jack, mate!' Pete said, 'You've got two gorgeous women on your lap, try to look 'appy. That's better.' He dashed to his position behind the sofa and the camera flashed seconds later.

Lizzie thought she felt Jack's hand tighten on her hip as she went to stand up but she could have imagined it.

'Punch anyone?' Jane said.

'What's in it?' Jeff asked.

'Cider, brandy, apple juice and a few secret herbs and

spices.'

Jeff wrinkled his nose but took a glass anyway, as did all the others.

'That's not bad actually,' Phil said. 'Bit of a kick to it.'

They chatted, drinking wine and punch for about fifteen minutes during which time, Lizzie couldn't help but notice, Jack did his best to avoid her.

'I think Fraser's here,' Jane said. 'I'm sure I heard an engine.' She pulled back the curtains which had been closed against the cold night air and nodded. 'Yes. It's Fraser. Shall we go?'

'I'll just check on Alastair,' Lizzie said.

Jack watched her walk towards the door and swallowed the lump in his throat. 'Shit!' he said, briefly closing his eyes and shaking his head as if trying to clear an image from his mind.

Iain Hamilton's farm was much larger than Lizzie's, being a working farm and from the outside, the farm house looked quite austere. His wife died shortly after Fraser, their only son, was born and Iain had brought him up whilst running the farm, with only part time child care from friendly and willing neighbours. Now twenty four, Fraser had returned, after university and some time travelling, to help his dad run it.

Lizzie met Iain when she was thinking of buying Laurellei Farm and he seemed both friendly and distant at the same time. He was clearly one of those rare people who were happy to do anything for anyone but he wanted to keep his private life, private. To her knowledge, there had been no women in his life during the two years she'd known him apart from Valentine's night two weeks ago when she'd seen him and Jane having sex in the barn.

'Don't let me do anything too stupid tonight Lizzie,' Jane said after Fraser had helped them down.

'Same here! I'm feeling a little tipsy to be honest. I

knocked back a couple of glasses of punch to settle my nerves but it hasn't worked. I hope everyone else has dressed up or we are going to look like we're really on the pull.'

They exchanged glances and sniggered nervously. 'I thought we were!' Jane said.

'Pretending to be,' Lizzie corrected. 'That way we won't get into any real trouble.'

'I wouldn't bet on that.'

Lizzie shook her head, 'Nor would I – and trouble is heading in our direction already.'

Jane turned and her large green eyes fell on Iain Hamilton, striding towards them, his raven black hair, with just a hint of grey at each side, blowing in the chill March night air. 'Oh God!' she said, watching his six feet two frame closing in on her and realising that the minute he opened his exquisitely curved mouth, she'd be a jabbering idiot. 'Help!'

'You okay love?' Pete asked, just as Iain came into earshot and it were as if a juggernaut had slammed on its brakes.

Lizzie saw Iain's welcoming expression disappear and his deep hazel eyes cloud over as they flitted from Jane to Pete, then to Lizzie as Jane slipped her arm into Pete's.

'I am now,' Jane purred, avoiding Iain's grim stare. 'Let me show you that there are other things up here just as lovely as my rolls.' She laughed coquettishly. 'Oh! Hi Iain,' she said as if she hadn't seen him and flounced past him, her arm still in Pete's and her head seductively leaning in towards him.

Iain watched them head towards the barn, on the cinder path he'd made earlier so that his guests would not slip on the icy snow, then turned back to Lizzie as he realised she was speaking to him.

'Sorry Lizzie, what were you saying?'

'I was just saying thanks and going to introduce you to the guys. That was Pete and these are Jeff, Phil, Steve, Ross and Jack.'

Iain nodded. 'Welcome.'

'Thanks,' Jack said. 'It was really good of you to include us.'

'More the merrier. Come on now and have a wee dram. It's a cold one out here that's to be sure.'

Iain held out his arm for Lizzie and she took it gratefully. Even with the cinder path, she didn't feel that steady in her boots but that was more to do with the punch she'd consumed than anything else. The other five guys followed them towards the barn. Iain opened a door to one side of the building and ushered them in.

Inside, Jack was surprised to see there were bales of hay, covered in tartan blankets, an impromptu dance floor covered with a dusting of sand, several small tables and upturned barrels, two stoves providing heat, a long table bowing under the weight of bottles of wine, spirits, and food, and party lights strung from the rafters and support beams, the whole length of the building.

'And this is a working farm?' Jack said to Lizzie.

Lizzie grinned, pleased that he had at last spoken to her. He hadn't said a word all the way here and had made a point of sitting as far away from her as he possibly could. He clearly had had second thoughts about breaking off his engagement – and about kissing her.

'It is,' she said, 'but because this barn is attached to the house, Iain uses it more for community things than for the farm. The village has all sorts of things here, especially in the tourist season. They put on displays of the old ways, you know, weaving, spinning, knitting, that kind of thing and it's where nearly all the ceilidhs are held. Iain's family have lived here for generations and he's seen as a sort of head man, although he's not the Laird.'

'I'll put these on the table shall I Lizzie?' Fraser asked holding the various plates and boxes he'd brought from the trailer.

'Oh yes. Thanks Fraser. I'll come and set it all out. We

brought a few bottles with us as well and some of my punch. Oh, there they are.'

Ross was holding a bag containing the bottles and Phil was holding a large thermos jug of warm punch.

'We'll put them on the table. It's help yourselves to food and drinks, guys and join in the dancing. I'll introduce you to a few people and –'

'No problem Lizzie,' Phil said, 'we can do that ourselves. It's pretty obvious who we are I think, despite the kilts. You just enjoy yourself. You've done enough for us today already.'

'Oh! Well, if you're sure. I would like to have a chat to a couple of friends from the village thanks.' She didn't want to point out that it was probably because of the kilts that it was obvious who they were. Apart from the six of them, only a couple of the old local die-hards were wearing theirs and there was no way they would be mistaken for guys from London on a stag do.

Jack watched Lizzie walk towards a couple of people on the other side of the barn, then followed Fraser, Phil and Ross to the end table to help put out the food and drink.

'This looks like it might be fun mate,' Phil said. 'I'm surprised how many people are here. I thought it was a small village. Must have come from miles around.'

'Yeah.'

Jack wasn't really listening. He was watching Lizzie, a frown forming as he saw her hand brush the arm of a tall, dark haired man who bent forward and kissed her on the cheek. The man said something and Jack could see that Lizzie blushed. Then she smiled up at the man and he put one hand on her shoulder, took her hand in his other and led her on to the dance floor, sliding his hand down her back and around her waist as he did so. Jack felt a surge of jealousy well up inside him and clenched his fists without even realising he was doing it.

'She's a good-looking woman and no mistake.'

Jack turned, startled. He hadn't seen Iain standing beside

him. 'Who?' he asked foolishly.

'Auch! Like that is it? Well don't worry, your secret's safe with me. Best take care though. That husband of hers wants her back and he's not the type to give up easily. Might be a long, hard struggle. Need to be sure you want that. Why don't I introduce you to some available women?'

What was Iain saying? Did he too, think Jack had fallen for Lizzie?

'I'm engaged! It's my stag weekend!' It didn't sound convincing, even to him.

Iain raised his eyebrows. 'My mistake,' he said.

They stood side by side, Jack watching Lizzie, Iain watching Jane, both pretending they were just watching the dancing in general but anyone watching them would have seen the occasional flash of their eyes, and gritting of their teeth when some man or other got too close or a little too familiar with either Lizzie or Jane.

Jeff, Steve, Phil and Pete joined in the dancing. Steve in particular looked to be enjoying himself. He was with a very pretty blonde who was smiling up at him as if he were a Greek God. When they whirled near Jack at one point in the dance, he mouthed the word 'single' to Jack and winked. Jack almost felt sorry for the girl.

'Are you not gonnae dance?' Iain said, after a long silence.

Jack shook his head, 'Not really in the mood.'

'Come and have a wee dram instead then?' Jack followed Iain through the barn and into what looked like a snug, between the barn and the main farmhouse. There was a roaring log fire in a huge stone hearth and four aged leather wing chairs formed a semi circle in front of it.

Jack smiled. It was a rural gentleman's club, or at least, that's what it looked like. He felt he could be happy spending winter evenings in such a place.

Iain grabbed a bottle and two glasses from the top of a small cupboard just inside the door and sat in one of the chairs beside the fire. He poured an amber liquid into the two glasses and held one out to Jack.

'May I?' Jack pointed towards a chair opposite Iain's.

Iain nodded and Jack took the glass from him.

Jack sat, and stretched his long legs out in front of the fire. He gulped at the drink then shook his head. 'Wow! This is bloody good stuff! What it is?'

Iain grinned. 'Home brew.'

'You have got to be kidding. I've had twenty year old malts that aren't a patch on this.'

'Great, great granddaddy's recipe. What do they say? I could tell you but then I'd have to kill you.'

Jack grinned. He liked this man. Iain may be ten years or so older but Jack instinctively felt he could be friends with him. They sat in silence sipping their drinks and watching the fire crackle.

After several minutes Jack said, 'Have you known her long?'

Iain raised his eyes from the fire. He didn't need to ask who Jack was referring to. 'Since just before she bought Laurellei. I'd met her a few times with Jane but when she decided to make an offer on Laurellei she came and asked me about the place. That was over two years ago. Been friends ever since. She's a bonnie lass and that doesn't mean just looks.'

Jack nodded. 'Do ... do you know her husband well?'

'Auch no! Met him a few times but didn't take. Comes up every so often and tries to persuade her to go back but she won't budge. She's a tough one when she needs to be. Laurellei was a wreck when she bought it but she's done wonders with the place. Her and Jane. Jane moved up here about a year before. Took over her aunt's old place.'

Jack noticed there was something about the way he said Jane's name but let it slide. It was none of his business.

'Had one of the worst winters in years the first year Lizzie was here and we all thought she and Jane might head back south but they toughed it out. We knew, if they stayed through that they'd stay through anything. A word of advice Jack. If you're interested in her and willing to take on the husband you'd best be deciding whether you want to live north of the border. There'll be no budging the lassie now.'

Jack gulped and coughed. 'I'm not! I told you, I'm engaged!'

Iain eyed Jack thoughtfully. 'Your mouth says one thing but your eyes say another.' He refilled his glass and handed the bottle to Jack.

Jack leant forward and took it, refilling his glass and handing it back.

'I hardly know her. I only met her yesterday.'

Iain stood up and threw a log on the fire where it spat and crackled before flaring up, the flames dancing in intricate patterns.

'That's all it takes Jack. One look at a woman and if she's the right one, a man can run through hell and high water to get away from her and lie to himself until he's blue in the face and tell himself all the reasons why it'll never work but, like it or not, he'll find himself running back to her before too long.' Iain let out a heavy sigh and dropped back into his chair.

Jack screwed up his eyes and scanned Iain's weathered features. 'You sound like you've tried running.'

'Still am Jack. Still am.'

They drank in silence, each deep in their own thoughts. Jack wasn't really sure how he felt. He knew he didn't want to marry Kim – although he wasn't ready to make that public knowledge just yet – and he knew he was seriously attracted to Lizzie, but as to having a relationship with her, well, how would that work? She lived in Scotland and clearly wanted to stay here, he lived in London. Would he consider moving?

'Do ... d'you know why they're separated?' Jack asked tentatively. For someone who was denying an interest he knew he was asking a lot of questions.

'Found him with another woman. Don't know the

94

details. Only know Lizzie walked out and came up here to stay with Jane. Laurellei had just gone on the market. She'd bought the place, left her job and moved up within a matter of weeks. He's been here several times trying to get her back but so far ...'

Jack screwed up his eyes and shook his head as if he were having trouble focusing. 'What is this stuff? I think it's blown my head off.'

'Auch no! Your head's still there. I can see it plain as day. Your sense ... well ... that's a different matter.'

'So this is where you're 'iding?' Pete said, poking his head round the door, closely followed by Ross and Phil.

Iain glowered at Pete.

'Don't think we've been introduced mate. I'm Pete.' Pete held out his hand.

Iain put his empty glass in it. 'Fill that if you don't mind, there's another bottle in that cupboard and get yourselves some.'

Pete grinned and did as he was asked. He filled Iain's glass and handed it back to him then poured some for Ross, Phil and himself. Pete downed his in one long swallow then made a gagging sound. 'Jesus Christ! That's strong stuff. What is it?'

'Home brew,' Jack grinned.

Ross and Pete fell into the two empty chairs and Phil pulled up a stool.

'This is my kind of home,' Ross said raising his glass to his lips.

Jack sighed deeply. 'I've just been thinking the same thing mate.'

Jane poured herself another drink from the makeshift bar and looked for Lizzie. She was on the dance floor and Jane waved at her to come over.

'What's up?' Lizzie asked, seeing the look on Jane's face.

'Nothing! That's the point. Have you seen Iain? I can't

find him anywhere.'

'No. The last time I saw him, he and Jack were headed off in the direction of his snug. That was almost two hours ago.' Lizzie didn't add that she'd been watching for Jack every few minutes since.

'Well, this playing hard to get game is working a treat isn't it? I've been flirting for ages and he hasn't even been around to see it. Clearly doesn't give a damn about me. Might as well get drunk and shag someone else instead.'

'Jane!'

'Well. What's the point? Obviously I was just a one night stand.'

'Actually, I think we both may have misjudged Iain Hamilton. You should have seen the look on his face when you flounced off with Pete when we arrived. He was ready to commit murder I swear.'

'Really?'

'Really! Maybe he thinks you're with Pete and he's keeping out of the way because he's jealous. Perhaps you do need to flaunt yourself with him a bit. You know, show him you're really keen on him. You *are* really keen on him aren't you?'

'Of course I am! You know damn well I am! I would have jumped on him when he walked up that bloody path if you hadn't told me not to.'

'My mistake. Sorry. Okay, plan B. Find Iain Hamilton and turn on the charm.'

'And how do I do that if he's secreted himself with Jack in his snug? You know they'll be drinking his home brew. I can't just walk in and sit on his lap now can I?'

Lizzie grinned. 'Actually, I think that's exactly what you should do. We've been drinking, and nothing brings out the protective instincts in a man like a tipsy woman.'

'Really? I thought it just brought out the, she's drunk I can screw her, instinct.'

Lizzie sighed. 'Yeah. Well. I think that depends on the man. Are you saying that you think Iain might have had sex with you because you were both drunk?'

'No! Well ... I've never seen him drunk and he seemed perfectly sober. I'd had a couple but oh, I don't know. I did it because I really like him but who knows why he did. You know what men are like, especially if it's offered to them on a plate, you're right about that and it was me who started it but ... well, I thought there was something between us, you know? Something had been sort of developing for ages and I thought that Valentine's was it. I thought he'd call after. I honestly did.'

'So why didn't you just call him?'

'What and make myself look even more stupid? No way. He should've called me.'

'Yeah. I do agree with that. There is a chance though that he thought you might not want him to. How did you leave it after ... well ... after ... you know?'

'After screwing you mean?' Jane threw Lizzie a mock shocked look. 'I don't remember exactly. We were in the barn and –'

'That part I remember, thanks.'

Jane sneered. 'Well, we were just lying there, cuddling, you know and then we heard Fraser call Iain. He got up and went into the snug and I remember he was gone for ages so I got dressed and ... well ... I went home.'

Lizzie was horrified. 'Why didn't you tell me this earlier? You went home? Without telling him?'

'He'd left me in the barn!'

'Yes but he could hardly tell Fraser that he'd left you there could he?'

'Why not? Oh, I don't know. I just expected him to call.'

'Okay. I think we may all have got our wires crossed. This needs sorting out. Come on.' Lizzie took Jane's hand and headed towards the snug.

'What are we going to do?'

'We're going to make it clear to Iain that you'd like a repeat performance.'

'I'd like several actually!'

Chapter Eight

'There you all are,' Lizzie said, peeping round the door of Iain's snug. 'We've been wondering where you'd got to.' She pulled Jane into the room with her and noticed both Iain and Jack sit up and fidget like naughty schoolboys caught up to no good.

Iain's eyes shot to Pete's face but he saw Pete was more interested in the contents of his glass than he was in Jane. He watched to see what Jane would do but she had her head slightly bowed and he couldn't see her eyes.

'We've come to say we may need looking after,' Lizzie said. 'We've had a little bit too much to drink and ... oops!'

Lizzie nudged Jane in her side making Jane stumble. Iain was on his feet and had caught her in his arms before anyone else even noticed.

Jane's surprise was genuine and when she cast her startled green eyes up to Iain's anxious hazel ones, she was so glad Lizzie had gone to plan B. She smiled invitingly and slid her arms around him as if to steady herself. 'Thanks,' she whispered, 'I do feel a little tipsy.'

He didn't speak but swallowed a lump in his throat and stared down at her, his eyes now filled with love and longing, his arms still firmly wrapped around her.

'I think she may need to lie down Iain. Could ... ooh!'

Lizzie watched as Iain swept Jane up and carried her towards the sitting room. She saw Jane grab the newel post at the foot of the stairs and shake her head.

'Bedroom,' Jane whispered.

Iain Hamilton didn't need to be told twice.

Lizzie beamed then realised Jack was staring at her. She met his eyes and a tingling sensation shot through her. She could feel the colour rushing to her cheeks and quickly lowered her gaze.

Jack screwed up his eyes. 'If I didn't know better, I'd

say that was planned.'

Lizzie raised her brows and cocked her head to one side. 'I have no idea what you mean.'

'I bet.' Jack pushed against the arm of the chair and slowly raised himself to his feet. He sauntered towards Lizzie, his eyes firmly fixed on her face and she felt like a sixteen year old with a crush.

Ross and Phil were snoring and Pete was still intent on staring into his glass.

Jack stopped within inches of her, towering over her. 'So,' he said his voice as soft as a down duvet, 'you may need looking after. I'd like to apply for that position.'

He raised one hand and pushed back a stray strand of brunette hair from Lizzie's face, holding it between his finger and thumb for what seemed to her an eternity.

'Um. No. I ... I'm fine. It ... it was Jane I was concerned about.'

The devilish grin, she'd come to recognise, spread slowly across his face.

'Clearly no need to be,' he drawled.

Lizzie's heart raced. She could feel his warm breath on her face. Smell a hint of his aftershave. Feel the heat from his fingers as they twisted in her hair like a curling brush. He moved closer so their bodies were almost touching. Almost, but not quite and Lizzie had to summon every ounce of her strength not to lean into him, wrap her arms around him and pull him to her. Oh God. She must keep in control of the situation. She could so easily get lost in his touch.

'I ... I ... '

He lifted her chin with his other hand and gently forced her to look at him. Those sapphire eyes held an entire galaxy of emotions and she felt as if she were being sucked into a maelstrom of whirling planets and exploding supernovas. This would outdo The Big Bang, she was sure of that.

'Jack,' she moaned as her arms slid around him. She

needed to hang on to something even if it was the cause of her dizziness.

'Yes,' he whispered kissing her forehead, his lips moving slowly to her eyelids, then her nose.

She parted her lips expectantly, wantonly. God she wanted him to kiss her again. So much so, that it physically hurt when he moved away from her.

'Not here,' he said his eyes now dark as a moonless night sky.

Lizzie gasped for breath. She hadn't realised she'd been holding it, waiting for his kiss.

'Wait here,' he said.

Lizzie slumped back against the wall as he left the room, her head still spinning. Pete briefly raised his eyes from his glass, nodded towards her, then stared into the glass again. Seconds later, Jack had returned, the keys to one of Iain's Land Rovers in his hand.

'Fraser said we can borrow it. I'll drive along the field track; he said it's easy to follow.' Jack took Lizzie's hand in his and led her out through the main front door so that they avoided the throng in the barn.

During the five minute drive to Laurellei Farm neither of them spoke. Jack seemed to be concentrating on driving and Lizzie's mind was racing with conflicting emotions.

What was she doing? She was going home alone with Jack and she knew what was going to happen. She wanted it to. God how she wanted it to. Ever since that moment on the station platform she'd felt drawn to him, swept up by him. And last night when he'd kissed her, she hadn't wanted him to stop.

This was madness. He was engaged, even if he did intend to break it off; she was still married. This could not happen.

Jack pulled up outside the farm and helped Lizzie down, his eyes scanning her face. She kept her head bowed, too frightened to look into those eyes that she knew would reflect her own wild passion.

He swept her up in his arms and she gave a little shriek.

'It worked for Iain,' he said, grinning.

Lizzie knew she should demand he put her down but the devilish grin seemed to reach his eyes and for some reason, she just couldn't get the words out. His eyes held hers and she knew the battle was lost before it had even begun. She wanted him, and if she said no now, she felt she would regret it for a long time to come. She had never felt like this about a man before – not even Max.

Jack pushed open the front door; no one locked their doors in Kirkedenbright Falls, and took the stairs two at a time, despite having Lizzie in his arms. He strode down the hall to his room and gently placed her on the bed, lying down beside her and slipping his arm around her to pull her close.

He leant in to kiss her and she parted her lips expectantly. Again, he pulled away from her. It crossed her mind that he might be playing a game at her expense and she tried to regain her composure. She was astonished when he spoke.

'You are sober really aren't you?' he asked, his lips only inches from hers.

'What?'

'Last night when I kissed you I'd had too much to drink and I wasn't really sure what was happening or why. I didn't think; I just acted on impulse. Today, once my memory came back – despite you trying to pretend none of it had happened – I knew why. That's why I told you I plan to break off the engagement. But I can't do it over the phone so I am still engaged.'

He had drawn slightly away from her, a concerned look etched on his face.

'I understand,' she said, not really sure she did, only knowing that every inch of her was screaming out for his touch.

'I really want you Lizzie. I've never wanted anyone so much in my life but ... I don't want to take advantage of you. I want you to know what you're doing. I ... I want you to be sure you want to do this.'

He brushed a finger across her face to push back a strand of hair and all her nerve endings seemed to react at once.

'I'm sure,' she gasped.

A deep sigh escaped him. 'From that moment on the platform it's as if ... well ... this sounds really corny but ... it feels as if this was meant to happen. I can't stop thinking about you, Lizzie. I even doodled a bloody heart on the window pane and –'

'You did that?'

'You saw it.'

'Yes but ... I thought your friends had done it as a joke.'

He shook his head. 'Nope. It was me. I'm like a besotted school boy. Can't remember the last time I felt like this. No. I can. I've never felt like this. This is crazy isn't it? Are you really sure?'

'I'm sure,' she said, a little testily. 'Are you?'

He had moved towards her but stopped as she spoke.

'Absolutely,' he said his eyes expressing a mixture of concern and growing passion.

'You seem to be doing everything possible not to.'

He lifted himself on to his elbow. 'What?'

'Well look at you. You carry me in here consumed with passion and lie down beside me then suddenly, it's as if you've dipped your toe in the water and discovered it's too cold to jump in. All you've done for the last five minutes is talk!'

He looked stunned. 'Well forgive me! I take this sort of thing seriously that's all and I've never cheated on anyone before. It ... it feels wrong and –'

'Well then don't! I'd hate you to do something you might regret.' Lizzie sat up with a jerk.

'I won't regret it! I was going to say, if you'd let me finish instead of jumping down my throat, that it feels wrong and yet so right. God, I've thought about nothing else since the first moment I saw you.'

'Really? And yet when you got back from the pub today you seemed to be doing everything you could to avoid me.'

Jack let out a sigh. 'I was. No. Let me finish. Steve said something on the way to the pub that ... well that made things awkward.'

'Oh?'

'He said it was obvious to everyone that I wanted to ... that I fancied you.'

'Wanted to ... what?'

'Oh come on. You know what guys are like.'

'Yes,' she said. 'I know exactly what guys are like. You're right, this is wrong. I'll leave.'

She wriggled to the edge of the bed but Jack grabbed her arm and gently pulled her back towards him.

'Don't go.'

And there was something in his tone that made her stay.

'I'm sorry Lizzie. My problem is I think too much.'

'Your problem is you talk too much.'

His eyes shot to her face. 'I really do want you Lizzie.' His voice crackled with emotion as he slid his arm around her waist and lifted her to him as if she were a feather.

She could see from his eyes that he did. 'Just shut up and kiss me.'

He bent his head towards her and this time, he didn't pull away.

When Jack's lips met hers Lizzie's senses reeled making her cling to him so tightly he could hardly move. She felt like a starving woman, being given food for the first time in days. The more he gave, the more she wanted. When he slid his tongue into her mouth her heart seemed to be pounding in her ears.

The deeper he kissed her the more she clung to him. Her entire body tingled as if a thousand tiny needles were embedded in her skin, sending little waves of electricity through all the meridian lines from the roots of her hair to the tips of her toes.

'Jack,' she moaned as his mouth moved to her neck. 'I

103

want you so much it actually hurts.'

His mouth came back to hers and his kiss was possessive, all encompassing, demanding. Lizzie couldn't stop now even if she wanted to; but she didn't want to. She felt him harden against her as his hand found her breast and caressed it.

He slid her dress down a few inches revealing her black lace strapless bra; his mouth leaving hers and his lips kissing their way down towards her breast. His fingers found the front fastening and he popped open the hooks. He lifted his head and gazed at her for a few seconds. Agonising seconds, whilst every fibre of her being seemed to be vying for his attention.

'You are so beautiful,' he said.

'So are you,' she moaned. 'Kiss me ple .... ase!'

His breath came in gasps. 'God Lizzie.' His mouth came down on hers possessively, passionately and with such longing that he lost all sense of reason.

Lizzie tugged at his shirt, her fingers fumbling with the buttons then pushing it off his shoulders as he moved one arm at a time to rid himself of it. Then her hands moved down to the kilt. She brushed her hand over him and he groaned before his lips crushed hers and his hand slid up her thigh and between her legs.

Lizzie had never wanted anything so much in her life and she tore at the buckle of his kilt as if her life depended on removing it. It fell away from him and she tossed it to the floor.

Lizzie wrapped her arms around him pulling him close and as he kissed her, his tongue probing, hers encircling his, shivers ran through her and she responded to him, leaving him in no doubt of what she wanted.

Jack slid his finger inside her and her nails dug into his back. Her head fell on to the pillow and she arched her back to move closer to him.

'I want you so badly Lizzie.'

His lips covered hers whilst his fingers sent a whole new

rush of emotions surging through her. 'Jack,' she gasped, between kisses, 'please!'

He slid inside her and she wrapped her legs around him pulling him deeper into her as they moved together in a frenzied rhythm until Jack lunged forward and gasped her name.

Lizzie heard it first; a faint buzzing sound. It stopped, then it began again. She blinked several times and tried to see the clock, suddenly realising she wasn't in her bed and her eyes shot to Jack's sleeping body.

Faint specks of daylight crept in above the curtain rail and she knew it was morning. She curled into Jack sighing heavily. They'd made love four more times last night and each time had been better than before. Each time giving and taking just a little bit more. For the first time in over seven years, she had made love with someone other than Max and it was a feeling of freedom and jubilation.

She heard the buzzing again and this time, she lifted her head from the pillow to look on the bedside cabinet. It was a mobile phone, and it sent a flashing beam towards the ceiling like a tiny searchlight. It was looking for Jack.

'Jack,' she said, shaking him awake, 'I think that's your phone.'

Jack turned to her and smiled. 'Morning gorgeous,' he said sleepily then lifted his head off the pillow. 'Shit! Sorry.'

He lent across her and she shifted beneath him so that they could change places. He grabbed the phone without looking to see who was calling and bent his head and gave Lizzie a quick kiss on her lips before answering it. The smile on his face quickly faded and he sat bolt upright.

'Shit! ... You're kidding? ... No! ... No! ... Of course ... .Is she okay?' his eyes met Lizzie's and held them. 'I'll get the first train back – or plane – if that's faster. Um. I'll let you know ... Where is she? ... Right ... Okay ... What?' He looked away from Lizzie. 'Yes ... yes I'm still here ... Fuck!

I mean ... Are they sure? ... Okay ... Yeah ... I ... I understand ... Okay ... I'll be there as soon as I can.'

Lizzie felt queasy. She scanned his profile. He didn't look at her.

'What is it?' she asked, not wanting to hear the answer.

'It's Kim,' he said, an odd inflection in his tone, 'my fiancée. She's been in an accident and is in hospital. I ... I have to go back!' His eyes flicked to hers briefly before he turned away. They were full of sorrow and his face wore an expression of guilt.

Lizzie gulped. She thought she'd throw up if she opened her mouth, so she didn't. She just nodded.

'Lizzie I ...' he tossed his legs out of the bed and sat on the edge, his back to her.

A dreadful feeling ran through her and her mind raced. It was as if he had turned his back on her emotionally as well as physically and it suddenly hit her that she had indeed been a one night stand. Even if Jack had meant what he said yesterday, which she very much doubted, that phone call had clearly made him realise his mistake. She had never seen anyone look so distraught.

She pulled back the covers and slid out of bed, grabbing her dress from the floor and hastily pulling it over her head.

Jack didn't move. He sat with his head in his hands.

Lizzie started towards the door, too upset to speak.

Jack's head shot up. 'Lizzie wait!'

Lizzie shook her head and held up her hand but she kept her back to him.

'Please Lizzie. You must understand. Last night was –'

'I know what last night was,' she snapped, grabbing the door handle and yanking it open. 'It was a final fling. You're engaged. I knew that.'

'No I ...'

Jack's voice trailed off, confirming her fears.

'That's okay,' she said struggling to keep her emotions in check. 'It was great fun but it's over. I don't have a problem with that. I don't know what the time is but there's a train around eleven, depending on the condition of the tracks I guess or you can get a plane from Inverness. I'll go and get changed.'

Lizzie dashed from the room. She'd thought last night was special; that it had really meant something; but clearly she'd been wrong. Jack had been about to tell her that it had just been a fling and although she realised that, and could just about say it, she couldn't bear to hear it from him.

As she reached her room, part of her hoped he would come after her, tell her she was wrong. Tell her last night really had been special and that they'd have a future together.

She sneered at her own stupidity. This was real life – and things like that didn't happen in real life. She couldn't blame Jack though, not really, even if he had lied. She'd known what she was getting herself into and she had jumped at it. She'd had several chances to back out, to walk away, but she hadn't. It was her fault as much as his, maybe more, she'd asked him to kiss her after all, she'd asked him to make love to her, and now she must suffer the consequences.

Jack let Lizzie go without saying another word. He was in shock, both from the call and from what Lizzie had said. Was that all it had been to her? A fling? He didn't know why he was so hurt. That's what he'd been telling himself for most of the last two days but last night in her arms, making love with her. It had been so much more to him. So much so, that it could have changed his life, until that call.

Jack collapsed on the bed and stared at his phone. He had to go back of course. Especially after what Kim's mum had just told him. Kim was very lucky, the doctors had said. It was a miracle.

Shit what was he going to do now? Did he still want to call off the wedding? No, of course not. He couldn't. He did love Kim and even if last night he'd seriously thought there might be a future for Lizzie and him, he realised now there wouldn't be.

He didn't know how but somehow he'd got to get back to Kim and put the last two days very firmly behind him. Whatever he thought he felt for Lizzie was over and whatever happened now, his future was definitely with Kim. So why did he feel as if his heart had just been ripped out?

Jack showered and dressed then threw his things in his bag and took one final look around the room. He'd felt more at home in this place over the last two days than he'd felt anywhere for a very long time. Leaving here would not be easy and he'd never forget Laurellei Farm – or Lizzie.

He swallowed the lump in his throat. Should he tell her how he felt? Tell her about Kim. Tell her last night had meant something to him. What was the point? She'd made it clear last night meant nothing to her. It was just sex. But the things she'd said, the things they'd shared. He'd never had sex like that. So all consuming, so intense, the need for one another so all encompassing. Surely she couldn't fake that, could she?

God, how had his life got so complicated in such a short space of time? Lizzie was right about one thing, as much as it hurt him to think it, last night was all they had, all they'd ever have and the thought depressed him more than anything had ever done before.

But his future was with Kim. He knew that now. Her mum's call had shocked him to his very core; knocked him for six and he still couldn't quite get his head together. This would take some getting used to but get used to it he would. Kim needed him – and he had to be with her.

He glanced at the window; the doodled heart with Lizzie's initial in it had almost completely disappeared. Perhaps that was some sort of sign. He shook his head, crossed the room to the door and closed it behind him as he left.

Downstairs, Lizzie was in the dining room talking to Pete and Phil but they all stopped talking and looked up as Jack walked in. She'd made toast and coffee and there was orange juice on the table.

'Shit mate,' Pete said. 'I'm so sorry. She's okay though?'

Jack was trying to catch Lizzie's eye but she was avoiding him.

'Yeah. Um ... some broken bones but she'll live. Look, I've got to go back obviously, but you can all stay on and –'

'Don't be mad mate. We'll all come back with you,' Phil said. 'Ross is calling the airport and station now to find the quickest way home and we've got an eight-seat cab on standby to take us to the station or drive to Inverness.'

Jack nodded. 'Okay. Thanks. Um, Lizzie. Lizzie!'

Lizzie left the room without looking back and Jack dropped his bag and followed her into the kitchen.

'I need to tell you something. I need to explain.' What was he doing? This was madness but he couldn't stop himself. 'Please Lizzie. I don't want to leave things like this. There's something you don't know ... we ... we need to discuss this –'

'No! We most definitely do not.'

'Yes we do!' I ... I'

'Jack. Please. You've got your life and I've got mine. You're engaged and I'm married –'

'I know but ...'

Lizzie sucked in her breath. 'There's no need to feel guilty about last night and don't worry I won't tell K ... your fiancée. Although I'm sorely tempted.'

Jack looked stunned.

'Do you know who I am Jack? Is that why you slept with me?'

Jack's brow creased. 'What ... what do you mean?'

'I'm Max's wife.'

Jack looked confused. 'Yeah I know. Lizzie listen –'

'No! You listen. Marshall is my maiden name. I used it when I started the business here. My husband is Max Bedford. Phil's colleague and, more importantly, the man your fiancée Kim Mentor had an affair with for several

109

months just over two years ago. She's the reason Max and I are separated!' She almost spat out Kim's name, this was the first time she'd used it in two years.

Jack felt for the second time this morning he'd been hit by a truck. Slowly it dawned on him. No wonder Lizzie could dismiss last night so easily. It really hadn't meant anything to her, well nothing more than getting her own back in some small way on her husband and Kim.

She was a bloody good actress. She'd actually made him believe she felt something for him. What a mug he was. She'd played him like a violin, then cut his heart strings and tossed him aside. She'd obviously planned the whole thing; probably before he even stepped off the train. Kim had slept with Lizzie's husband – although this was the first he had heard of it – so Lizzie had slept with him. All's fair in love and war.

'Humph! Well, I'm glad we've got that cleared up. Happy to have been of service to you. And there's no need to tell her. I'd planned to tell her myself anyway.'

Lizzie was confused. What did he mean? "Happy to have been of service to you." She'd only just found out who his fiancée was from talking to Phil and she'd been as shocked as Jack had seemed just now.

'You've got a bloody nerve! You're the one who lied to get me into bed.'

Jack looked enraged. 'I lied! Shit! You missed your calling. You should have been on the stage. I've never seen such good acting. You really sucked me in with all that "I'm so confused Jack. I want you Jack" I actually believed you cared!'

'I do ... did! It was you who pretended you were going to break off your engagement. You're not are you?'

Jack opened his mouth then closed it.

Lizzie turned away to try to hide the tears pricking at her eyes. She only just heard him when he answered.

'No. I'm not.'

'I knew it!' she hissed, her back still turned to him.

'What are you so angry about? You just slept with me to get revenge on Kim and your husband. Hardly makes you an angel.'

Ross burst in looking flustered. 'Jack! There's a flight from Inverness in an hour and a half. If we leave now we can make it. I've booked seats and the cab's on its way. Jack. C'mon mate.'

Lizzie swung round to face Jack. 'I did not! I ... oh what does it matter? I'll refund some of the money you –'

'Don't bother! You earned every penny believe me.' Jack spat out the words, his eyes travelling the length of Lizzie's body and his lips curled up at one side as if he had a nasty taste in his mouth. 'It's been a real experience.' He turned to leave.

'Jack!'

'What?' his voice was cold and his sapphire eyes were molten steel.

What could she say? He was going back to his fiancée. Lizzie turned away. She felt crushed. 'Nothing. Goodbye Jack.'

Jack turned and stormed from the room, slamming the door behind him.

Lizzie grabbed the table for support. It felt like Jack had stabbed her through the heart then twisted the knife for good measure. The last time she had felt like this was when she found her husband and *that woman* in bed together.

Pete knocked then peered round the door. 'We're off ... oh ... you okay? You look like shit.'

Lizzie forced a smile. 'Thanks,' she said, 'but I'm fine.'

'Okay. Look. We're really sorry about this but we can't let 'im go back on 'is own. It's 'is stag do after all.' Pete grinned sheepishly.

'I understand and don't worry. It's not a problem. I hope Ki ... she's okay.' She couldn't bring herself to say *that woman's* name again. 'I told Jack I'll refund some of the money.'

'Nah! You're okay. 'e's got plenty. We all 'ave. That's

one of the good things about working in the City.'

Lizzie nodded. 'But I'd like to.'

'Nah! Really. Don't. Tell you what. If you like. When Kim's better and all this is sorted, maybe we can call you and come up for a few days or something.'

Lizzie gulped. The thought of seeing Jack again was both a pleasure and a torture, although, she didn't think he'd come anyway after the way he'd just left. She nodded. 'Anytime. I am quite booked up in the summer but let me know and we'll sort something out.'

'You're on,' Pete said as Phil poked his head round the door.

'Cab's here. Bye Lizzie and thanks for everything.'

'I didn't do much,' she said.

Phil shrugged. 'You'd be surprised. I think once the dust settles we'll see you did a whole lot more than any of us expected. See you soon.'

Lizzie frowned. What the hell did that mean? Jeff and Steve popped their heads in.

'See you,' Jeff said.

'Thanks, and say goodbye to Jane,' Steve said.

Lizzie went to the window and watched as they got in the cab. Jack seemed to be lingering and Lizzie began to hope. Would he come back and take her in his arms again, just for a moment? Would he say he hadn't meant the things he'd said and he would end his engagement? Would he give her that incredible grin? Would he ...? God she really was stupid. It had been a one night stand. When would she just accept it?

Large white flakes fell from the sky and Lizzie watched as Jack raised his head and looked up at the snow-laden clouds. She found herself hoping that he wouldn't be able to leave, that the flight would be cancelled, trains would stop running, but what good would it do. It would just be delaying the inevitable. Still, she hoped he would look back, just once, even if he didn't smile. She held her breath.

Jack put his hand on the top of the cab door but still he

seemed to hesitate. Slowly, he began to turn his body back towards the farm, then stopped, his head still facing the cab. He made a decision and in one swift movement, he bent his head and got in the cab without looking back.

Seconds later, it pulled away taking Jack, and all Lizzie's fragile hopes, with it. Restraining an irrational urge to run after him, she watched until it disappeared into the distance, shrouded by a veil of snow, then, she slid to the floor and sobbed.

Chapter Nine

Iain Hamilton sat on the edge of the bed and watched Jane sleeping. He still found it hard to believe that such a gorgeous, vivacious young woman could possibly be in love with him but last night, she told him she was; had been for some time and even as she said it, he couldn't take it in. Part of him was sure he'd wake and find last night had all been a dream.

He wasn't sure when exactly he'd realised he was in love with her; shortly after she'd moved up from London, he suspected. But he'd kept his feelings hidden. He was, after all, thirteen years older, a working farmer with a grown up son – who would one day take over the farm, he hoped – and a fairly run down farmhouse that, he was convinced a young ex city girl like Jane, would want nothing to do with.

When Lizzie moved up, they had grown closer. Lizzie and Jane invited him to lunch or dinner at regular intervals and the three of them had become good friends. Still, Iain held back. He didn't want to ruin their friendship by making a stupid pass at her.

Then Fraser had come home and somehow, that had made Iain feel very old. Fraser and Jane got on like a house on fire and, Iain realised, they had much more in common than he and Jane; so he kept his emotions firmly in check.

There had been brief relationships since his wife had died but he had put his love life on hold for so long, that he didn't really know how to restart it in any case, and if Jane hadn't come on to him, he would still be doe-eyed watching her from afar.

At the Valentine's Day dance, it had been Jane who had made the first move – and the second and third, if he was honest. Even when they were kissing, Iain couldn't believe he could be this lucky and kept his hands firmly on her back, his arms tightly wrapped around her. Only when Jane took his hand and placed it on her breast did he realise that something else might happen between them. And something certainly had. Then she'd left without saying a word.

When he went back into the barn that night and she was gone, he thought she must have regretted it or that it was just meaningless sex to her, and he had just happened to be in the right place at the right time. After all, why would a woman as gorgeous and clever as Jane Munroe be interested in a forty-five year old farmer?

Every day he dialled her number then hung up without pressing the call button, and he'd driven to her croft or to Lizzie's at least twice a day but had always turned back, unable to think of an excuse to go in.

Before he made love with Jane, he wouldn't have needed a reason, he was always welcome. Now, he felt awkward and self conscious and he couldn't bring himself to face her, so he stayed away.

When he heard that six men from London would be staying at Lizzie's though, he knew he had to act. These were the sort of men Jane would be attracted to and he knew one, if not all of them would be attracted to her. How could any man not be? So he'd discussed it with Fraser, and Fraser had suggested the ceilidh.

Jane wriggled under the covers and Iain bent forward and kissed her gently on her lips. She opened her eyes and smiled.

'Good morning,' she purred, then saw he was dressed. 'How long have you been up? What time is it anyway?'

He kissed her again, this time lingering before answering. 'Good morning to you sweetheart. I've been up for an hour or so but I didnae wanna wake you. You look so gorgeous lying there that I let you sleep. It's about ten and, I hate to tell you this, but it's been snowing again for the last two hours.'

Jane sat up revealing her breasts and Iain sucked in his breath. It would take him a very long time to get used to that sight without it having a direct effect on him. He shifted slightly on the bed.

'I've made some coffee,' he managed to say. 'What would you like for breakfast?'

Jane rose up to her knees exposing her full nakedness and she leant her body against him. 'You!' she said, sliding her hand down to his lap then raising her eyebrows, 'and it seems we both have the same thing in mind.'

'Good Lord! You're insatiable woman,' he said, his eyes filling with longing for her.

'Are you complaining?'

'Definitely not,' he said, gently pushing her back on to the bed and kissing her, no longer needing any encouragement to put his hands on her breasts.

It was almost eleven thirty when Iain dropped Jane at Lizzie's and Jane rushed into the kitchen, shaking the snow from her hair, half expecting to find Lizzie slaving over the stove. She stopped in her tracks when she saw her sitting at the kitchen table, staring into space.

'What's going on?' Jane asked making her way to the Aga as usual. 'Why's it so quiet? Where are the guys?'

'Gone,' Lizzie said.

Jane switched on the kettle. 'Gone? What d'you mean, gone? Gone out for the day?'

'Precisely that. Gone. No longer here. Ran back to London. Well, flew actually but who cares?'

Jane picked up on Lizzie's tone and knew something bad had happened. 'Why did they go? Why didn't you call me?'

Lizzie sighed deeply and rubbed at her eyes and Jane could see she'd been crying. She rushed to her side and threw her arms around her.

'What's happened? Are you okay? Tell me Lizzie!'

Lizzie gulped. 'Oh God!' she said, 'where do I start? I told you this bloody booking was a mistake and would end in disaster! Why do I always let myself get talked into things I know will come back and bite me? If I had just said

116

no to Max when he asked me to take the booking, none of this would have happened.'

'Lizzie! What's wrong?'

Lizzie shook her head. 'It's not your problem Jane. I'll deal with it.' She forced a smile. 'Would you some like coffee? I'll make some then you can tell me all about last night and –'

'I'll make it and last night can wait. Tell me what's happened right now!'

Lizzie sighed again. 'Well, needless to say, like the idiot I am I ended up in bed with him.'

She didn't need to say his name, Jane knew she meant Jack.

'And ... that was bad because ...?'

'Actually it was bloody magnificent. That's the problem. Everything was going so well – or at least – I thought it was; then his phone rings this morning and all hell breaks loose.'

The kettle boiled and Jane made herself a cup of tea. She filled the coffee machine and switched it on for Lizzie. Lizzie always drank coffee in the morning. 'What do you mean, all hell breaks loose?'

Lizzie shoved her hair back from her face and rubbed her eyes. 'It seems his fiancée has been in an accident – no don't worry, she's alive, just a few broken bones, but he says he's got to go home and naturally, they all go with him.'

'Oh my God! Poor Jack. That's only to be expected I suppose,' Jane said cautiously. She pulled out a chair and sat next to Lizzie.

'Oh I know. It's just ... well ... I know it's my fault and everything but I really didn't think it was just a one night stand and when he said it was I just ... flipped.'

Jane took Lizzie's hand in hers. 'Bloody Hell! It's my fault. I persuaded you it wouldn't hurt. I'm soooooo sorry. Did ... did he actually come right out and say it? The shit!'

'What? No. Actually it was me who said it, but he was

going to, I could tell, he was trying to build up to it, you know, let me down easy and I couldn't deal with that so I said it had been great but I knew it was only for one night. I may have said something else. I'm not sure really. I was so stupidly upset, I'm not totally sure who said what, or when, to tell you the truth. But I am sure of one thing. He lied about breaking off the engagement, either that or when he got the phone call this morning and found out she was hurt, he realised he didn't want to. I don't know, but he did come right out and say that! I asked him and he said he wasn't going to call it off!'

'The bastard! And I thought he was a saint.'

'Oh and you haven't heard the best bit. Guess who his fiancée is?'

Jane screwed up her eyes and shook her head.

'Only Kim fucking Mentor!'

Jane's mouth fell open. 'You're kidding?'

'Nope. Phil told me just before they all left. Apparently, it was Phil who introduced Jack and K ...*that woman* two years ago, well they were in the pub and she joined them or something. Must have been just after Max ended it with her. How bloody ironic.'

'Bloody Hell! Can you believe that? You couldn't make this stuff up.'

'I know. It's as if that bloody woman is my nemesis or something. This sounds awful I know but part of me wishes she had more than a few broken bones.'

Jane nodded. 'Couldn't agree with you more.'

Jane got up and poured Lizzie a coffee. She sat back down and they sipped their drinks in silence both deep in thought.

'So ... how was it left then? Between you and Jack I mean?'

Lizzie bit her bottom lip and rubbed one eye. 'Badly. I'm not really sure what happened. I ... I thought that telling him I knew it was a one nighter would sort of, I don't know, ease things, you know? Instead, it seemed to get

118

worse from there. He came into the kitchen just before he left and I thought he was trying to make peace or something then I told him about her and Max – no Jane, don't say it – I didn't do it to be bitchy, it was before he was going out with her so it wouldn't matter to him but, well, everything happened so fast and we were both angry and said things and ... and he seemed to be saying that I had used him to get back at her and Max! And, that I was the bad guy in this whole bloody thing, not him. Oh Jane I'm so confused.'

'You're confused! Why didn't you tell him it wasn't like that? You didn't know who she was when you slept with him did you?'

'No! I would have stayed well clear if I had, believe me, even though I couldn't stop thinking about him.'

'So why didn't you say that?'

'I did! Well. Maybe I didn't. It all seemed to get so out of control, you know, me saying one thing and him hearing something entirely different. How does that happen? How can two people hear the same words and get totally different meanings from them? One minute I was in his arms blissfully happy, the next, the whole world's come crashing down on me. God! If you'd seen the look he gave me when he walked out. I wanted to curl up and die.'

'That bad?'

'Treble it and you wouldn't even be close to how bad!'

'So ... what are you going to do?'

Lizzie looked perplexed. 'Do? Nothing. What can I do? It was a fling. We both knew it, except I saw the rose petals and champagne as usual whereas he just saw a cake on a plate.'

'Oh Lizzie. I really am sorry.'

Lizzie shrugged. 'C'est la vie – and all that crap. I'll get over it I guess.' She let out a strangled laugh. 'It did one bit of good though, I suppose.'

'Yeah. What's that?'

'It made me realise I'm no longer in love with Max. I couldn't have done it if I was.'

'Well. Thank heavens for small mercies. At least that's something right?'

Lizzie glanced down at the wedding band and diamond solitaire, sparkling mockingly up at her from the third finger of her left hand. She took a deep breath and in one swift movement, she pulled the rings from her finger and shoved them on to the third finger of her right hand. Then she let out the breath she was holding in a long, deep sigh.

Jane looked doubtful. 'Are you sure?'

Lizzie nodded. 'It's time. And it's time I stopped being so stupid about men. I've got a good life here – when the roof's not leaking – and I must put the past behind me once and for all. I still love Max but I'm no longer in love with him and there's no going back. It's time we both accepted that and moved on.'

'Good for you!'

Lizzie stood up abruptly, almost knocking the chair over in her haste. 'And I'm not going to put it off for a moment longer.' She strode towards the hall.

'What are you going to do?' Jane asked, concerned by her friend's sudden rash behaviour.

'I'm going to call Max and tell him.'

'Over the phone?' Jane was a little surprised, although she completely understood that it might be easier that way.

'Of course not. I'm going to see him in London.'

Jane jumped up so quickly that her chair did fall over and the loud thud it made when it hit the floor made Alastair jump from his basket and give out a loud, startled bark.

'Sorry boy,' Jane said, ruffling his furry head, then racing into the hall after Lizzie. 'Lizzie wait! Don't do something you might regret later. It's been snowing all morning so there's going to be transport problems before too long. Why not think about it – just for today and if you still feel the same tomorrow – I'll go with you if you want, for moral support.'

Lizzie hesitated, her hand on the phone.

120

'Please Lizzie. You're really upset and you're angry. Don't take out your anger on Max when it's directed at someone else.'

'You've changed your tune. You're the one who's always telling me I should end it with Max once and for all.'

'Yes, and I still think you should but not like this. Not today. Look, it's twelve o'clock. Let's open a bottle of wine and get drunk watching weepy movies.'

'Thanks but no thanks. I'm having enough trouble keeping it together sober. I suppose you're right though, it can wait until tomorrow.'

Lizzie didn't want to say that part of the reason she had decided to go to London today was because she didn't want to be in the house. Jack's face seemed to be everywhere she looked and in just two days he'd created more memories for her than Max had done, visiting her over the last two years. She really must be losing her mind.

'It'll be okay Lizzie. Everything will work out fine, you'll see.'

'You always say that and it never does. No, I've just got to keep busy that's all, keep my mind off it and focus on something else. I'll start cleaning their rooms and washing the bedding and ... oh Hell! No I won't. Open the bottle. And then, tell me all about last night and Iain. I take it this time he will call.'

Jane beamed. 'Abso..bloody..lutely!'

'Hello-o!'

Iain Hamilton's deep voice startled both Jane and Lizzie. They were curled up on the sofa in the second sitting room which housed the television, tartan throws wrapped over their legs, boxes of tissues balancing on their laps, tears streaming down their faces.

'We're ... in ... here,' Jane called out between sobs.

Iain stood in the doorway, his solid frame almost filling it.

'I knocked but no one ... Oh God! What's happened? What's the matter with you?' He rushed to Jane's side.

Jane sobbed again and pointed to the television. They were watching "The Last of The Mohicans". She pressed the pause button.

Iain relaxed visibly. 'A film! I thought something had happened! Where are the men?'

Lizzie let out a strangled sob and Jane put her arm around her.

'They've gone back to London. I'll explain it later,' Jane said, shaking her head to warn Iain off the subject. 'What are you doing here anyway? Don't you have a farm to run?' She was grinning between her tears.

'Seems I couldnae keep my mind on it. Fraser can cope for a wee bit. Thought I'd pop over and take a look at the boiler Lizzie said was playing up.'

Another strangled sob as Lizzie remembered the radiator, the heart, Jack naked, Jack ... the flood gates opened and Lizzie got up and fled from the room with a handful of tissues pressed firmly against her nose.

Iain looked stunned. 'What did I say?'

'She just needs a bit of time on her own I think,' Jane said, patting the sofa to indicate he should sit next to her and when he did, she curled up to him and he put one strong arm around her and kissed her on the forehead.

He still couldn't believe how good it felt to put his arm around this beautiful woman who loved him and it sent a strange sensation shooting through him. A mixture of pride, love and pure, raw passion.

He lifted her chin with the fingertips of his free hand and stared into her huge, green, watery eyes. He brushed a stray tear from her cheek with his thumb and an overwhelming urge to kiss her took him almost by surprise. He bent his head and his mouth came down on hers in a gentle kiss, slowly building into something more. He remembered where he was and reluctantly pulled away, his hazel eyes filled with longing.

'Seems I cannae keep my hands off you woman,' he said, his voice thick with passion.

Jane smiled at him and he nearly threw caution to the wind but what she said stopped him.

'Lizzie is really upset over Jack. I won't go into details but something happened between them and now this morning, it seems as if it meant nothing to him and he's gone back to his fiancée in London.'

Iain was silent for a moment. 'Well, I only met the man last night but, apart from myself,' he kissed Jane on the forehead again, 'I've never seen anyone so besotted with a woman as he was with Lizzie.'

Jane glanced up at him. 'Really? Well, I thought so too. I think we all did. But either he's a really good actor or he was besotted and then this morning when he heard about the accident, he realised he loved his fiancée more.'

Iain held her away from him, his eyes filled with concern. 'What accident?'

Jane shook her head. 'Oh, of course, you don't know. Well Jack's fiancée was involved in an accident and she's in hospital. She's okay but Jack had to go back, which I think was the right thing to do but Lizzie said he said he isn't going to break off the engagement now so –'

'What? Are you saying he told Lizzie he was calling off the wedding – for her?'

'Yes and no. I mean, he had told Lizzie that he was going to call off the wedding but he didn't say it was because of her, he said he'd realised he didn't love his fiancée enough to marry her or something, which I also think makes sense but Lizzie thinks he lied and used it to get her into bed ... oh!'

Iain's face darkened with rage. 'You mean the man took our Lizzie to bed then ran back to his other woman this morning?'

Jane looked sheepish. 'Yes, but I hadn't meant to tell you that bit. Don't tell Lizzie I told you, she'll be so embarrassed, you know what she's like ... and ...

123

technically, Lizzie was the other woman and –'

'Auch. It doesnae matter who was the other woman. What matters is the man shouldnae ha' done it. I wouldnae ha' believed it of him!'

Jane loved the way Iain reverted to his Scottish tongue when he was really fired up. Last night when they were in bed he'd said several things to her in his Scots drawl that she couldn't quite understand but which had sounded really sexy in the heat of passion.

'I agree with that ... but ... actually, it does matter who the other woman was – and you're never going to believe this – you know Max had an affair with his secretary ...'

'Aye, that's why Lizzie came up here two years ago.'

'Well ... and even I still can't believe this ... it was the same woman. Kim Mentor, the woman who had the affair with Max is now Jack's fiancée!'

Iain blinked several times in disbelief. His voice now calm he said, 'What the hell do they put in the water down there? I've only been to London the once but it's a pretty big place. There must be more than one woman to choose from.'

Jane shook her head. 'I know. It seems bizarre but actually, the City's a pretty small place. Everyone seems to know everyone else – or at least, someone who does, if you see what I mean. Kim was Max's secretary so that's how they had the affair and Phil, one of the guys on this weekend, works with Max at the bank, so he knows Kim and from what little sense Lizzie was making earlier, Phil told Lizzie today that he and Jack were in their local pub and Kim came in and joined them. It must have been just after Max had ended the affair with Kim because Lizzie had found out.'

'Clear as mud,' Iain said, pulling Jane back into his arms and hugging her tightly to him. He was very glad she had left London. 'So, Phil knew Lizzie was Max's wife and he knew Kim was the bit on the side and now Jack's fiancée and he still came here?'

'Oh. Um No. I mean. I don't think Phil knows about the affair. They had booked somewhere else but it burnt down or something so this was a last minute thing. I think Max was just being Max and trying to be the hero. He knew Lizzie was a bit short of cash and he knew the guys were looking for somewhere to go so he suggested here. You know, Max saves the day as usual, and I don't believe for one minute that Max knows Kim is Jack's fiancée. There's no way he would have let the guys come here if he knew that. Bit too close for comfort, especially as he's trying to get Lizzie to go back to him.'

'So it's all just one huge coincidence, is that what you're saying?'

'Or fate ... '

Iain tipped his head to one side so that he could see Jane's face. 'So you believe in Kismet sweetheart?'

Jane glanced up at him. 'Don't you? If my aunt hadn't left me the croft and if I hadn't spent the summers there as a child and had happy memories of it, I wouldn't have come up here and if I hadn't come up here I wouldn't have wanted to live here and if I hadn't decided to live here – I wouldn't have met you, and last night wouldn't have happened, or Valentine's night, and –'

Iain's kiss interrupted her. 'Well,' he said, several minutes later, 'then I'll believe in Kismet too and I would have asked you over for a repeat performance tonight, only Fraser –'

'Oh God! Is Fraser upset? I didn't think –'

'Sweetheart, no!' He kissed her on her nose. Fraser is very happy for us both. In fact, his very words were, "I don't know what took you so long, dad, Jane's perfect for you" and that's a direct quote.'

Jane's mouth fell open. 'Fraser said that? Really?'

Iain stroked her cheek with his fingers. 'Really. What I was going to say was, that Fraser's invited some friends over tonight – one of whom is a wee lassie he's definitely got his eye on, and if last night was anything to go by, I don't think having his dad and his dad's sweetheart upstairs making love all night is going to work somehow.'

Jane smiled coyly. 'You could always come over to me,' she said, fiddling with the top button of his shirt.

Iain shifted his position and started to get up, pulling Jane to her feet and wrapping his arms around her. 'That's exactly what I was hoping you'd say, sweetheart,' he said, kissing her again. He took her hands in his to stop her undoing his shirt button. 'Now you keep your hands to yourself until tonight lassie or I'll have no option but to ravage you here and now.'

Jane grinned devilishly. 'I rather like the sound of that,' she said, leaning her body into him.

Iain's eyes were dark with passion. 'I'll be round at six,' he said reluctantly pulling himself away. 'I don't suppose Lizzie will want me messing around with the boiler right now. Tell her I'll do it whenever she wants.' He blew Jane a kiss from the doorway and turned to go, then turned back. 'Will Lizzie be all right though? On her own I mean. As much as I love you, if she needs you to be here I'll understand. I can spend the evening under a cold shower.'

Jane's eyes filled with love for the large, rugged man. For someone built like a mountain and with hands to match, he was incredibly gentle and kind.

'Do you know how much I love you Iain Hamilton?' she said huskily.

He was across the room in one second flat and had swept her up in a kiss so passionate it made her head spin.

'As much as I love you,' he said when he finally pulled away. 'And Fraser's right – about everything.'

'Oh God, Iain,' Jane gasped still getting her breath from that kiss. 'I'll speak to Lizzie and call you but either way, if you don't make love to me at some point today, I think I'll go mad.'

'Me too sweetheart. I want to make love to you every day for the rest of my life. Call me as soon as you can. I love you Jane Munroe.' And with that, he was gone.

Jane stared after him for at least ten minutes. She felt enveloped in love as if some fairy godmother had wrapped an invisible cloak of it around her. Unless she was very much mistaken, Iain Hamilton had just told her he wanted to spend the rest of his life making love to her. That was almost as good as a marriage proposal and it took her a further five minutes before she had her emotions under control enough, to go and find Lizzie.

Chapter Ten

Lizzie had made a decision. She knew what Jane and Iain were like and she knew that they would be worried about her and that wasn't fair to them. She could see how much in love they were and was astonished that she hadn't seen it before.

Jane had always been there for her; a shoulder to cry on every time Max came up to visit and Lizzie had ended up sleeping with him, then getting mad at herself for doing so when the whole sordid business of the affair came back and hit her like a punch to her stomach.

When Lizzie had discovered Max and *that woman* in bed together, she'd instinctively fled to Jane and Jane had taken her in without a second thought, had comforted her through the long and lonely nights when Lizzie felt as if her entire body was being physically ripped apart, limb by limb and jealousy was eating at her soul.

Jane had never judged her, even though Jane thought Lizzie should end things with Max, she had never criticised when Lizzie had fallen back into his arms. Jane was a true friend and Lizzie loved her for it. Now Lizzie should be a true friend to Jane and give her and Iain time to be together, without Lizzie wallowing in the background, like a moody child.

She had checked with the airport; planes were still flying despite the snow, although they were subject to delays. If she didn't leave soon, she might not get away and although she'd told Jane she would think it over, she knew she couldn't spend the night alone at the farm. Not tonight. Neither would she ruin Jane and Iain's night by asking Jane to stay.

No, Lizzie had decided. She would go to London and she would talk things through with Max and, if she was feeling really brave, she might even visit her solicitor to start the divorce proceedings. Oddly enough, the thought of this made her feel slightly better and by the time Jane came into the kitchen, Lizzie's mood had lifted enough for her to smile without forcing it. 'Iain looks like a love sick puppy,' she said, teasingly.

Jane grinned, 'More like a love sick bear, although I'm not sure "love sick" is totally flattering. Sounds like he's caught some disease.'

Lizzie grinned back. 'I've made tea if you want some – and I've made a decision but I need to ask you a favour.'

Jane poured herself some tea. 'Sure, what is it?'

'Will you look after Alastair for a few days and pop over and feed the animals. No, don't say it. I know you think I should wait but I've calmed down now and thought it through and it really is the best thing for me to do. There are flights, and if you're okay with taking Alastair, I was thinking of getting one this evening. That way, I can talk to Max tomorrow and if things go well, I can go to the solicitor first thing Monday morning to start the divorce proceedings.'

Jane nearly spat out her tea.' My God Lizzie! You really are going for it aren't you? Of course I'll take Alastair and feed the animals but ... are you really, really sure?'

Lizzie nodded. 'Yes. Deep down, I know that even if I can forgive Max – which I still can't and it's been over two years already – I'll never fully trust him again and it would never work. I think I've been clinging to our relationship because I didn't think I'd ever fall in love again but ... and I know this is even more stupid ... this business with Jack has shown me that I will, or at least, I can.'

Jane squeezed her friend's hand across the kitchen table. 'That's good. So something positive has come out of it. Are you sure you don't want me to come with you? Iain will happily look after Alastair and the animals. I would be happy to go.'

'I know you would and I really appreciate that but it's time I started standing on my own two feet. I'm a thirty-two old woman, as you constantly remind me,' Lizzie said, grinning at Jane, 'and I need to get on with my life. Things didn't work out with Jack and it's going to take me a little while to deal with all that but if, no, when, I do meet someone else, at least I'll be free, both emotionally and literally to start a real relationship. As you said, a wedding and engagement ring don't exactly shout, "I'm free", do they?'

Jane got up and walked round the table to hug Lizzie. 'Things will work out Lizzie, you'll see. It'll be fine.'

Lizzie raised her eyebrows. 'I told you Jane, you always say that and it never is.'

'Oh I don't know, Iain Hamilton has just said he wants to make love to me for the rest of his life, so I'd say that's working out pretty well, so far.'

Max was lounging on the balcony of his penthouse apartment which overlooked the Thames, enjoying the March sunshine. He was reading The Times as he always did on a Saturday afternoon and he'd seen the article about the snow they were having in Scotland.

His mind wandered back to the Christmas and New Year holiday he'd recently spent with Lizzie and how they'd been snowed in for several days. Several sex-filled days when Max had begun to hope that, at last, Lizzie had forgiven him and would come back to London so that they could resume married life.

He wasn't sure why those days had felt different, to be honest, whenever he'd gone to visit Lizzie they'd always ended up having sex, great sex but then, sex had never been their problem, at least, sex between them had never been a problem. What had been a problem was that for some reason, that even Max couldn't quite understand, he still wanted sex with someone else too.

When he'd fallen in love with Lizzie – and he definitely had fallen in love with her – he'd never have married her if he hadn't, he'd only wanted to be with her, day in, day out, for the first two years at least, but he still turned to look when other women walked by.

By the third, although he still loved Lizzie and wanted to make love to her, he'd also started wondering what it would be like to sleep with some woman or other who happened to cross his path and whom he found attractive. He never did anything about it though, they were just thoughts.

In the fourth year, Kim Mentor came to work for him and Max found her very attractive. Not in the same way as Lizzie, Kim and Lizzie were about as opposite as they could be, but in a base, animal instinct, sex driven way.

Lizzie was sensual and sexual in an understated way. Kim was sex on legs. Nothing more, nothing less. Everything about her oozed sex, from her tiny waist to her shapely, swaying hips and her long gym toned, spray tanned legs but mainly it was her voluptuous breasts, all natural and not an ounce of man-made synthetic fibre in them. Just thinking about them now was enough to give him the start of an erection.

He shifted uncomfortably in his reclining chair and adjusted his jeans. He was definitely a boob man. Lizzie's were nice, a shapely 34D but they had nothing on Kim's. Kim's were enough to drive a man wild.

He could remember the first day he'd seen them. It was July, a hot sticky day outside even at nine in the morning but cool and pleasant in his air-conditioned office and he was reclining in his chair, feet on his desk, closing a deal over the phone.

He was irritated that his new temporary secretary was late. He demanded all his staff be in the office by eight-thirty at the latest and was going to call personnel and give them a bollocking just as soon as he finished this call. He was just about to hang up when there was a knock at his open, glass door and Kim sashayed in, like a snow-queen on heat.

Tall, waist length blond, almost ice-white, hair, long white painted fingernails, white stilettos and a tight fitting, fairly short, fairly low cut white cotton dress, belted at her tiny waist. The dress had two thin straps about an inch wide, under which he could make out the straps of her white lace bra and as she leant over his desk to pass him a cup of espresso, the straps pulled against the pressure of her ample breasts like restraining ropes on heavy cargo; he actually thought they might break under the strain.

Max got an eyeful. His feet slid off the desk, taking a file of papers with them and he dropped the phone. Kim didn't say a word. She put the coffee on the desk, glanced up at him under heavy mascara coated lashes and smiled through generous, glossy, blood red lips, exposing just a hint of perfect white teeth. It was both an invitation and a challenge and Max swallowed the lump in his throat.

Kim sauntered seductively around his desk, bent down; causing the already short dress to ride higher up her long tanned legs, bent forward and picked up the file and the phone. Again that look, again that smile, the glossy, blood red lips only feet from his crotch and Max had to grab his Financial Times from his desk to try to cover his erection.

In his haste he knocked over the coffee she'd just brought him. He jumped up, bumping chests with the now standing Kim as he did so and her breasts brushed against the fine cotton of his shirt. She didn't move away and for the first time in his life, Max felt cornered, but the proximity of her body sent a rush of heat coursing through every last inch of him. They should take whatever Kim had and bottle it – it would outsell Viagra.

It was like leading a lamb to slaughter. Less than two weeks later Kim had taken Max to her bed and Max's new temporary secretary had become Max's new permanent secretary – and a lot more besides.

Max had improved Kim's dress sense. Kim had subdued Max's commonsense and the affair went on for almost six months until that fateful day when Lizzie had come back early from a weekend staying with Jane in Scotland and had found Kim Mentor with Max, in Max and Lizzie's bed.

The telephone rang bringing Max back to the present. He fidgeted to try to get comfortable and picked it up.

'Hi Max. It's Lizzie. Can you spare me a minute? Max? Are you there?'

'Sorry. Yes. Miles away. I was just thinking about you actually. I read you've got snow up there. Not like last time I hope.'

'Um. No. No it's not too bad. Um. Are you free tomorrow?'

He sat upright. 'Yes. Why? Is there a problem? Are you okay? Do you want me to come up?'

Lizzie sucked in her breath. This was going to be more difficult than she thought.

'Yes and No. I'm okay but Ja ... the guys have gone back to London. The bridegroom-to-be's fiancée was in an accident and is in hospital so Ja ... they've all gone back.'

Max picked up on her strange tone. There was something she wasn't telling him. 'Oh. That's a bit of bad luck. Will it affect you, financially I mean? If you're going to be out of pocket I'll see you right, sweetheart. You did this for me after all.'

'I did it for the money Max.' How like him, she thought. 'I have offered to refund them part of it but they refused.'

'Quite right too. It's not your fault after all. So ... why do you want to know if I'm free tomorrow?'

'I'm coming down and I'd like to talk to you tomorrow, if that's okay?'

Max tossed his newspaper on the floor and swung his legs off the recliner. At last! He thought. She was coming back to him at last.

'Of course it's okay darling. You should know you don't have to ask. I'm here for you. I'll always be here for you. What time do you get in tomorrow? I'll pick you up from the airport.'

'Actually, I'm coming down tonight but I'll grab a taxi and stay in an hotel -'

'You'll do no such thing! I'll pick you up and you'll stay

133

here. Don't argue. I insist.'

'Max! Please. I really think it would be better if you didn't and I'm staying at an hotel. This ... this is going to be difficult and ... well, I think it's best if we have our own space.'

Max felt like he was a car in a crusher. He'd thought she was coming home but now ... well ... it sounded as if she was going to be delivering unpleasant news. Had she really meant what she'd said on the phone only a few short weeks ago, that it was finally over? He should have taken her away for Valentine's instead of just sending flowers and perfume. An entire room full of flowers and a Valentine's Gift Set of her favourite Chanel No 19 perfume but just flowers and perfume nonetheless.

'Well. That sounds ominous! All the same Lizzie, I will pick you up and you will stay here. You can't afford to be wasting money on hotels, unless you let me pay for it. I'll pay for the flight too.'

'Max no!' One thing she had to say for Max, he was generous with money. When she told him she'd decided to buy Laurellei Farm, and he'd realised he couldn't talk her out of it, Max insisted on buying her share of their home in Blackheath for an overinflated figure so that she would have cash to buy the place outright and pay for the work to be done. It was even enough to leave her a reasonable amount to tide her over until she got the business up and running.

'Lizzie yes! Now stop arguing with me and go and get yourself ready. I know what you're like; you'll have to check everything four times before you leave. Is Jane looking after Alastair?'

'Yes.'

'Good. Then go and get your flight and text me the details. I'll pick you up and we can take it from there. Here or an hotel is up to you − but I'm paying for everything either way. See you soon sweetheart and safe journey.'

Lizzie hung up. If only Max hadn't cheated on her. In

every other way, he really was the perfect man – apart from Jack. No! Jack was definitely not the perfect man and she must stop thinking that he was.

So, Max thought, after hanging up the phone. It seems there's a chance that I'm going to be a single man again and for some reason, that didn't give him any pleasure at all.

He hadn't been a saint since Lizzie had left him. He was a man after all and he had needs. Seeing Lizzie every few months wasn't nearly enough and he took his pleasure where he could get it.

He'd even considered seeing Kim again but he soon put that out of his mind. If Lizzie discovered that, she'd never take him back so he got Kim transferred to the legal department, far enough away not to be a distraction but close enough so that he could get the occasional look. A sort of pleasurable torture.

He'd heard from someone but he couldn't remember whom, that she had started dating and she'd told him herself a few months later, that it was pretty serious. He couldn't help but feel just a twinge of lust for her exquisite body. When she'd come to his office, late one evening, just before last Christmas to tell him that she was getting engaged, he wasn't sure whether it was to gloat, to give him a chance to prevent it or just to have one final romp for old time's sake.

She'd flirted with him, there was no doubt about that and he'd been sorely tempted, especially when she'd joked about being his "Christmas stocking," but it just so happened that he had planned a surprise visit to Lizzie for the Christmas holidays and he was leaving the next day, so he'd told her he was very happy for her but he had to dash and he'd run like hell as if a pack of wolves were chasing him.

When he reached the lift and took a quick glance over his shoulder, he could see through the glass panels of his office that she was leaning back provocatively against his desk, legs slightly apart and those incredible breasts of hers, standing out like an oasis to a parched man in a desert.

The lift bell pinged and he stepped through the opening doors feeling he'd had a lucky escape and also, feeling a small twinge of sympathy for her fiancé to be. Kim, he'd realised, was one of those women who would never be satisfied with her lot, no matter how good it might be.

Jane called Iain to tell him Lizzie was going to London and he insisted on taking them to the airport.

'There's something I need to get in Inverness so I'll drop you and then pick you up a wee bit later if that's okay. You can have coffee with Lizzie whilst she waits for her flight.'

'If you don't mind, that would be great. We've both had a few glasses of wine and whilst I don't mind driving home across the fields after a drink, I won't drive on public roads and I'd hate Lizzie to have to get a taxi.'

'Auch I wouldnae hear of it woman. What time's her flight?'

'Six.'

'Perfect. Then I'll come straight back to yours, if that's still okay?'

Jane smiled even though Iain couldn't see it over the phone. He seemed to be taking a while to accept that she wanted him as much as he wanted her, no matter how many times she'd told him last night, that she had loved him for almost three years, since shortly after they'd met, in fact.

'I wouldn't say it's okay Iain,' she said in her sexiest voice, 'I'd say it's an absolute necessity.' She heard him suck in his breath on the other end of the line. 'And Iain,' she purred, 'have something to eat in Inverness, the only thing your mouth will be touching tonight ... is my naked body.'

She was sure he dropped his mobile phone; in any event, the line went dead.

Iain pulled up at Jane's house at six thirty. Lizzie's flight had been on time so they'd left her just after five – Iain had got back from Inverness in time to wave her through the departure gate with Jane – and the traffic from Inverness had not been too heavy.

They'd stopped to pick up Alastair, his basket and a few of his favourite toys from Laurellei Farm and after several kisses in the kitchen and the hall and leaning against the Land Rover, they had eventually made it to Jane's still fully clothed, if a little dishevelled.

Inside, Jane settled Alastair whilst Iain lit the fire, bringing in extra logs to put beside it so that he wouldn't have to stop what he was doing and go and get some more. He also brought in a shopping bag from the boot that Jane hadn't noticed earlier and his overnight bag.

'What's in there?' Jane was curious to see what he'd gone to Inverness shopping for.

He grinned. 'I have a wee surprise for you.'

She shimmied towards him, 'Now Iain,' she said provocatively, 'we both know it's not wee.'

His hazel eyes lit up but he held her off with one hand. 'Auch. You're sex mad woman. Can you no think of anything else?' He smiled. 'Not that I'm complaining mind. Now close your eyes and you dunnae open them till I tell you.'

Jane was intrigued but she did as she was told. Five minutes later, he spoke again and his voice was warm and filled with love.

'You can open them now, sweetheart.'

Jane was stunned. In front of the fire was a brand new luxurious tartan blanket of the softest wool, several plump cushions, also new, a bottle of champagne and a hamper containing strawberries, truffles, mini cakes and pastries – and in his hand he held a jar of chocolate body paint.

Her eyes shot to his face. 'Well, a man's got to eat,' he said as Jane threw herself in his arms and kissed every inch of his rugged face.

Several hours later, they were still wrapped in each other's arms – naked under the tartan blanket, watching the fire crackle and flare.

'Tell me again that you love me,' Jane said, 'I'll never tire of hearing it.'

Iain kissed her on her forehead. 'You might after fifty years – but I love you Jane Munroe.'

Jane pushed herself up on one arm and ran a finger across his muscular chest. Her eyes focused intently on what she was doing. 'That's the second time you've said that,' she said softly.

Iain tilted his head to try to see her face but her head was bowed and she didn't look up. His voice sounded strained. 'Auch woman. I've said it a damn sight more than that. What's wrong?'

'I meant the fifty years bit,' she said hesitantly. 'Earlier, you said you want to make love to me for the rest of your life.'

Iain didn't answer but his arm tightened around her.

Now she did look up and her eyes sparkled a little nervously in the glow from the fire. 'Do ... do you mean it?'

He looked away from her to the fire and when he spoke his voice cracked with emotion. 'I was married once, but when Alice died not long after Fraser was born, I vowed I wouldnae wed again –'

Jane felt deflated. 'I understand,' she interrupted him hurriedly. 'Forget I said anything.' She buried her head in his chest and screwed up her eyes. It was too early to think of such things anyway, she thought. Why had she been so stupid?

Iain took her gently by the arms and moved her away from him. He stood up, without saying a word, walked over to where he'd thrown his trousers and bent down to pick them up.

Panic raced through her. She had ruined everything.

Lizzie was right. Why did she keep throwing herself at Iain Hamilton. She'd made him feel cornered and now he was going to leave. She felt her heart slowly shattering, like the icicles outside dropping from the roof of the croft and smashing to the ground below.

'I'm sorry, Iain!' she almost shrieked. 'I'm an idiot! Please don't go!' she scrambled to her feet and ran to him, standing naked before him, her eyes pleading, tears forming at the sides.

Iain's expression went from flustered to horrified in two seconds flat.

'Good God what are you talking about?' He brushed a stray tear from her cheek and cupped her face in his hands. 'Sweetheart!' his voice was soft and soothing. 'You dunnae understand a thing, you crazy woman!' he used the words lovingly. 'If you had let me finish instead of interrupting me.'

He kissed her on the tip of her nose.

'I'm sorry I –'

'Auch! For heaven's sake woman,' he said and smiled down at her. 'Will you let me finish? Aye! I had vowed never to wed again – until I met you. For the last three years I've been like a man possessed. Wanting you, loving you, being too scared to tell you or ask you out because I was sure you couldnae be interested in a man like me.'

'But –'

Iain put his finger on her lips. 'Hush,' he said. He brushed his lips against hers, 'On Valentine's Night I couldnae believe it when you kissed me and when you ... well ... there's no other word for it ... seduced me!' He laughed lovingly. 'I felt like the luckiest man alive. Then Fraser called out and I went in to see him and when I came back, you'd gone. I thought ... well I thought you regretted it so I didnae call you or come to see you – but I told you most of this yesterday.'

Jane nodded but stayed silent.

'I told you what Fraser said today but I didnae tell you

everything he said. Don't look so worried sweetheart, it's all good. Apart from saying you were perfect for me – which you are by the way – he also said, and I'll try to get it exactly as he said it, "I don't know why you don't just marry her. You've been crazy about the woman for the past three years and you're not getting any younger. If she loves you, and any fool can see she does, stop wasting time and marry her before she changes her mind." I think that was almost word perfect. Auch no! He also said, "It would be good to have a step mother but maybe you shouldn't tell her that bit" – but I have.'

Jane's mouth fell open but no words would come out.

Iain held up his trousers, reached into the pocket and pulled out a small box covered in blue velvet. He got down on one knee, leant forward and planted a kiss on Jane's naked stomach.

'So Jane Munroe, I know we've only been dating for less than twenty four hours but I've loved you since almost I first laid eyes on you and I'll love you for the rest of my days – and nights,' he grinned and winked up at her. 'Will you do me the greatest honour a man can ask and be my wife? If you need time to think that's fine and –'

'Hush man!' Jane said, putting her finger on his lips as he had on hers. A huge smile spread across her mouth and tears of joy rolled down her cheeks. She tossed her copper-coloured hair from her face. 'I think it's rather humiliating to discover that Fraser is the most sensible one of the three of us. I adore you Iain Hamilton and I'd be honoured to be your wife.'

Iain got to his feet and swept her up in his arms to kiss her but she held him gently away. 'Aren't you forgetting something?' she said, waggling the fingers of her left hand in the air.

He smiled, pulled the ring from its box and placed it on her third finger. 'Now can I kiss you?'

Jane shook her head her eyes filling with tears. 'Not until I tell you that I would also be very happy to be Fraser's step

140

mother. He really is a very bright young man.'

'I'm sure he'll be pleased,' Iain said. 'Now I'm gonnae kiss you whether you like it or not.'

'Oh I like it. I like it very much indeed,' Jane said grabbing Iain's hands before he had a chance to put his arms around her, and leading him back towards the fire and the tartan blanket, 'and you'll be doing a lot more than kissing me.'

Iain's mouth came down on hers and nothing else needed to be said.

Chapter Eleven

'Thanks for this Max.' Lizzie leant back against the elegantly covered restaurant seat and took another sip from her glass of vintage port.

'My pleasure,' he said, grinning, 'you always did love a glass of port.'

Lizzie shook her head and pursed her lips, in mock rebuke. 'You know I didn't just mean the port, Max. When you suggested we come out for dinner I really didn't want to, but, well, it's done me the world of good. This used to be my favourite restaurant.'

'I know,' he said, his eyes twinkling, 'that's why I chose it.'

Max reached out a perfectly manicured hand across the table and took Lizzie's left hand in his.

Lizzie knew she should have pulled away but she didn't. She waited for the usual rush of emotion and was surprised when it didn't come. For the first time since she'd known him, Max's touch had no effect on her.

'Lizzie,' his eyes, now serious, Max searched her face, 'I was kind of hoping that you were thinking of coming back to me but ... I think you've come down to tell me something entirely different, something I know I'm not going to want to hear.' He rubbed his thumb over the pale lines on her third finger, where her wedding and engagement rings used to be. 'You've taken them off ...' His voice trailed off but his green eyes met hers and held them.

'Not completely,' she said, lifting her right hand. 'I wanted to ... but I couldn't.'

'So ... is there still some hope for me ... for us?' His fingers tightened around hers.

A small crease formed between her soft blue eyes. She gave a little shake of her head and sighed. 'I don't think so Max. I've tried to put it behind me, to forgive you and move on, but every time I think I have, it comes back to bite me. It's like some poisonous snake hiding in the grass in a summer meadow.'

Max flinched, 'Wow. That paints the picture perfectly, I guess. Look Lizzie, I know I was a fool and I know I was totally to blame but I've told you before and I swear to you now, if you'll just give me another chance – give us another chance, I will never, ever do anything like that again. I promise.'

Lizzie could feel the tears pricking at the sides of her eyes and blinked them away. 'I do believe you mean that Max, really I do. But you see, the thing is I just wouldn't trust you again and it would always be there, between us. Every time you looked at another woman –no. don't say you wouldn't, I know you too well for that – I'd start to wonder and that's no way to live.'

'But ... but surely, there's no harm in just looking? Are you saying you don't look at other men and think they're attractive?'

'No, of course I'm not and no, there isn't any harm in looking but you did more than look Max and that's the problem. Maybe, if it had just been one night, oh, I don't know, after a drink or a dance or something and you'd acted out of drunkenness or ... or lust even, then perhaps I could forgive you and move on but it wasn't one night was it Max? It was almost six months and that ... that I just can't forgive.'

Max fell back against the seat but still held Lizzie's hand by his fingertips. 'I still don't know why I did that Lizzie and that's the truth. Things were just crazy. We were both caught up in our careers and had moved into the house in Blackheath. We ... we were talking about starting a family, you remember and –'

'I remember,' Lizzie said, her eyes dropping to focus on the left-over crumbs of stilton cheese on her plate.

'Well ... it's not an excuse and don't think for one minute I'm suggesting that you were in any way to blame but ... well, I think it all terrified me a little, you know, the thought of parenthood and –'

'Oh come on Max! You said you wanted it too. We discussed it.'

'I know we did and I did want it ... I still do Lizzie but, well I think in the whole scheme of things, I saw myself sitting in front of the fire with grandchildren on my knee and that freaked me out.'

Lizzie's eyebrows shot up. 'You saw that as a bad thing? Us growing old together with a family?'

'No! ...Well, maybe a little ... then ... oh I don't know. All I know is, I felt my youth slipping away from me. I had just turned thirty and I was seeing myself with wrinkles and a pipe or something.'

'You don't smoke Max,' Lizzie said unable to hide the hint of sarcasm in her voice.

Max tutted. 'You know what I mean Lizzie. It's a pretty scary image for a guy who's only thirty I can tell you. We all freak out about it.'

'So you're saying that this is a natural phenomenon, all men, when they reach their thirtieth birthday see this, freak out, rebel against the inevitable and have an affair with their secretary! Really, you're saying that? Men have no choice in the matter? I rather thought it was just your dick telling you to have some fun and not get caught!' Lizzie yanked her hand from his.

Max opened his mouth to speak but thought better of it and instead, knocked back his port in one swallow. After a minute or two he said, 'Lizzie. Don't get mad. I'm not trying to make excuses. I didn't when you found us ... well, when ... '

'Oh just say it Max! When I walked in and found you in bed with that bloody woman!'

Max was startled by the hatred in her voice.

'Okay. Well, I didn't make excuses then and I'm not making excuses now. It was me – my fault entirely. A woman threw herself at me – literally – and I should have

144

thrown her back but I didn't and yes, I should have ended it before it got out of control – but I didn't. I tried, but I didn't, so I have no one to blame but myself. I was a fucking idiot!'

'What an appropriate way to put it!'

'God Lizzie, stop it. Stop being sarcastic. I know I hurt you, really hurt you but it hasn't been all sunshine and roses for me either you know. Every day I think about what our life might be like if only I hadn't done it. Every day I miss you and wish I could take back all the hurt. Every time we make love again I pray that it won't be the last and that you'll come back to me. I love you Lizzie. More than I've ever loved anyone, I love you!'

Lizzie stared at him for two whole minutes during which neither of them spoke then she leaned forward and looked him straight in the eye.

'Tell me Max,' she said, 'and believe me, I'll know if you're lying. How many women have you slept with since we separated? I don't need precise numbers – a ball park figure will do.'

Max felt his mouth go dry and he licked his lips. Christ. What was he going to say? He couldn't lie, she'd know, she was right about that.

'Lizzie I –'

'I rest my case.'

'Lizzie! I'm only flesh and blood for Heaven's sake and I'm not a bloody saint. I missed you. I was lonely. None of them meant anything –'

'None of them? So, clearly there were several. No, Max. Don't. Don't say anything else. God what a fool I've been. Don't you think I missed you too? That I was lonely? But until last night I've been totally faithful to you, d'you know that? I kept telling myself that somehow, things would eventually work out between us and every time you came to stay I really thought ... well, it doesn't matter does it? I knew, deep down, it was over. I wouldn't have moved to Scotland if I hadn't. I told myself I needed space but the truth was, I needed to be so far away that things could never go back to the way they were. We've both been hanging on to something that died a long time ago. Our marriage is like our favourite dead pet that we can't bear to lose so we have it stuffed and put it beside the fire and think it looks real and alive but really all it is, is a dead dog.

'Humph! Well, thanks for the analogy.' Max dragged his hand through his thick, blond hair.

'I think it's time to go,' Lizzie said.

'Wait!' Max's eyes formed small slits and he leant forward so their faces were only inches apart. 'You said, "until last night" what does that mean? Have you ... Christ Lizzie! You didn't fuck one of the guys did you?'

Lizzie hadn't even realised she'd said it and now her cheeks flushed crimson. 'I ... I ... it doesn't matter who it was. What matters is, it was the first time for me!'

'Oh really! That's what matters is it? Not that you screwed someone I know, someone I may work with. That's just fucking great. How's that gonna go on Monday. "Thanks for fixing us up for the weekend Max – oh , and thanks for letting us screw your wife!"'

Lizzie threw her napkin on the table-cloth. Some of the other diners were casting startled looks in their direction, as their voices grew louder. Lizzie noticed and blushed even more.

'Keep your voice down Max. People are looking at us. It wasn't like that and ...' and what? It was exactly like that. Jack had lied to get her into bed and she'd gone, willingly and enthusiastically. Oh God! Did Jack know Max really? Maybe it was Jack who used Lizzie to get back at Max. "You've screwed my fiancée, I've screwed your wife. Now we're quits". Oh Shit.

'And what? Don't tell me, I know. It's true love!'

'Now who's being sarcastic? Jane said you'd act like this.'

'Oh, so Jane knows too? Why don't you just put a notice in The Times?'

'Max stop it! This is ridiculous. I really think we should go.'

'Not until you tell me who it was.'

Lizzie's eyes grew wide in horror. 'No! It's none of your business. You don't own me.'

'You're still my wife.'

'Only on paper – and we can soon change that! I'm not getting into this Max. I haven't asked you the names of the women you've slept with since we separated and I'm not going to tell you his!'

'Was it Phil?'

'No! I'm not saying.'

'It wasn't Phil then? Well that's one good thing at least. He's the one who works with me so that would have been gross but the others, well I don't know any of them except Pete Towner and I've only met him a few times. Don't think Phil will spread gossip though. He's not the sort.'

'My God Max! That's all you're worried about. You're not so concerned about the fact that I slept with someone else as you are about your bloody reputation! Do you ever think about anyone but yourself for longer than a minute a day?'

Max was stunned. 'Now that's not fair. I've done nothing else but think about you for the last seven years!'

'Oh come on Max. That's a bit strong. Were you thinking about me when you were screwing Ki ... *that woman* and were you thinking about me when you were screwing the various, um, companions over the last two years since we've been separated?'

Max glowered at her. 'You may find this hard to believe but actually, yes, I was thinking about you – and the guilt's been killing me.'

Lizzie looked startled, then, she burst out laughing. 'You poor baby. It must have been hell. No wonder you look so tired.'

'I look tired.' Max snapped, 'you look like death warmed over. For someone who's just had a night of passion and found "true love" you look pretty fucking dejected.'

They glared at one another across the table in silence. A waiter approached them and stood beside their table.

'How is everything this evening, Mr. Bedford? Anything I can get you?'

Neither Lizzie or Max had seen him and they simultaneously raised startled eyes to his sanguine face – and simultaneously burst out laughing.

The waiter didn't bat an eyelid; he merely waited.

Max looked across at Lizzie. 'Truce?'

Lizzie nodded. 'Truce.'

'Then we'll have some more of this port, please and ... and some of the Amaretto pancakes.'

'Oh!' Lizzie sucked in her breath, they too, were her favourites. 'No Max, I mustn't.'

He grinned wickedly at her and put on his best dismissive tone. 'They're for me actually, your minute was up a long time ago, I'm back to thinking about myself now.'

Neither did the waiter bat an eyelid when Lizzie threw her napkin in Max's face.

Max's eyes softened and he smiled at Lizzie. 'I'm sorry, Lizzie. Not just for tonight but for all of it.'

'I know,' she said, 'me too.'

'I really shouldn't have eaten those,' Lizzie said half an hour later when they'd eaten the Amaretto pancakes and drunk more port. 'I'm so full up I might burst.' And a memory of an inflatable doll and a gorgeous man flashed into her mind unbidden.

Max saw something flash across her eyes. 'You okay?'

'Yes,' she said after a few seconds, 'I'm fine.'

'Well that's good because there's no way in hell I'd be clearing up that mess!'

Max's eyes met hers and they smiled at each other.

'Lizzie, I still love you, you know that and I still want

you back but, I can see we're never going to be able to put this behind us. You're right, every time it looks like we might, it all comes up again. We're both hanging on, I'm not sure I like the dead dog bit, but I do see what you mean. Maybe it is time we accepted it and tried to rebuild our lives – God, even the thought of that depresses me. Oh well, bite the bullet. Do ... do you want a divorce?'

Lizzie studied his handsome face. Throughout their marriage it had been like this. They hadn't rowed often – before *that woman* – but when they had, they'd been like tonight. Short, sharp bursts of anger, followed by long, passionate nights of making up. Tonight though, there'd be no passionate making up.

'I think it's for the best, don't you?'

Max sighed deeply. 'I suppose so. We ... we'll still be friends though, right? I mean, we'll still keep in touch and ... maybe have dinner occasionally?'

Lizzie smiled and nodded. 'I don't think I could cut you out of my life completely Max. I do still care for you a great deal and I want you to be happy ... it's just not with me.'

Max nodded in agreement. 'Your new man might not like it, though.'

Lizzie bit her lower lip. 'There is no new man Max, it ... it was a mistake ... just one of those things that happen after a few drinks.' She shrugged.

Max regarded her for several seconds. 'You okay?' he said, his voice tender and soothing.

Lizzie nodded and hoped the floodgates wouldn't open. 'Yeah. I'm fine. It's just been a long – and very exhausting few days.' She had been tempted to tell him about Jack and about, *that woman*, but she'd thought better of it. What difference would it make anyway? Jack didn't seem to know Max and Max didn't know Jack so it was better to leave things as they were.

'Shall we go to the solicitor's on Monday?' Max was asking. 'It'll be pretty straightforward I guess so I suppose it'll be fairly quick, even if not painless.'

'I ... I had thought about that but there's no rush Max if ... if you'd rather leave it for a few days.'

Max shook his head. 'No. Best to get things rolling. Otherwise I might start to hope again and get difficult and try to delay things.'

Lizzie smiled at him. 'You wouldn't do that Max. I ... I'm sorry about saying you don't think about anyone but yourself. That isn't really true.'

Max grinned sardonically. 'Yeah it is, kind of. Anyway, let's not drag it out, that won't do either of us any good. Say, why don't we just have a lovely day tomorrow, go to Hampton Court or Kew or something, like we used to. I promise I won't try and change your mind or beg you to take me back, more than thirty times, okay?'

Lizzie laughed, she knew he wasn't serious. When Max made a decision, he stuck to it, it just sometimes took him a long time to make one, that's all. 'Okay,' she said, stifling a yawn.

'Do you want to go to bed?' Max asked.

Lizzie tipped her head to one side and raised an eyebrow.

'Sorry, didn't mean it like that. You know what I mean. Do you want to go home to sleep?'

Lizzie grinned. 'Yes please. As I said, it's been a very long few days and I'm absolutely shattered – and, if I'm honest, a little bit tipsy to boot.' Another memory flashed through her mind of the last time she was tipsy and Jack kissing her and...

Why wouldn't that man just get out of her head? She stood up and walked a little unsteadily from the table. She had high heels on and it had been a while since she'd worn those. The drink didn't help and after Max had helped her on with her coat and held the restaurant door open for her, she stepped out on to the pavement and her ankle twisted beneath her.

'Ouch!' she yelped, stumbling into Max who grabbed

her in his arms.

'You okay? Have you hurt yourself?'

'It's my ankle.' She was balancing on one foot. 'I think I may have twisted it or something.'

'Lean on me,' Max said, bending down to examine the ankle whilst Lizzie leant on his shoulders.

'Owwww!'

'Sorry. Didn't mean to hurt you. I don't think it's broken but I'm no expert. We'd better call a cab and get you to hospital.'

'No! I'm sure it'll be fine. Just take me home, please. If it still hurts in the morning I'll go to hospital then.'

'Are you sure, Lizzie?'

Lizzie nodded. 'Yes. Spending hours in accident and emergency really doesn't appeal to me tonight. I don't think I can walk though so may I just lean on you?'

'Of course you may, sweetheart! Sorry, force of habit. It'll take a while to get used to not calling you that.'

Lizzie smiled, 'Don't worry about it, Max.'

He put his arm around her waist and Lizzie leaned in to him. The pain in her ankle was worse that she'd admitted and it was making her feel slightly nauseous. Her head began to swim and she thought she might pass out. She closed her eyes and rested her head against Max's chest whilst they waited for a cab.

Jack's journey, from the moment he left Laurellei Farm, was torture. He felt as if he'd been put on a rack and was being pulled from limb to limb in different directions.

From time to time, one of the guys spoke to him but he just nodded or shrugged until eventually, they left him in peace. Peace, huh, that was a joke. It would be a very long time before he ever felt at peace again, he was certain of that.

His mind kept going over the night he'd spent with Lizzie, how she'd felt in his arms, how she'd responded to his touch, how she'd blown his mind. Sex had never been like that with Kim or anyone else as far as he could remember. Lizzie just had to touch him or even look at him and all the blood rushed to his groin. Even now, with everything else that was going on, just the thought of her was starting to arouse him.

He'd call her, he thought, as soon as he got a chance to get away from the guys and he'd tell her everything. Tell her how he felt, tell her why he'd left; tell her about Kim. Then what? Tell her he couldn't break off the engagement and that he intended to marry Kim. So what good would that do?

At least she'd understand. At least she'd know he hadn't lied. Hadn't made up an excuse to get her into bed and then toss her aside the following day like a used condom. Oh my God. Condom! What was the matter with him? Last night he'd made love with Lizzie five times – and not once had he used a condom!

Jack's mind raced. Was she on the pill? Had she said she was? Had either of them even thought about it? He'd have to find out. He'd have to call her and ask her? Yeah right. How would that go exactly, "just calling to ask if you're on the pill 'cos I forgot to ask last night before I made love with you ... five times!"

It was as if he'd lost all sense of reason. Must have been that home brew of Iain's. He wouldn't normally have made love to someone without checking, then again, he wouldn't normally have made love to anyone other than Kim.

Oh God. Kim! Jack felt as if his head would explode. This was all just so unbelievable. Only two days ago, his life had seemed so simple, so straightforward, now it was like he was on a runaway train full of explosives and every so often, one went off, one by one until the whole bloody thing blew up in his face.

He closed his eyes and it was Lizzie's face he saw. He remembered the last time he'd seen her in the kitchen when she told him that Kim was the reason for her separation from her husband. It all came flooding back to him. Lizzie

152

had used him! How had he managed to forget that part of this saga? How stupid was he? She'd even told him it was nothing more than a one night stand.

It hadn't felt like a one night stand though and he tried to remember exactly what had happened that morning. Before that phone call, everything had been wonderful. He was happy – and so was Lizzie. He hadn't imagined that. Neither had he imagined the things they'd said to one another the night before. It had been more than just a fling, he was sure of it and maybe the only reason Lizzie had said the things she had today was because he'd said he was going back to Kim.

On and on it went, over and over in his head until, by the time he finally reached St. Thomas' Hospital four hours later, he felt he was the one in need of medical attention.

The guys went with him. They wouldn't leave until they were sure everything was really okay but even when Kim's mum met them in the corridor as she was getting herself some coffee, and told them Kim was fine, Ross still insisted on staying. The others made their way to the nearest pub after giving Jack express instructions to call them if they could do anything at all and to join them later for something to eat. Jack didn't think he could face food but he agreed, just so that they would go.

Jack hesitated before he went to see Kim. He needed to be fully in control of his emotions when he finally faced her. Ross was almost as bad as him and Jack sent him off to get coffee, he had to do this alone. Jack forced a smile to his face and pulled himself up straight then marched to Kim's bedside. To his utter relief, she was sound asleep.

Jack hung around alternating between pacing up and down and sitting beside her, willing her to open her eyes. Nothing settled him and when his stomach started rumbling from hunger he decided he may as well meet the others for some food. The company might do him good. Ross had hardly spoken a word to him for the last half hour. Ross seemed to want to stay but Kim's mum was there and she promised to call Jack if Kim woke up so he and Jack headed for the pub.

A good meal and a pint of beer made Jack feel better and an hour later, when he headed back to the ward to see Kim, he was feeling as if things might not be quite as black as he'd painted them. He had a good job, good friends and a lovely fiancée. Soon he'd be married and ... and Lizzie and Laurellei Farm would be firmly in the past. Locked away in a box in his mind marked "things that might have been".

Kim still wasn't awake and her mum told him there really was no point in him hanging around. He should go home and get a good night's sleep. Jack got the distinct feeling that she was trying to get rid of him and he wondered why. She was obviously distressed – she had a right to be, Jack reasoned. Maybe she just wanted some time alone with her only daughter. He could understand that. Mrs. Mentor promised she'd call him if there was any change or when Kim woke up.

Jack went back to the pub; he couldn't face being alone with his thoughts after everything that had happened. He didn't leave until eleven and by then, he had phoned Laurellei Farm six times even though he had no idea what he was going to say. He was both glad and annoyed that the phone went unanswered.

In the taxi home, Jack vaguely wondered where Ross had gone. He had left without saying good bye, which was a bit odd but then, Ross had been a bit odd for a while now and Jack realised that he really should ask his friend if there was something worrying him.

Ross was usually the life and soul of the party but, thinking about it now, since Jack had got back from Hong Kong, Ross had been decidedly off par. Jack had been so consumed with his own doubts and fears that he hadn't even thought about his friend. Tomorrow, before he visited Kim, he'd go to Ross's and have a man to man talk with him.

Jack settled back against the seat of the cab and peered

out of the window. The streets were half empty for just after eleven on a Saturday night but it was quite cold out so most people would be inside the pubs, bars and restaurants. The cab pulled up at a set of traffic lights and Jack's eyes settled on a couple standing by the side of the road. The guy was tall, about Jack's height, blond and, Jack thought, looked like he'd stepped from the pages of a magazine advert. The woman was petite, not much above five feet and a few inches probably, and had the most amazing brunette air, almost exactly the same as Lizzie's. Jack stared at them and over the juddering of the cab's stationary engine he thought how incredibly like Lizzie the woman looked.

Jack was only a few feet away in the cab and he saw the man's arm tighten around the woman's waist as he planted a quick kiss on her head. She seemed to be balancing against him, one small foot lifted slightly off the pavement, her head resting on the man's chest. He said something that Jack couldn't hear but it made the woman raise her eyes to the man's face.

The traffic lights changed from red to amber to green. As they did so, the woman laughed and shook her head and her brunette waves bounced around her shoulders. Jack twisted on the seat of the cab as it drove away from the couple. Peering out of the rear window he saw a cab pull up in front of them and watched in disbelief as the man swept the woman up in his arms and placed her gently on the seat then dashed around the other side and got in beside her.

To his astonishment and horror, Jack realised the woman didn't just look like Lizzie, the woman *was* Lizzie! And even though he told himself again and again that it couldn't be because Lizzie was miles away in Scotland, the woman's silent laughter and the unanswered phone at Laurellei Farm, taunted Jack's brain for the duration of his journey home.

Chapter Twelve

Ross knew he had to talk to Kim. When he'd heard about the accident from Phil he felt as if his throat had been slit. Horrific pictures of her twisted, mangled body instantly flicked through his mind and he almost blurted out everything then and there. Almost, but not quite.

Phil said Kim was okay and Ross regained his composure, he knew once he'd said it, there would be no going back and he was glad that he could delay it for a little while longer. But that was all he could do. The shock of thinking Kim might be seriously hurt was a real wake-up call and clarity finally dawned.

No matter how much it may hurt Jack and no matter what happened from here, the truth must come out. There was no way Ross could just stand by and watch Kim marry Jack.

Ross loved Kim, had probably always loved her, even before she had started dating Jack. He had seen her a few times when he'd gone to meet Phil after work at Brockleman Brothers Bank and once, he'd considered asking her out, but she seemed to be with some guy so he'd held back.

Ross was in New York on a business trip when Kim had started dating Jack and he couldn't help but feel that if only he'd been in The Mucky Duck that night, (The Black Swan was its actual name but the regulars all affectionately called it The Mucky Duck) things might have turned out differently.

For two years, Ross put his feelings on the back burner and watched Kim and Jack's relationship develop, always hoping it would come to nothing, but when Kim announced after Christmas, that they were engaged and were getting married in March, it were as if Ross had been struck by lightning. Ever since, he'd struggled to keep it together.

Then, almost six weeks ago, Jack went to Hong Kong for three weeks and Ross took Kim out for a drink and that, as they say, was that. Ross couldn't hold back anymore and two years of lust and longing and love burst out of him like an eruption of a long dormant volcano.

Guilt inevitably set in and Ross vowed it wouldn't happen again but his flesh was weak and almost every night for three blissful weeks Ross and Kim made love – until Jack came back.

They'd talked about telling Jack but Ross knew it would destroy their friendship and he thought it would devastate Jack. He couldn't do it and so he ended things with Kim and tried to fade into the background but that hadn't worked. All he could think about was Kim and his resentment grew and festered until it felt as if his heart was rotting away.

Ross realised if he didn't say something now he would probably stand up at the church and yell out that he objected, that it should be him marrying Kim and not Jack! Marry Kim, Ross hadn't thought about that. Did he really want to marry her? Even as he asked himself the question he knew the answer. Yes, he most definitely did.

When they had arrived at the hospital and the guys went to the pub, Ross stayed with Jack, hoping to get a chance to see Kim. It hadn't worked though, Jack sent him for coffee and Kim just slept. Kim's mum was constantly by the bedside and Jack paced up and down like a bear with a sore head.

Finally, Jack decided to go to the pub and Ross went too – but Ross didn't stay. When Jack came back after his second visit to the hospital, saying Kim was still sleeping and he'd see her tomorrow, Ross decided this was his chance. He'd gone back to the hospital and found Kim slowing waking up.

'I really need to talk to Kim alone Mrs. Mentor,' Ross said sheepishly.

Mrs. Mentor glared at him. 'So, you're Ross,' she said.

Ross was taken by surprise. 'Um, yes. I'm Ross.'

'Well then, yes Ross, you really do need to talk to Kim. I won't call Jack. You two need to sort out this sorry mess.' She turned to Kim and squeezed her daughter's hand, 'I'll be back before visiting hours end love and don't you take any nonsense from this one, you hear me. I've told you what I think and whether you heed it, is up to you, but this is your life and your happiness we're talking about, so you decide what you want and everyone else can go hang.'

Mrs. Mentor turned back to Ross and poked him in the chest. 'As for you, young man, you need a good kick up the back side. You either love my daughter or you don't, only you know the answer to that, but if it's yes, then stop being a wimp and do something about it – or you'll have me to answer to.'

She raised her hand and for one dreadful moment, Ross thought she was going to slap his face. He probably deserved it. To his surprise, she took his chin in her hand and gave it a little shake, then, she smiled and left him alone with Kim.

Ross took Kim's hand in his left one and stroked her bruised face gently with his right. 'Are you okay?' he asked.

'Do I look okay?' she said, a little testily.

He bent down and brushed his lips against her forehead and when he stood up, Kim thought she could see tears at the corners of his eyes.

'Compared to the horrific images that had been driving me crazy all day, frankly, you look wonderful. Shit Kim, at first, I thought you were dead!'

'Well, that would have made things easier for you wouldn't it?' she snapped.

'Easier for me? What the hell d'you mean, easier for me?'

'Well, then you and Jack could carry on being best buddies and he would never know about us, would he?'

Ross let out a deep sigh. 'Don't even think like that Kim.

I've been going crazy with worry all day, Christ, when we got here, I almost barged Jack aside and told him you were mine.'

Kim eyed him between swollen lids. 'Almost,' she said, 'but you didn't.'

'No ... but I will. This has made me realise one thing Kim. I really do love you and there is no way I can just stand by and watch you marry Jack – or anyone else for that matter.'

A tiny smile hovered on her cut lip. 'Ross, do you mean it? Really?'

Ross nodded. 'I mean it. Really!'

Kim swallowed a lump in her throat and tears slid down her puffy cheeks. 'There ... there's something you need to know.'

Ross wiped at her tears with his thumb. 'Don't cry Kim. Everything'll be okay now, I promise. I'll talk to Jack. Don't worry. I'm sure he'll understand but even if he doesn't, I don't care. You and me'll be together no matter what.'

Kim shook her head and sobbed. 'He won't and ... and you won't want me when you know.'

Ross furrowed his brows. 'Of course I'll want you! What are you talking about Kim? When I know what?'

'I'm pregnant – and I don't know who the father is!'

For the second time that day, Ross felt as if his throat had been cut.

Jack opened the door to his apartment and threw his weekend bag on the floor. He'd unpack later. Right now what he needed was a drink – a strong one, and he headed to the drinks cabinet and poured himself a large, single malt. He held the crystal tumbler to his mouth and gulped down the contents, then poured himself another.

Grabbing the bottle by its neck he trudged to the sumptuous sofa and dropped on to the black plump cushioned seat. He poured another glass full and tossed the contents down his throat as if it was water. His features tightened and he clenched his jaw, gritting his teeth.

On Wednesday evening, when he and his mates had boarded the Caledonian sleeper, the only thing troubling him was a niggling feeling that he wasn't quite as happy as he should be, at the prospect of his impending marriage.

Now here he was, at eleven thirty-five on Saturday night drowning his sorrows with his finest 20 year old single malt – and not even that tasted like it should.

On Wednesday, on his way to Scotland to spend a long weekend of fun and relaxation on his stag party, he'd been engaged to a woman he thought he loved.

By Saturday, he'd slept with a married woman, realised he didn't love his fiancée, decided to call off his wedding and was dreaming of the possibility of a future with another man's wife.

By Saturday night, he was trying to get so drunk, that he could forget the married woman had only used him – and he'd just seen her in someone else's arms, possibly her husband's; his fiancée had been in a car crash and there was no way in hell he could now call off the wedding.

As the clock struck midnight and the whisky was having no effect whatsoever, Jack realised that, two weeks from now, he'd be married to a woman he didn't really love, a woman whom, in less than eight months time would give birth to a child, his child and he'd be tied to her for the rest of his miserable life.

Lizzie woke early, the pain in her ankle a little less piercing this morning and she swung her legs from the bed, carefully putting her feet to the floor. So far, so good.

Gingerly, she pulled herself upright. Arrows of pain shot up her leg and she buckled under the onslaught. Gasping, she dropped back down on the bed. She was going to have to go to the hospital.

Max knocked on the door. 'Lizzie, are you awake? May I come in?'

160

'Yes, Max. Come in.'

He saw her perched on the edge of the bed, hands gripping the sides. 'You okay?'

Lizzie shook her head. 'Afraid not. I thought my foot was better but when I put weight on it, the pain was excruciating.'

A concerned expression hovered over his face but he made light of it. 'You shouldn't have had those Amaretto pancakes last night.'

She grinned, in spite of her throbbing ankle. 'Your fault,' she said.

'As usual. C'mon then, let's get you to A&E. Shall I carry you? I think my back can just about support your weight.'

Lizzie threw him a quelling glare; she'd like to have thrown a pillow. 'I think I'd better get dressed first,' she said.

'Oh yes.' He realised she had a long T-shirt nightdress on. 'Would you like me to help you with that? I'm generally better at taking them off but I'm willing to give it a go.'

This time she did throw the pillow.

Half an hour later, Max had carried her down to the waiting cab and they were on their way to St. Thomas'. He carried her in and sat her down in the waiting room which was surprisingly empty for a Sunday morning.

'Must all be in church,' he joked.

'Or dead,' she hissed. Lizzie hated hospitals.

He was told they'd have at least two hour's wait but Max wasn't used to waiting. He pulled out his iphone and touched the screen. Fifteen minutes later a nurse called Lizzie's name.

'How did you do that?' she asked.

'Contacts,' he said and smiled.

The receptionist glared at him and he wished her a good day.

'Well, I'm pretty sure nothing's broken and it's just a

sprain,' the doctor said after examining her swollen ankle. 'A few days rest should help but I'm afraid you won't be dancing on it anytime soon and it could take several weeks to heal properly. I'll send you for x-rays just to be sure and then we'll bandage it up and give you some crutches.'

'Thanks,' Lizzie said. 'Will I be able to travel? I'm down from Scotland and my return flight's on Tuesday.'

The doctor shook his head. 'I wouldn't, but I suppose if you've got someone with you, you'd be able to manage. You won't be able to put weight on it for some time though.'

'Oh,' Lizzie said, casting her eyes to the floor. Either she was going to have to stay with Max for the next few days – or he was going to have to take her back to Scotland.

'No broken bones,' the doctor confirmed half an hour later after her foot had been x-rayed. He bandaged it up and organised crutches, checking she could manage to get about with them, adjusting the hand holds to allow for her five feet two height.

Lizzie had to hand it to Max. She'd had first class treatment all the way. St. Thomas', she knew had one of the best A&E departments in London but even she knew she'd had special treatment because of Max. A thought suddenly hit her. This was the hospital Ross or Phil or one of them had said that *that woman* was in and the temptation to go and try to find her, to get one look at this nemesis of hers, was almost overwhelming.

When she'd found Max and *that woman* in bed together she hadn't really focused on the woman, hadn't really focused on anything, all she'd seen was her husband naked and very obviously making love to someone else. It could have been an inflatable doll for all the impression she'd left. Another vision, another inflatable doll. Oh god. She needed a drink.

But just one look. One real look. She'd fled to Scotland the day after the discovery and although she'd asked Max once or twice – actually more like thirty or forty times – to

162

describe her because all Lizzie could remember was her long blond hair, he'd refused. "It doesn't matter and it wouldn't help to know" was all he'd say, which to Lizzie meant "She's absolutely stunning in every way and you'd feel like an ugly duckling in comparison."

Lizzie was tempted to tell Max about the accident and who Jack's fiancée was but she had a feeling that if she did, everything else would come out too and that was better left where it was, so she quashed her curiosity, limped out of the hospital and got into the waiting cab, with a little help from Max.

The minute they got back from the hospital, Lizzie called Jane to tell her what had happened and to ask how things were going.

'Hey Lizzie! You must have read my mind. I was just about to call you. Things are pretty damned good, actually.'

Lizzie adjusted the position of her raised ankle on the footstool and took the glass of wine Max held out to her. 'Anything you want to tell me – or is Iain there?'

'Yes to both!' Jane couldn't contain the excitement in her voice. 'You'll never believe this Lizzie – I'm engaged!'

Lizzie almost spilt her wine. Max spotted her astonished look and gave her a quizzical glance. She smiled up at him.

'Jane's engaged to Iain Hamilton,' she said to Max. Then to Jane, 'Congratulations! I assume it is to Iain and that you haven't run off with someone else.'

'Very funny. Who're you with? Max?'

'Yeah. I'm staying at his place. He says Congratulations too.'

Jane hesitated for a moment. 'Is that wise?'

Lizzie watched Max as he set the table for lunch. He was a good cook and liked to eat meals at the table, none of this on your lap stuff for him.

'Actually, yes, but there is a bit of a problem and I need to ask yet another favour, sorry.'

'What's wrong?' Jane's voice echoed her concern.

'I've sprained my ankle and the doctor says I've got to

rest it, so Max has kindly said I can stay here. Do you mind keeping Alastair and feeding the animals for a bit longer? Shouldn't be more than a week.'

'I bet he did!' Jane said. 'Are you okay though? You know there's no problem about Alastair etc but are you really sure it's sensible to spend a week with Max? I could come and get you if that helps.'

Lizzie waited till Max had gone back into the kitchen. 'No. It's fine. We had it all out last night and we are going to see the solicitor tomorrow; although with my ankle, I'm not sure that'll be happening. I'll tell you all about it when I get back. Bit difficult now. But anyway, tell me all about the proposal. Did he get down on one knee? Set a date?'

'Oh Lizzie! It was soooooo romantic. He'd bought a hamper and champagne and he set it all out on a blanket in front of the fire and ... oh, hold on, I think he's getting embarrassed. Go and do something darling, I want to tell Lizzie all the details.'

'Not all of them, I hope,' Lizzie heard Iain say and she heard him give Jane a kiss.

Jane giggled. 'I'll spare your modesty, don't worry, now go – but not too far, I'll need more kisses in about five minutes. Ouch!' Iain had smacked Jane's bottom.

'You sound really happy Jane, I'm so pleased for you,' Lizzie said and meant it.

'Oh God Lizzie, I am! He's just so unbelievable – and I don't just mean the sex – I mean in every way. I fall more in love with him by the minute. We haven't set a date yet but I don't think it'll be too far away. I can't wait to be Mrs. Hamilton.'

'I bet he can't wait for you to be Mrs. Hamilton either. I'm so happy for you both and thanks for Alastair and everything. I'll be back by next weekend at the latest and we can have a proper celebration then but tell me about the proposal and the ring.'

Jane told Lizzie all about it.

'So, Jane and Iain Hamilton eh?' Max said when Lizzie eventually hung up the phone, twenty minutes later. 'Didn't see that coming. Have they been dating long? Can't remember them being a couple at Christmas.'

Lizzie held her glass up for the refill Max was offering and shook her head. 'Neither did I, which doesn't say much for my powers of observation. I only found out this week that they've been crazy about one another for years. They sort of got together on Valentine's Night but it only really came to anything on Friday. I can't believe he's proposed so soon.'

Max sat opposite her and stretched out his long, lithe body in the chair. His green eyes were studying her in a way she found a little unsettling, like she used to not so very long ago. He ran a finger round the rim of his glass, then took a slug of wine.

'It doesn't take long if it's the right woman Lizzie. I knew within a week of meeting you that I was going to ask you to marry me.'

Lizzie didn't try to hide her surprise. 'Seriously?'

Max smirked. 'Seriously.'

'Then ... how come it took you over a year?'

Max's eyes held hers, then he shrugged and looked away. 'I didn't think there was any rush and, I guess, I wanted to be sure.'

Lizzie felt an urge to say something sarcastic, like, 'that worked well', or something but there really didn't seem any point. Instead she said, 'That's strange, I hadn't even thought about marrying you, until you proposed.'

Max's eyes formed tiny slits. 'Even then, you weren't sure; it took you about ten minutes to say yes.'

Lizzie's eyes shot to his face. 'It didn't!' she said, but as soon as she said it, she realised it had.

Max saw from her subdued expression that she was remembering too. 'Oh well, water under the bridge now,' he said. 'Which reminds me, you obviously won't be able to make it to the solicitor's tomorrow, shall I arrange for him to come here, it's all pretty straightforward, just a matter of going through the motions really so we could probably just do it all over the phone.'

'Yeah, it's so amazingly simple these days. Family Law wasn't my field but I could do it and save some money, I just thought it's ... less emotional if someone else handles it.'

'I'll pay for it anyway, so don't worry about that. No! Don't argue Lizzie. I'm the one who broke it, I'm the one who should pay to clear up the mess – in a manner of speaking.'

Lizzie knew there was no point in arguing over this so she just said, 'Thanks Max.'

'Okay, I'll get him to come here at say five-ish tomorrow. I'll leave the office early.'

'Okay but he may not be free at five.'

Max looked at her as if she was being ridiculous. 'Of course he'll be free,' he said.

And Lizzie knew – for Max – he would.

Chapter Thirteen

There was no time like the present, Ross told himself. When he left Kim's bedside last night he should have gone straight back to the pub, hauled Jack outside and told him the truth but as usual, he'd put it off.

Telling your best friend outside a pub that you've slept with his fiancée is not a good idea. Telling your best friend in his own apartment that, at least he'll get to have the place back to himself as his fiancée would be moving out, was much better – wasn't it?

Ross summoned all his courage. It wasn't that he was frightened of what Jack might do to him – he'd actually feel better if Jack beat him to a pulp, not that he thought for one minute that he would, Jack just wasn't a violent man – it was that he was worried about what he might do to Jack.

Ross, Phil and Jack had been best friends since they were five and the knowledge that Ross had betrayed him would hit Jack hard. Two things were important to Jack, friendship and fidelity and Ross had torn them both to shreds then set fire to them for good measure.

When Kim had announced the engagement and Jack had to choose his best man, Phil and Ross had drawn straws because Jack wasn't prepared to pick one over the other, even though Ross had said it should be Phil and he was happy to stand aside. When Jack discovered it was because Ross hadn't wanted to be the one standing beside him as Kim walked down the aisle, he would feel doubly betrayed.

There was no way to sugar coat it. Ross loved Kim, Kim loved Ross and although they both loved Jack, they loved each other more, so Jack had to go. Ross now wished he'd had the courage to tell Jack two weeks ago, things would have been so much easier then. Now there was a baby involved and that brought a whole new pram load of problems.

Kim assumed the baby was Jack's but Ross thought there was a slight chance it might be his, so that meant waiting for the results of a paternity test, and then what? How would they cope if Ross wasn't the father and Jack was? Jack wasn't the sort of man who would just walk away and let someone else raise his child. He'd want to be involved.

Ross had gone from being a jealous bachelor to a possible husband and part time father of another man's child in a matter of five minutes last night. Once he'd recovered from the initial shock of Kim's pregnancy – and it had been one hell of a shock – he realised very quickly that even if the child wasn't his, he still wanted to marry Kim.

He'd taken off his signet ring, got down on one knee beside Kim's hospital bed and asked her to marry him. It was an odd scenario as she was already engaged to Jack, but her ring had been removed by the nurses in accident and emergency and was now safely wrapped in tissue in her mum's handbag. When Kim said yes, Ross slipped his signet ring on the third finger of her left hand and promptly kissed her full on the lips.

'Well thank heavens that's one thing sorted out at least,' Mrs. Mentor had said as she got back just in time to witness the proposal. 'Now all you've got to do is tell the other fiancé, move out of his flat, reorganise the wedding, and find out who's baby it is and it'll all be plain sailing from there on in!' Mrs. Mentor always looked on the bright side of life.

It was Sunday and Sunday was a good day for a confession. Some people went to church to confess, Ross went to Jack's apartment. As he walked the few blocks between his place and Jack's, Ross went over what he was going to say. He'd been up most of the night thinking about it and had even written some notes, ironically on the same notepad as he'd been writing his best man's speech but the irony didn't occur to him, his mind was in too much turmoil.

The day was bright and sunny, much warmer than it had been of late and Ross saw this as a good sign. He still had no idea how Jack would take the news and had considered for just one moment, asking Phil to go with him, not for support but in case Jack freaked out and shouldn't be left alone after.

He realised he was being a bit dramatic, 'Stop being such a girl,' he told himself, 'Jack will take it like a man, he may throw you out of his apartment straight into the Thames but he won't shed any tears or throw a tantrum whilst he's doing it.'

The one thing Ross was more concerned about than anything else though, was losing Jack's friendship and the thought of it hurt him as much as the thought of not being with Kim had done. He wondered if it was possible to retain just a scrap of what they had and tried to put himself in Jack's shoes but it didn't help so he decided he'd have to wait and see. He pressed the buzzer to Jack's apartment and held his breath.

Jack saw it was Ross via the video and buzzed him in.

'Come in mate,' Jack said from the open door of his apartment, 'I've just been calling you but your phone's off.'

Ross took his phone from his pocket. Jack was right. Ross had switched it off last night at the hospital and he'd forgotten to switch it back on. He did it now and three messages flashed on the screen. He scrolled through them, they were all from Jack.

'What's up mate?' Ross asked, half dreading the answer.

'I need to ask you something and it's going to be awkward but I need to know the truth, okay?'

Ross tried to swallow but something stuck in his throat, unable to speak, he nodded instead.

'D'you want coffee? I've made coffee,' Jack said pacing to and fro. 'Had a bit of a session last night and needed it. Think I'll have some more. Want some?'

Ross felt Jack had had enough for both of them already

but he nodded and managed to get out a strangled, 'Yeah.'

Jack poured the coffee, handed one to Ross, gulped his down in three swallows then dropped on to the sofa. He got up again so quickly he startled Ross and almost made him drop his cup.

The door buzzer went and Jack raced across the room to answer it. 'Yeah, come up mate.' Jack turned back to Ross. 'It's Phil,' he said, seconds before Phil tapped on the half open door and stepped in.

'Ross just got here,' Jack said to Phil. 'Must have read my mind 'cos his phone was off. Coffee mate? There's some in the pot.'

Phil nodded to Ross, strode across the room and poured himself some coffee.

'Pour me one mate, I'm gasping,' Jack said.

Phil glanced at him over the top of the Ray-bans he was still wearing.

'You sure you haven't had enough already Jack, you look a bit wired.'

'I'm wired all right – but it's not from coffee. I think Kim's having an affair!'

Luckily for Phil, he had moved towards the chair beside the fire so that when Ross spat his coffee out in total shock, it didn't hit him, only the coffee table.

Two pairs of eyes focused on Ross.

'I know mate,' Jack said, 'that's just how I felt when I realised.'

Phil put down his cup and went into the kitchen for some kitchen paper, as he came back he noticed Ross was fiddling with the neck of his T-shirt as though it were too tight and was throttling him. Jack had resumed pacing.

'So,' Phil said, wiping up the coffee, 'what makes you think Kim's having an affair?' He glanced at Ross and in that split second, he had an uneasy feeling that Jack might just be right.

'Kim's pregnant!' Jack said, standing still for the first time since either Ross or Phil had arrived.

This time it was Phil who was shocked and he couldn't help but notice that as far as Ross was concerned, it was old news. Perhaps Jack had already told him, then again ... Phil dropped on to the chair beside the sofa as if all the stuffing had been knocked out of him. He had the weirdest feeling that things might get a lot worse from here on in.

No one said a word for at least two minutes. Then Phil said, 'I'm not sure if I'm meant to say congratulations or not and perhaps I'm missing something but why does Kim being pregnant make you think she's having an affair? Have you been told you can't have kids or something?'

Jack shook his head, 'No! I can have kids. Well, I assume I can, never needed to find out. It's not about me, it's about her.'

Phil looked perplexed, 'Sorry mate, you've lost me. Bit hung over this morning,' he said, finally removing his sunglasses and squinting in the morning sunshine as he did so.

Jack dropped on to the chair beside the fire. 'Mathematics mate, pure and simple,' he said.

Phil shook his head again. 'I know I shouldn't be saying this as I'm a banker, but there's nothing simple about mathematics Jack and certainly not when I'm hung-over. Just tell me in layman's terms.'

Ross was now coughing repeatedly and still tugging at the neck of his T-shirt.

'Well, Kim's crap at remembering to take her pill so I've got in the habit of reminding her every morning ... '

Phil waited for Jack to continue but he didn't. He looked like his brain was churning something over.

'Well, that's good to know,' Phil said, 'but I still don't see what makes you think she's having an affair.'

Ross didn't say a word. His head was bowed and he seemed to be wringing his hands.

'Because ... it means I know her monthly cycle as well as she does. Better in fact and she had her period just before I left for Hong Kong.' He saw Phil cringe. 'Sorry mate, too much information?'

'Just a tad. I still don't get it though.'

'Nor did I, at first. Then I did the maths.'

Ross stopped wringing his hands and he lifted his head, 'Maths?' he said.

Jack and Phil both glanced at him as if they'd forgotten he was there.

Jack nodded and a huge smile softened his taught face. 'I was away for just over three weeks and I've been back for just over two, making it almost six weeks right?'

'Right,' Phil said, no nearer understanding.

'Well, she wasn't pregnant when I left and ... I'll spare you the details ... but either she should only be at the most, ten days pregnant or she slept with someone else or it's an immaculate conception and we all know the third option's hardly likely.'

'So ... how many days is she pregnant?' Ross asked, a tiny light shining at the end of what had seemed a very long, dark tunnel.

'Not days Ross, weeks. The doctor told me she is five weeks pregnant! I phoned again this morning and checked. He's absolutely certain. Apparently, you can almost pinpoint it to the very day. It's unbelievable.'

'But ...?' Phil still wasn't sure he understood. 'Are you saying then, that there's absolutely no chance the kid could be yours?'

'None whatsoever!'

Ross's sigh of relief echoed throughout Jack's spacious apartment.

Phil's eyes shot to Ross's face then darted to Jack's. Jack seemed oblivious.

'Forgive me mate,' Phil said hurriedly 'but ... you don't seem ... well, disappointed. In fact, I'd say quite the opposite. You look like a man reprieved.'

He beamed at Phil. 'And that's exactly how I feel. I can't say I'm happy about her sleeping with someone else behind my back, obviously, but believe me, I completely understand how that can happen and, well it doesn't matter why,' his voice lowered an octave, 'and the reason's not relevant anymore but I realised when we were in Scotland that I didn't want to marry Kim.'

'Shit!' Ross said.

'I know it's bad,' Jack said, totally misinterpreting Ross's remark, 'especially with the kid and everything but, hey, that's not my fault.'

'So, is she trying to make out it's yours then?' Phil asked a sudden thought occurring to him.

'No idea,' Jack said, 'She was asleep yesterday so I haven't spoken to her yet and I don't know if she knows the doctor's told me. Her mum told me when she called Saturday morning that Kim was pregnant and it was a miracle the baby was okay but she didn't say how pregnant and to be honest, I was in such a state of shock and ... well anyway, I didn't ask. It was only when we got down here and the doctor said she was five weeks, that I knew how far along she was. Even then, I didn't think anything of it. It was only when I was mulling things over last night that something kept niggling at my brain. And I didn't need a super-computer to work out that ten days is nowhere near five weeks, in actual time. I ... I didn't tell you guys about the baby yesterday because, well, there were some things I needed to sort out with Kim first, before we broke the news, but now ...'

'So, what are you going to do?' Phil asked, stunned by these latest revelations. He'd realised for a while that Jack wasn't totally happy but he'd thought it was just nerves. When he saw how Jack reacted in Scotland every time Lizzie came near, he began to wonder whether it was something more and after just one day, he'd started to think that Jack might have fallen head over heels in love with another woman.

'I'm going to talk to Kim today ... and I'm going to call off the wedding.'

'Don't ... don't you want to know who the other guy is?'

Ross asked unable to stop himself.

Jack looked him squarely in the face. 'You sound as if you might know,' he said tentatively.

Ross's eyes darted from Jack to Phil and back to Jack. 'No mate! Haven't got a ... oh fuck! I can't keep this up.' Ross rose to his feet and paced the floor then stopped in front of Jack. 'Don't hate me mate. I mean, of course you'll hate me but it wasn't like I planned it, you know ... it ... it just kind of happened and ... oh shit Jack. I love her! I loved her before you two even started dating.'

Phil spoke first. 'You fucking bastard! You've been screwing her behind Jack's back all this time. You little –'

'No! ... No. It was the first time five weeks ago.'

'The first time?' Jack said, recovering from the shock of Ross's confession. His voice was as cold and hard as marble.

'Christ! What can I say Jack? There's no excuse. We ... went for a drink the night you left, I don't know why. She ... she didn't want to be alone or something but, well I've been crazy about her for as long as I can remember and ... one thing led to another and ... '

'Shit you didn't rape her?' Phil hissed.

'What the ... of course I didn't! What kind of guy do you think I am?'

'At this precise moment, I'm not sure you want me to answer that.' Phil stood up and glared at him.

'So, the minute I got on the plane then? You certainly didn't waste any time mate, did you? But, you said "the first time", so I'm assuming it happened more than once. I don't want numbers, a yes will suffice.'

Ross nodded. He was feeling slightly queasy. 'Yes,' he said, 'but not since you've been back.'

'Well, thanks for that. Why not?'

Ross was confused. 'Why not what?'

'Why not since I've been back?'

'Because ... because I couldn't do it, not like that, not anymore. I ... I was going to tell you the minute you got back but ... well ... you seemed so happy so ... so I ended it.'

'You ended it?'

'We ... we both did.'

'Somehow, I'm not sure I believe that. So ... were you ever going to tell me? I mean, let's just suppose none of this had happened. Not the accident, the baby, me working it out, would you have told me or were you planning to just let me walk down the aisle in ignorance?'

'Honestly? I don't know. I didn't want to. Even though Kim said we should. I ... I didn't want to hurt you and –'

'Bit late to be thinking like that afterwards mate, should have considered that whilst your trousers were still zipped.'

'I know. I told you. There's no excuse and believe me, I hate myself for it. But the thing is, I really do love her and ... well, I don't think I could have let you marry her.'

Jack let out a derisory laugh. 'What? Pistols at dawn?'

'Course not! I ... I think I just would have told you, eventually. If you want to thump me, do it. I deserve it.'

Phil punched him squarely on the jaw and Ross reeled backwards, sprawling across the sofa.

Jack gave Phil a sardonic look.

'Well he's right. He did deserve it. Someone had to do it and let's face it Jack, you didn't want to.' Phil reached out and pulled Ross to his feet.

'Thanks mate,' Ross said sarcastically, swishing his jaw from side to side to check it wasn't broken.

'My pleasure,' Phil said, slapping him hard on his back.

'So ... are you thinking of marrying her then?' Jack asked, flopping down on to the chair and stretching his long legs out in front of him.

'Um ... if ... if that's okay with you.'

Jack smirked and shook his head. 'I think you'd better ask Kim that.'

'Well ... um ... I already have.'

Jack's eyes opened wide. 'You continue to amaze me. What did she say?'

Ross grimaced, 'She said yes.'

Jack leapt to his feet and Ross involuntarily took a step backwards.

Jack noticed and grinned. 'Don't worry mate,' he said reassuringly, 'Phil's already done it. I'm going to get the champers out. I suddenly feel like celebrating.'

He headed towards the kitchen whilst Phil and Ross stared after him in disbelief.

'So ... are we okay Jack?' Ross asked anxiously when Jack returned, champagne bottle and three glasses in his hands.

'Well, I think it'll take me a while to forget what you did and I don't think we'll be sharing cosy nights by the fire anytime soon but, yeah, we're okay. As a matter of fact, if you had told me two weeks ago, things might have been different, but now, well, I sort of understand what you were going through and whilst I don't condone it – you shouldn't ever betray your mates – I can see how it happened. Let's just put it down to life and drink to better times ... and new beginnings.'

Jack handed Phil the glasses and poured the champagne. Phil gave a glass to each of them and they all raised them in the air.

'To better times and new beginnings,' Phil said.

'Oh and Congratulations, I guess Ross,' Jack added, 'you're going to be a father.' They clinked glasses then gulped down the champagne as if they were dying from thirst.

Chapter Fourteen

Lizzie glanced at the clock and saw it was four-thirty. The solicitor would be there soon – Max had called her to confirm that five was fine – and she began to feel odd, like she was losing something and she'd never get it back. She felt the same way when she bought Laurellei Farm, not moving to Scotland, but leaving London. She felt as if it was the end of an era and this felt the same.

It was, of course. It was the end of her marriage to Max. It wouldn't be finally over until the Decree Absolute came through, she knew that, but here, today, was the death knell. Once this ball started rolling, she knew she wouldn't stop it and she asked herself, one final time, if she was really sure.

Max had been so good to her. After lunch, yesterday, they'd read the newspapers then watched movies on Max's enormous 3D television, then played scrabble and it had felt as though they'd turned back time. Only when Max carried her upstairs, deposited her in the spare room, kissed her lightly on the forehead and said goodnight, did reality kick back in.

This morning, he'd brought her breakfast in bed, then carried her downstairs before he left for work and this afternoon, on his way to a meeting, he'd dashed in, given her a huge box of chocolates and dashed out.

He was perfect in so many ways, so many, except one. He'd cheated and no matter how many times he apologised or how many wonderful gestures he made, nothing could ever counteract that in her mind.

Max was feeling stressed. Monday was a busy day for him. He had back to back meetings and had to get his secretary to rearrange the last two so he could get home in time for the solicitor at five. He didn't want to leave Lizzie on her own all day either, so he arranged for his daily help Susan to spend a few extra hours at his place for the duration of Lizzie's stay and, on his way from one meeting to another, he'd dashed in to tell Lizzie and to give her a box of chocolates he'd got his secretary to pick up. He thought it might cheer her up.

Lizzie had been dosing in an armchair when he'd rushed in and she'd looked so gorgeous, so vulnerable, and so sexy that he'd had to fight back an urge to sweep her into his arms and make love to her.

Those days were gone though, he had to accept that but he was amazed at how much the thought tore him apart. Then he remembered what she'd said about sleeping with someone else and jealousy shot through him like blood poisoning. He kept wondering who it was and what exactly had happened. She'd said it was a mistake so it sounded as if she wouldn't be seeing the guy again but still ...

Just after four, Phil knocked on Max's open glass door. Max was on the phone to Lizzie but he gestured to Phil to come in.

'I'll be home by four forty five at the latest Lizzie,' Max said. 'There's champagne in the fridge and we'll order in something really special, okay? After all, it's not as if something like this happens every day is it?'

Phil heard the name and his head shot up. He couldn't hear what Lizzie said but Max laughed in response.

'Well, it's an important day and I think we should treat it accordingly.'

Again Lizzie said something Phil couldn't hear.

'Okay. See you later sweetheart.' Max hung up and glanced at Phil.

Phil was staring at him curiously. 'Um...I...was that Lizzie?' he asked, 'sorry, couldn't help but overhear.'

Max smiled and leant back in his chair. He put his feet up on the desk and linked his fingers putting his arms up and his hands behind his head. 'That's okay Phil. Not a problem. She's staying with me. Came down Saturday night.'

'Saturday! S...she's here?' Phil couldn't hide his surprise.

Max picked up on it. 'Yeah. She told me about the weekend. What a disaster?'

Phil's eyes met his. 'Yeah. One of those things I guess.' He scratched his chin. 'Look I ... I just wanted to say thanks for arranging it anyway and ... um ... well, I didn't know she was your wife. You didn't say.'

Max studied Phil's face. He seemed anxious. 'Didn't I? Well, I guess I just assumed you knew. Lizzie uses her maiden name for the business. Was that a problem? Lizzie being my wife I mean?'

'No! No, of course not. Just ... just a surprise that's all. Um ... we had a great time. She's a really lovely lady.'

'Yes,' Max said, his voice cool, his eyes penetrating. 'She is. Did she tell you we were separated?'

Phil picked up the word "were". 'I ... I think it was mentioned, although at the time, we didn't know it was from you.' He could hear the rising panic in his voice and tried to stay calm. He knew something had happened between Jack and Lizzie, something serious. He just didn't know what.

'Oh well. Not an issue any more. At least you got two days there. Did your mates have a good time?'

Phil licked his lips. 'Yeah. Yeah they did. Anyway, Max. Just wanted to say thanks and please tell Lizzie we ... we're all really sorry about having to dash off like that.'

Max's eyes narrowed. He wanted to ask Phil which one of them had screwed his wife but he wouldn't. 'No problem Phil. As it happens, it's given us the push we needed to sort things out. I'll give her your ... regards shall I?'

Phil met his eyes. 'Yeah. Please do that.'

Max swung his feet down. 'Talking of which, I've got to dash. Promised her I'd be home at four forty five and it's almost four fifteen now.' He grabbed his case and his newspaper and headed towards the door.

Phil stood aside for him.

'See you later Phil,' Max said tapping him on the arm with the newspaper and he dashed towards the lift.

It definitely wasn't Phil, Max thought, but Phil sure as hell knows who it was.

'I didn't know whether I should tell you or not,' Phil said later that evening. He and Jack were in The Mucky Duck having a pint after work and Phil told Jack about the phone call he'd overheard and his conversation with Max.

Jack's hand tightened around his glass and his jaw clenched. 'So it's true then.'

His voice was calm but his face wore a dejected expression. 'I saw her with him on Saturday night. Didn't know it was him, of course. Assumed it might be. Couldn't really believe it was her. Thought it was her doppelganger or something but I knew. Somehow I knew.'

'Don't know what to say mate,'

Jack shrugged. 'Nothing to say. These things happen.' He raised his glass to his lips and sneered. 'It was a stag do after all.' He gulped his Stella.

'None of my business but ... ' Phil hung his head and twisted his glass in his hands, 'did you –'

'Yes mate,' Jack interrupted. 'Like the bloody mug I am, I did.' Jack emptied his glass. 'Another?'

Phil nodded and Jack went to the bar. He returned with two pints and four whiskies. Phil gave him a quizzical look.

'Need them,' Jack said, 'You can either join me or watch me. Up to you.'

'Jack, if there's anything I can do I –'

'Thanks! But there's nothing. I'll get over it.' A twisted smile formed on his lips. 'Won't be calling me Lucky Jack anymore though.' He knocked back one of the whiskies in one gulp.

Phil gave him a wry smile, 'Don't know about that mate, you've got out of marrying Kim. I'd say that was pretty lucky.'

Jack shot him a sideways look, then smirked. 'You're

180

right Phil. That was pretty, damn lucky. You don't really like her do you?'

Phil shook his head. 'Nope. Just something about her. I don't know what. Odd really as I normally go for the blonde bombshell type – and I will say that for her – she is definitely a blonde bombshell.'

'Definitely a bombshell, anyway,' Jack said, picking up one of the pints.

They grinned at one another.

'I actually feel sorry for Ross now. Don't think he has any idea what he's getting himself into. Especially with a kid and everything. Somehow don't see Kim as the stay at home mum type.'

Jack shook his head. 'Me neither.' His brows knit together. 'D'you know, I have absolutely no idea why I ended up being engaged to her. Actually, I don't even know why I started dating her. What the hell was I thinking?'

Phil sniggered. 'I don't think you were thinking, mate. That's something else I'll say for her. When Kim's around men don't think – well, not with their heads anyway.'

Jack's brows shot up. 'You seemed immune. Or did –'

'No mate!' Phil shook his head. 'Thought about it, just like every other male who got within fifty feet of her but I worked with her don't forget, and I soon realised that was one web I didn't want to get tangled in.'

'That was it!' Jack thumped his glass down. 'That's how I started dating her. You introduced us. You shit! Why didn't you warn me off?' Jack's words belied the wry smile he wore.

Phil shook his head. 'I did, actually. And I didn't introduce you. She came over to us and introduced herself as my work colleague. When she asked you to see her home, I remember distinctly telling you to come back with me but you wouldn't have it. Couldn't let her go home on her own.'

'God, I remember. I was just going to see her home 'cos we'd all been drinking quite a bit. Didn't even fancy her, well, not as a girlfriend, if you see what I mean.'

Phil nodded. 'I see exactly what you mean.'

'It was a Friday, wasn't it? Christ, next thing I know, I've spent the whole bloody weekend in her bed. I remember she got really upset 'cos, I don't know, I must've made it obvious I wasn't that interested or something, not in a relationship anyway and I felt guilty and ... God, we just sort of went on from there.'

Phil nodded again. 'That's what I meant about the web. She sort of entangles you. Even the guys at work, they ... I don't know, they sort of pander to her, you know? Mind you. I was still bloody astonished when she announced your engagement. Didn't see that coming at all.'

Jack picked up his glass and stared into it. 'Don't think I did either.' He cast his mind back to Christmas. 'One minute we're talking about Christmas presents and she says she wants a ring, so I say fine, pick one, next thing I know she's got a bloody engagement ring and she puts it on, on Christmas day at my parent's house! What could I say? Take that off, I never proposed! I'd been in Hong Kong the fortnight before, negotiating that deal I finalised a few weeks ago. Huh! Hong Kong's got a lot to answer for. First time, I'm engaged, second time, she sleeps with Ross. Oh well. Anyway, when I get back the ring's under the tree all wrapped up and the first time I see it is when she opens it Christmas morning and shoves it on her finger!'

'Shit!' Phil said. 'You should've said it was a mistake.'

'Yeah right! I think I tried to actually, you know, "I didn't mean that sort of ring" but mum was jumping up and down and dad was congratulating me and ... well, I did love her − or thought I did − so, I didn't see it as a major problem.'

'But why set the date then? Surely you could have delayed it? Thought about it? Got out of it.'

'Kim and her mum! Seems they have contacts. The date's set and everything's booked before I know what's happened. And don't forget. I thought I loved her so, what was the point in delaying? She seemed so happy.'

'Your problem is you're too bloody easy going.'

Jack's eyes clouded over, 'Really, I thought my problem was I talk too much.'

Phil shook his head. 'I'd say you don't talk enough. Why didn't you say something?'

Jack shrugged. 'Didn't seem much point. I was engaged to someone I thought I loved. Didn't really matter how.'

'So ... when did you realise you didn't? I mean, you didn't seem at all bothered when you found out about her and Ross. Christ, I would have killed him if it had been me.'

Jack grinned. 'No you wouldn't.' His face became serious and his eyes filled with sadness. 'I ... was having doubts before we went to Scotland.' He finished his Stella and put the empty glass on the table. 'Scotland made me realise I couldn't go through with it. Then I got the phone call and ... well anyway, as you said, a lucky escape.'

Jack picked up a whisky and gave one to Phil. 'Let's drink to lucky escapes.'

'Lucky escapes,' Phil seconded.

They both raised their glasses in the air and downed the contents in one swallow.

A week after Lizzie sprained her ankle, it was still no better and Max persuaded her she should stay with him for at least a few more days.

They had been getting on so well since they started the divorce proceedings that Max joked that, if he'd known this was how things would be, he'd have started them two years ago.

He left the office early every day and either he cooked or they ordered take out. He insisted Lizzie do nothing except rest. Every night, he carried her to the spare room and kissed her on the forehead. And every night, she tossed and turned and dreamt of Jack.

On the Thursday of the second week Max came home at

six, a little later than he had been of late but still much earlier than the hours he would have kept had Lizzie not been staying with him. He seemed preoccupied.

'Is something wrong Max?' Lizzie asked whilst they were eating the Chinese meal he'd ordered.

Max scowled. 'I heard something today and I'm not sure if I should tell you or not.'

Lizzie felt her insides churn. He'd heard about her and Jack. She held her breath. It had nothing to do with him anymore, she told herself. They were getting divorced but she still felt guilty somehow.

'Tell me ... please,' her voice sounded calmer than she felt. She took a swig of wine and waited.

'It ... it's about Kim – and I don't want you to go mad.'

Lizzie took another gulp of wine. 'Go on,' she said.

He looked her straight in the eye. 'Well, I don't know the whole story and this is really only gossip amongst the secretaries, although Martin Henderson in legal, confirmed it's true, well part of it at any rate.'

Lizzie held her breath.

'Y ... you know the stag weekend I arranged?'

As if she could forget. 'Yes.'

'Well – and I swear to you Lizzie I had no idea – it seems it was Kim's fiancé's and it was Kim who had the accident!'

Lizzie didn't say a word; she fiddled with the stem of her wine glass and dropped her eyes to the table.

'You knew!'

Lizzie nodded. 'I found out the day they were leaving. Phil told me her name and that she worked at the same bank as he did. That's when I realised he was the one who knew you. He ... he didn't know about your affair though, did he, or that we were married?'

Max eyed her thoughtfully, then shook his head. 'No. Kim knew she'd lose her job if that was made public. I did think I had told Phil you were my wife but maybe I just assumed he knew, anyway, it doesn't matter now does it?'

Lizzie shook her head. 'Not now.'

'It must have been quite a shock when he told you it was Kim who was getting married.'

Lizzie nodded. 'It was. That bloody woman seems to ...'

Max glanced at her over his wine glass. 'Seems to ...?'

'Nothing. It doesn't matter.'

Max sipped his wine. 'Did you also know she's pregnant?'

Lizzie almost tipped her wine glass over. The colour drained from her face and her mouth fell open.

'Obviously not,' Max said. 'Then again, neither did she, apparently. Only found out because of the accident.'

'How ... long?'

Max looked confused. 'How many weeks pregnant is she, d'you mean?'

Lizzie nodded.

'I think they said five weeks but I could be mistaken.'

'And ... she didn't know? Neither of them knew?'

'Total surprise. I assume you mean Kim and her fiancé? Kim didn't have a clue but then, she isn't the brightest lamp on the street.' Max poured them both more wine. 'The gossip is, apart from the pregnancy, that the wedding's off, or at least, it's postponed until Kim gets out of hospital. Not sure about that. Anyway, it was originally this coming weekend but now it's not – oh, and, she won't be coming back to work. Her fiancé, Ross insists she stay home and rest! Bit difficult with crutches anyway I would have thought. She's broken her leg or something –'

'Jack. Her fiancé's name's Jack.' Lizzie corrected him in a dazed tone.

'Really? I could have sworn they said Ross.' Max shrugged. 'Makes no difference. Anyway, I just wanted you to know I had no idea the stag do was connected with Kim in any way, shape or form. I wouldn't have got involved if I had, believe me.'

'I do believe you Max.' Lizzie rubbed her temples with her fingers. This news had stunned her. 'Would you mind if

I went and lie down? I've got a headache coming.'

'No, of course not. I'll take you up.'

Lizzie's sprained ankle wasn't giving her anywhere near the pain her broken heart was. She was being ridiculous, she knew that but she couldn't shake herself out of the lethargy she felt.

The weekend came and went. The weekend Jack would have been getting married. At least she didn't have to face that thought for now. Max had said it had been postponed but he hadn't said when to. Not that it made any difference. Kim was pregnant, Jack was going to be a father and whether he married Kim this weekend or three weekends from now, he would marry her and he'd be out of Lizzie's life forever.

Lizzie could picture Jack as a father and somehow, she knew he'd be great at it. She had visions of him playing in the snow with his son – it would be a boy, of course, Kim would naturally give him the son that every man secretly wanted.

Lizzie realised one strange thing. She no longer thought of Kim as *that woman*. It was as if she just didn't have the energy to hate her anymore or maybe it was because Kim was going to be a mother, *the* mother, of Jack's child. Maybe she just couldn't bring herself to think of Kim in her usual derogatory way.

It didn't matter what she called her anyway, in Lizzie's mind, Kim had ruined any chance of happiness Lizzie might have had. First, by having an affair with Max, second, by being engaged to Jack and third, by being pregnant.

Lizzie had thought about little else since Max had told her about the baby and she had suddenly realised something. Something that made her blissfully happy, then unbelievably sad. Jack had not lied. When they had made love on that Friday night, which now seemed so long ago, Jack had every intention of calling off his engagement.

Lizzie was certain of that. She now recalled with clarity everything they'd done, everything they'd said and how he'd behaved when he woke up that fateful Saturday morning – before he'd answered the phone. That call had changed everything and Lizzie now knew without a shred of a doubt that during that call, Jack had been told Kim was pregnant.

That was why he had turned his back to Lizzie, not because he didn't want to be with her but because he couldn't look her in the face and tell her that, whilst he was making love to her, his fiancée was lying in a hospital bed with his child inside her. It must have turned his world upside down.

One minute he'd been planning to end his engagement, the next, he'd been told he was going to be a father. All his words, all his looks came flooding back and she suddenly heard them and saw them in a totally different light.

But it didn't change the outcome and it didn't matter whether Jack had feelings for her or not. Lizzie may have only known him for a couple of days but she knew one thing about him. He was not the sort of man who would walk away from his own child – or the woman carrying it.

This knowledge did not improve her mood and by the following Tuesday, almost two and a half weeks after she'd arrived, Lizzie decided it was time to go home. Her foot was considerably better; she couldn't yet walk without crutches but the swelling had reduced and there was now very little pain, unless she put pressure on it.

Max insisted he would travel up with her and stay a few days to make sure she could manage.

'No arguing,' he said. 'I know Jane will happily stay with you Lizzie but somehow, I just can't see her carrying you upstairs to bed. I want to be sure you can manage.'

'I can't ask you to take time off work for me Max.'

'You didn't ask sweetheart, I offered.' Max still couldn't get out of the habit of calling Lizzie sweetheart.

'I know you did but that's not the point. You're busy and

it's not fair on you.' Lizzie hobbled to the kitchen on her crutches and made them both a cup of tea, balancing on one foot whilst she did so. 'You see. I can manage, honestly.'

Max stood in the doorway watching her. He leant against the frame, his arms folded in front of him, an amiable expression on his handsome face and just a hint of a smile at one corner of his mouth.

'And how, exactly, do you propose to carry even one of those cups into the sitting room, let alone two? Do you intend to balance them on your head?'

Lizzie frowned then her smile brightened her blue eyes. 'We'll drink them in here,' she said.

The grin spread slowly across Max's face and Lizzie got a flash of the man she'd fallen in love with, more than seven years ago. It unsettled her but a little voice in her head said, 'He isn't Jack,' and the moment was gone.

Max pushed himself away from the doorframe and strolled to the kitchen table. Pulling out a chair opposite Lizzie he watched her limp with one crutch and one cup at a time. She managed, with a little effort, to balance her crutches against the back of a chair and drag another out to sit on. Max seemed relaxed but he was poised ready to catch her should she fall.

Only when she was safely seated did Max sit down. 'Yes,' he said, 'I can see you can manage admirably – but I'm still going with you.'

Chapter Fifteen

Max booked their tickets for Thursday, giving himself a day in the office to get things organised for his time away. He had a lot going on and would need to delegate efficiently; he could stay in touch via his Laptop and video conferencing but there were some things that had to be dealt with in person. Not everything was handled electronically, even in a bank as cutting edge as Brockleman Brothers.

If he was honest, this wasn't really a good time for him to be away from the office but he'd let Lizzie down badly once and he had no intention of doing that again. Their marriage may be over and they might be in the process of divorcing but she was still his wife and she mattered more to him than a couple of multi-million pound deals. That was just money after all, and money could always be made in the City, especially if you were Max Bedford.

Despite the fact that she would be returning home tomorrow; or perhaps because of it, Lizzie felt she just had to get out of the apartment, even if only for a few hours. She could walk fairly well with the crutches and, providing she avoided stairs, she should be fine.

She wouldn't mention it to Max though; he was being very "mother hen-ish" and she thought he would either insist that she stay indoors or, on going with her, and that would defeat the object; she wanted some time alone in the fresh air. Well, maybe not "fresh air", this was the City after all.

Sitting on Max's balcony had been the only time she'd spent out of doors since the day she went to the hospital, seventeen days ago and she was craving freedom – in more ways than one. London couldn't offer her the wide open spaces of home or the breathtaking vistas or scent of pine on every intake of breath, but it could at least, give her a change of scene and for some strange reason that she couldn't quite fathom, today, she really needed that.

She could pack the few things she had tomorrow. There would be plenty of time before their flight and she didn't have much. Originally she'd only intended to stay for a few days so had brought just a couple of changes of clothes and underwear. Since she'd been here, she'd been washing and drying them to wear again or, more precisely, Susan, Max's daily help had.

Lizzie made it safely to the hall and dealt with the lift with no problem whatsoever. In the foyer, Preston, the concierge, called a taxi for her, then, when it arrived, he held her arm whilst she shuffled on to the seat. She hadn't realised that getting into a taxi would be such a problem but having started this little expedition, she was determined to go ahead with it and neither Preston or the taxi driver seemed to mind helping her – or that it took almost ten minutes to achieve.

She wondered whether she should have just taken a slow "limp" down to the river bank and sat on one of the many benches to watch life drift by on the Thames, but she wanted people, throngs of people and you didn't get that around Max's luxury apartment block.

Getting out of the taxi in Covent Garden, proved to be a little less fraught. She shuffled to the edge of the seat, placed one arm around the taxi driver's neck and he lifted her out. He kept his arm around her until she got her balance.

After click-clacking with her crutches around Covent Garden market, which was also more difficult than she had expected, she stopped at the Piazza cafe for a pot of tea and a cream cake. She felt she had earned herself a treat. The afternoon sun was gloriously warm for the end of March and she closed her eyes and basked in the soothing rays. By the time she was ready to move on; her cheeks had recovered their usually healthy glow.

She decided to surprise Max. It would prove to him that she was able to get about by herself and although she knew it wouldn't change anything and that he would still insist on going back with her, it would at least show him that she was determined to manage as much as possible on her own.

She hailed a taxi and with some assistance she took less than last time to get herself settled on the seat. Then she sat back and watched as they negotiated the busy streets of central London and headed towards Brockleman Brothers Bank in the heart of the City.

It was just before five when she arrived and for one dreadful moment, she worried that Max may have already left. She asked reception to call him and his secretary said he was still in the office but was unfortunately held up in a meeting.

As if on cue, Lizzie's mobile rang. It was Max.

'Where are you Lizzie? I've been worried sick. I've been calling home for the last fifteen minutes and keep getting the answering machine.'

She hadn't thought of that. 'I'm so sorry Max. I should have called you sooner but I lost track of time. I've popped out for a bit.'

'What ... what do you mean? Popped out for a bit.'

Lizzie sniggered. 'Precisely that. I wanted to get out of the apartment for a couple of hours. I've been basking in the sun in a cafe in Covent Garden.'

'Covent ... how the hell did you get there?'

'Well, it was a major expedition Max and I know I took my life in my hands but I was very brave and faced every danger that getting in the taxi and then drinking tea in the sun threw at me. You should be very proud of my achievement.'

'Yes. Very amusing. But you could have hurt yourself.'

'But I didn't.'

'That's not the point. Did Susan go with you?'

'Um. No. I asked her not to tell you so don't get stroppy with her.'

'Lizzie ...,' Max took a deep breath then let it out. 'Well, there's no point in telling you that you shouldn't have gone. You did and that's that, I suppose. At least you're home now ... you are home now aren't you?'

'In a manner of speaking.'

'What does that mean?'

'I'm downstairs. In the foyer.'

'That's good. Get Preston to help you to the apartment. He won't mind.'

'Not that foyer Max. Brockleman's foyer.'

It seemed to take a second or two for this news to register. 'What? You're here? Why didn't you say so?' Then the line went dead.

Less than a minute later Max appeared from the express lift and marched towards her, a less than pleased expression etched across his incredibly handsome face.

'You don't look very pleased to see me,' Lizzie said now wishing she had gone straight home.

'I'm always pleased to see you Lizzie, you should know that by now. The thing is, I'm stuck in a meeting and I won't be able to get out for at least another hour. That's why I was calling you. To let you know I'd be late.'

'Oh. I see. I'm sorry Max. I ... I just thought that perhaps we could go out for dinner tonight that's all. You know, last night in town and all that. Not a problem though. I should have realised you'd be busy. I'll go. Don't worry. I'll see you later.' Lizzie smiled then turned to go.

'Wait.' Max was beside her in a split second. 'Dinner would be great. If you don't mind waiting in my office for an hour we'll do that. I really can't get out of the meeting. I must get back to it actually, so if you want, I'll take you up to my office now and leave you in my secretary's capable hands ... What? You look annoyed. I'm sorry Lizzie but –'

'No. Of course you must get back and I'm not annoyed. I ... I'd just rather not wait in your office that's all. I haven't been in there since ... well since your previous secretary worked for you. I'd just rather not be there. Silly I know, but there it is. Why don't I wait in the pub? I've got a book with me so I can continue reading that and have a glass of wine – which I must admit I would kill for right now.'

Max's brows drew together but he didn't press the issue. 'That sounds like a plan; if you're sure you'll be okay in the pub for an hour on your own. I'll get someone to help you there.'

'Max! I can get to the pub on my own thanks. It's only round the corner, if I remember correctly. The Black Swan isn't it? And I'm sure I can handle an hour alone in a pub without some major disaster befalling me.'

The Black Swan, or The Mucky Duck, as the regulars called it, was actually an ancient Inn dating back to the fourteenth century that had been added to and extended over the years. On the ground floor was a large bar area and a cosy a la carte restaurant, together with a further brasserie-style restaurant. Upstairs were six en suite bedrooms; now mainly occupied by tourists.

Fortunately for both Lizzie and Max, Max had never told her about the afternoons he, and his former secretary, Kim had spent in one or other of the bedrooms there, on the pretence of being out of the office at a meeting.

Even when cheating on his wife and in a way, his employer, Max didn't like to be too far from his office – and the owners and staff of The Mucky Duck, where nothing if not discreet. At more than one time during its very long history it had also been affectionately known as Ye Olde Knocking Shoppe or something very similar; a fact that the current owners, seemed rather proud of.

Lizzie made her way to the bar and ordered a large glass of Chablis then she headed towards one of the booths which were half hidden towards the back of the pub – another reminder of its former past. One of the staff carried her glass over for her and put her crutches against the wall behind the high-backed padded seat, so they weren't sticking out of the booth for someone to trip over. Lizzie thanked him and settled down with her book to wait for Max.

She didn't know how long she'd been reading but she'd finished one glass of wine and a member of the staff had brought her a second – so somewhere in the region of thirty or forty minutes, when she heard a voice she recognised – and it wasn't Max's.

She scooted forward on the seat, half hoping, half dreading and saw three men and one woman standing at the end of the bar, farthest from her, all dressed in business suits. Two of the men were facing in her direction but she didn't recognise either their faces or their voices. The woman was facing the bar, so Lizzie could see her profile. She was young; probably little more than eighteen or nineteen and stunning with short, naturally curly, black hair and a perfect figure which even a plain dark suit couldn't hide. Lizzie didn't recognise her either.

The third man she would recognise anywhere even though he had his back to her. She recognised his height and his build and the way his clothes seemed to fit so perfectly they could have been made especially for him – and probably were; recognised the colour of his hair and the way he threw his head back when he laughed; recognised that laugh; recognised those hands, one of which was holding a glass of champagne and offering it to the stunning young woman, the other of which was on the woman's waist, gently coaxing her forward towards the glass of champagne – and towards him.

A river of fire swept through Lizzie's veins, followed swiftly by a glacial flow which seemed to freeze both her heart and her reason. So Jack Drake was in the pub with a woman, a stunning young woman and although Lizzie had only seen Kim Mentor for a split second that day she'd found her in bed with Max, she knew for an absolute certainty, this woman wasn't her.

Jack turned his body slightly and the woman raised one slim hand with long, red painted fingernails and placed it against Jack's chest in a feeble attempt to push him away. He laughed and drew her closer, planting a kiss on the top of her head then pulling her to his side and wrapping his arm protectively around her. She leant in to him, took the glass he proffered, raised herself on tip toe and planted a kiss on his left cheek. The group all cheered and laughed and the woman remained encircled in Jack's left arm until two other men Lizzie also recognised, joined the happy group.

Phil slapped Jack on the back and kissed the stunning woman on her cheek. Pete also leant over and gave her a quick peck. Jack released her and turned to the bar. Another bottle of champagne appeared and Jack handed glasses to Phil and Pete then filled them with champagne.

Lizzie was mesmerised. As much as her body seemed to be tearing itself inside out, she couldn't look away. Jack seemed so happy, so carefree and the look of pure unadulterated love on his face when his eyes rested on the young woman was clear for all to see. And yet, this woman wasn't his fiancée. Neither was she his sister – the only other reason a man would look at a woman with such a protective and loving eye; Jack was an only child, he'd told Lizzie that during their night together.

It seemed Jack Drake was no different from Max after all. Both of them wanted to have their cake and eat it. But Jack was actually far worse than Max. He was going to be married soon and more importantly, he was going to be a father. What's more, Jack didn't try to keep his bit on the side a secret; his friends all knew her and it seems, they liked her. A dreadful thought occurred to Lizzie. How long had he been seeing this girl? Before he went to Scotland? Before he and Lizzie ...?

A mixture of rage and jealously tore through her and she wished she could march over to him and slap his face then storm out in disgust, but she couldn't even walk without her crutches and storming anywhere was a step far, far away.

Instead, she sat in the booth watching him and seethed;

one minute wishing she could be in the young woman's shoes, the next, wishing she could tell him exactly what she thought of his philandering, but all the time, telling herself what a fool she had been – what a fool she still was – for falling for the charms of Jack bloody Drake.

Even when he moved away from the bar and headed in her direction five minutes later, she couldn't drag her eyes away.

Jack was in a good mood. It had taken him a while but he felt he had finally come to terms with the fact that, no matter how much he might wish it otherwise, Lizzie was lost to him for good. There really wasn't any point going over and over in his head what he could have said or done differently. Nothing would change the fact that she was reconciled with her husband. And nothing would change the fact that she had used him.

When it came down to it – other than as a blow to his ego – did it really matter whether she had meant any of the things she'd said to him during their incredible night together, even if only for a moment, or whether she was just playing him the entire time? Ultimately, all she'd wanted was to get some sort of twisted revenge on both her husband and Kim.

Oddly enough though, it did matter, but for the life of him, he couldn't understand why. Whether she had felt anything for him or not, she had gone running straight back into her husband's arms – and from what little he'd seen on that Saturday night – they both seemed very happy with the situation.

Phil was right; he had to put it all behind him and move on with his life. At least everything was sorted out with Kim now, so one good thing had come out of that weekend. He should be happy – things could have turned out a whole lot worse. A broken heart could mend. All it needed was good friends, a few drinks and ...

'Lizzie!'

Jack stopped so abruptly that the man walking behind him crashed into his back, spilling his beer down the back of Jack's charcoal grey suit.

'Shit! Sorry mate,' the man said.

Jack didn't hear him, nor did he feel the beer which had splattered his suit jacket, and after giving Jack a few odd looks, the man shrugged and carried on towards his friends.

Neither Lizzie or Jack spoke for what seemed like an eternity but Lizzie's mouth fell open, a hot red flush swept across her face and she eventually managed to drag her eyes away from his and cast them down at the table in the booth.

She fiddled nervously with the stem of her wine glass and tried to stop her eyes from darting a sideways glance at him.

Jack moved somewhat cautiously towards her, almost as though she were a rare bird and might fly away at any moment.

'Lizzie?' His tone was both questioning and disbelieving at the same time.

Lizzie tried to control her breathing; she felt she was gasping for air. After several seconds she managed a modicum of composure and slowly turned her head to face him, her blue eyes cold, hiding the anger and resentment threatening to explode from her at any moment.

'Hello Jack,' she said taking a deep breath.

'Wh ... what are you doing here?' he stammered.

Lizzie pursed her lips. She felt like saying, "Caught you in the act didn't I?" Instead she said, 'I'm having a glass of wine and reading my book. Do you mind?'

Jack seemed confused. 'Do I m...? Um ... no. Of course not. Why would I mind? It ... it's just a surprise, that's all. Um ... it's lovely to see you, Lizzie.' A smile began to form on his lips.

Her eyes travelled the length of his body and her lips curved into a tiny sneer. 'Really Jack? Somehow I doubt that.'

His brows shot together and his penetrating sapphire eyes seemed to drill into her, weakening the barrier she was trying so hard to construct.'

'I ...' His voice trailed off as his eyes seemed to search her face.

Lizzie felt herself wilting in the heat of his gaze. She must hold her ground; those hypnotic eyes could so easily entice her.

'Well, we did part on rather, shall we say, less than amicable terms.' She raised her glass to her lips in an attempt to appear uninterested but her hand shook and she found it difficult to swallow so she quickly put it down again.

Jack watched her. 'Yes,' he said, 'I'd almost forgotten that.'

Lizzie misread his meaning and instantly felt her hackles rise. 'Naturally! With so many women in and out of bed with you it must be difficult to keep track. Don't trouble yourself though Jack, it was hardly worth remembering. I'd almost forgotten it myself until I saw you again just now.'

'What the ...?'

His eyes flashed and she saw the colour drain from his face, then rise again, this time to an almost blood red fury. His lips formed a tight, hard line and she noticed his fists clench. For one dreadful moment she thought he might lash out and strike her, but deep down, she somehow knew he wouldn't.

She saw him take a deep breath and then his mouth curved into a grin; not the devilish grin she had come to know so well and love but a cruel, bitter grin that made the tiny lines around those exceptionally blue eyes, stand out.

'Well,' he said after a while, his voice now almost mellow 'at least we remember each other's name, that's something I suppose.'

Lizzie's mobile rang from inside her handbag but she made no move to answer it.

He glanced at her bag. 'Aren't you going to answer

that?'

'It's probably Max,' she'd said, before she could stop herself.

Jack's eyes glinted then he smirked. 'Well. Don't let me stop you,' he said, taking a step away from her towards the rear of the pub – and the gents' toilets. 'It was good to see you again Lizzie – for reasons you can't even begin to imagine.' And with that he was gone.

Ludicrously, she wanted to run after him. To ask him what he had meant by that. To ask him anything in fact, just to spend a few more minutes with him but of course, she could hardly even walk let alone run.

He'd have to come back though, she realised. He'd clearly headed for the gents, so he'd reappear sooner or later. All she had to do was wait. So she answered her phone – it was Max to say he'd be another fifteen minutes – and then she did just that.

Jack's mood had gone from good to bad in about ten seconds flat. Why could seeing Lizzie make him feel so unbelievably happy one minute and then angry enough to kill, the next? How could she do that to him? Until he'd met her he'd always been so easy going. Nothing much had really bothered him. Even finding out his fiancée and his best friend had slept together behind his back hadn't made him mad. Mind you, he might have felt differently about that if he hadn't met Lizzie and already decided he didn't want to marry Kim – though somehow, he knew he wouldn't have.

And how come he, who was never usually lost for words, could hardly manage to string more than one sentence together when he was talking to her? It was crazy. He was crazy – and that was the problem. No matter what he told himself or what he did to try to change it – there was one thing he had to accept – he was crazy about a married woman.

He couldn't face her again. He wouldn't describe

199

himself as a coward but subjecting himself for a second time to her contemptuous sneer and dismissive comments, wasn't his idea of bravery – more like suicide in fact; by a firing squad of looks and words. Then there was her husband. He'd no doubt be joining her and the thought of spending even ten minutes watching them all cosy together was even worse.

There was a side door between the gents and the main bar area. He could leave through that. He would call his friends and make some excuse, then meet them all later. Emma wouldn't mind – and if she did, he would find a way to make it up to her.

Chapter Sixteen

'Welcome home!' Jane and Iain yelled in unison. They were waiting in the hall for Lizzie when she opened the front door of Laurellei Farm on Thursday evening. Alastair, who didn't want to be left out, barked and wagged his tail, darting from Jane to Lizzie and back again as if he were on an elastic cord.

'Yes. I'm happy to see you too boy!' Lizzie balanced on her crutches and stroked Alastair's head. 'Go to your bed now, so I don't trip over you.'

Alastair raced to his basket but put his head on one side so he could still see Lizzie through the open kitchen door.

Lizzie hugged Jane and Iain in turn then Max helped her off with her coat.

'Oh it's so good to be home! I've missed you so much,' Lizzie said fighting back the tears pricking at her eyes.

'I've missed you too!' Jane said not bothering to fight hers.

They hugged again and Iain and Max nodded to each other over their heads.

'Go through into the sitting room,' Iain said, 'there're cakes and biscuits and I'll go and make some tea.'

'Thanks,' Max said.

Lizzie and Jane were already on their way through, Lizzie limping on one crutch with one arm around Jane. Alastair saw they were going into the sitting room and trotted in after them. Once Lizzie was seated, he curled up on the floor beside her feet.

'Show me the ring,' Lizzie said as soon as she was comfortable.

Jane held out her left hand and an intense green, oval cut emerald with a diamond either side sparkled up at Lizzie.

'It's gorgeous!' Lizzie said surprised that Iain should choose such a ring.

Jane beamed. As if reading Lizzie's mind she said, 'Iain chose an emerald because he said it matched my eyes.'

Lizzie glanced up at her. 'It does! Well. Who'd have thought Iain was such a romantic.'

'Oh Lizzie. You don't know the half of it! He is sooooo romantic and kind and gentle and loving ... and ... well, perfect!'

Lizzie hugged her again. 'I really am so happy for you Jane. So, have you set the date now?'

Max was hovering in the doorway when Iain brought the tea tray loaded with a pot of tea, milk and sugar from the kitchen and Iain gave Max a quizzical look.

'Women's talk,' Max said, nodding his head towards the sofa where Lizzie and Jane were huddled together giggling and holding hands.

'Aye. Best leave them to it. D'you want tea, or something a wee bit stronger?'

Max smiled. 'A wee bit stronger, please.'

'I'll give them their tea and we'll go back in the kitchen.' Iain took the tray through and laid it on the coffee table. He leant forward and kissed the top of Jane's head. 'We'll be in the kitchen if you need us, sweetheart.'

Jane beamed up at him. 'Okay love. Thanks.' Then to Lizzie, 'Well we've talked about it and obviously with the tourist season approaching and everything, we thought we'd wait until October.'

Iain smiled and left them to it.

'October! That's months away.' Lizzie said.

Jane grinned. 'I know but wait, I haven't finished. We discussed it with Fraser – well, actually that's not true. We told Fraser we were planning to wait until October and his reaction was the same as yours. He suggested we have a quick civil ceremony before the season starts and then a blessing and a formal reception in October. For a twenty-four year old that young man really has his head screwed on. Iain says Fraser just wants me to move in quickly so that he doesn't have to put up with his dad's cooking, but I know that's not true. Iain's a really good cook.'

Lizzie gasped. 'So, is that what you're doing, about the wedding I mean, not the moving in bit?'

Jane nodded. 'It's all arranged! I was going to tell you over the phone but I wanted to tell you in person. It's March 31st! That way we thought we could go away for a few days honeymoon and still be back in time for the Easter weekend. We had to give a minimum of fifteen days notice so we were cutting it fine but you'd said you weren't going to open again before Easter so we thought that would be perfect. Will you be able to walk without the crutches by then?'

'Oh Jane. It's so exciting! And I'll make damn sure I can walk without crutches. But you shouldn't have worried about me or the tourist season. This is your wedding and nothing else matters.'

Jane shook her head. 'D'you know something Lizzie. I always thought I wanted a big wedding, you know, church, bridesmaids, carriage, the whole enchilada but all I want, all I really want, is to be Iain's wife and I don't care if it's in the back of a tractor!'

Lizzie hugged her and neither of them tried to hold back their tears; they were tears of pure joy.

Lizzie and Max fell into a routine. At eight in the morning Max took her a cup of coffee in bed then he fed the animals – he asked Jane to show him what to do, animal husbandry was not his strong point – then he carried Lizzie downstairs after she'd showered and dressed, and deposited her in the kitchen.

He made them both breakfast and after that, he went to Lizzie's study at the back of the house behind the kitchen and did some work via his Laptop. Jane came and spent the morning with Lizzie, baking or just talking and then both Jane and Max did household chores.

'I don't know what's come over Max,' Jane said on Saturday morning. 'I never thought I'd see the day when

Max Bedford would be feeding animals and cleaning them out. And as for using the washing machine and vacuum, well, that's just unbelievable!'

Lizzie grinned at her. 'It has only been two days Jane. He'll soon get fed up with it. No. I shouldn't be mean, he's been brilliant. Especially bearing in mind that he probably hasn't even looked at a duster, let alone used one, for years. Actually, I think that's the one thing I miss; earning enough money to pay someone else to do the housework.'

'You pay me,' Jane teased.

'We share,' Lizzie countered. 'To be honest, he did suggest getting someone in but I reminded him that I'm not made of money and I won't let him pay, so I suppose he didn't really have much choice. I was surprised when he offered to feed and clean out the animals though. I half expected him to make some excuse and say you were so good at it and that he wouldn't interfere.'

'In typical Max fashion, you mean. Where he convinces you that he's actually doing you a favour, instead of the other way around. I did tell him I was happy to do them actually, but he insisted. You don't think he's doing this to try to get you back do you?'

'No! Well, I don't think so. The divorce proceedings have been started and he hasn't even brought up the subject – of us, I mean. No. I think he finally realised when I was in London that I'll never really get over his affair and that we both need to move on with our lives.'

'Hmm. Well let's hope so. I'm going to make some coffee. Do you want some?'

'Well that's a pretty silly question. Of course I do – and biscuits.'

They sat at the kitchen table drinking coffee and munching biscuits until Jane said tentatively, 'You ... haven't mentioned Jack since you've been back. Have you heard anything else? Has Max said any more about it?'

Lizzie's eyes misted over. 'No. Nothing since he told me about the pregnancy and the postponement of the wedding.

I thought about asking him but I don't want to stir it all up again. He knows something happened between me and one of the guys and if I seem too interested in Jack he may put two and two together. It doesn't matter anyway. It was a mistake.'

'I don't know Lizzie. When you told me what Max said about Kim being pregnant, it all sort of made sense somehow. Everyone thought Jack had feelings for you – even his friends. I really think if he hadn't got that phone call, things may have gone differently and –'

'But he did get the call and nothing's going to change that – or the fact that she's pregnant. I've gone over and over it all since Max told me and yes, I also began to think that maybe I'd misjudged Jack, and that it wasn't just a one night stand for him either – until I saw him in the pub. Whether I like it or not, I have to accept that Jack isn't the Knight in shining armour I keep making him out to be. He's a cheating, lying bastard who knows exactly what to do and say to get a woman into bed with him – and exactly what to do and say to get her out of it when he's finished!'

Jane shook her head. 'I still can't believe that. I really thought he was a decent guy after all. Are you sure she wasn't just a work colleague or something – or just a really good friend.'

'Yeah! A really, really good friend. Believe me, you don't look at friends the way he looked at her and certainly not work colleagues – unless something's going on. He loved her! Loves her, I suppose I should say. It was written all over his face.'

'But you can love friends Lizzie. We love each other and we're just friends. Iain loves you, and he's just your friend. You love –'

'Okay. I get it. There is a slim chance, I suppose that she was just a friend but I'm not sure I buy it. She was half his age – eighteen or nineteen at the most – unless she's had a bloody good facelift – and I just don't believe an eighteen year old girl and a thirty-five year old guy would be best buddies somehow.'

Jane tutted. 'You're getting cynical in your old age my girl. Of course they can! But the thing I still don't understand, out of all of it, is why he didn't just tell you about the baby when he got the call that morning.'

'Ah. That bit I do get. I think he was probably suffering from shock. He looked dreadful; the colour drained from his face. At the time, I thought it was just the shock of hearing about the accident but now I suspect it was the shock of being told he was about to be a father. I mean, he had just decided to end his engagement and spent the night with another woman – and it must have been one hell of a surprise, assuming he was telling the truth about ending the engagement, which, of course, I'm still not convinced he was.'

'Oh God. What a mess the whole thing is.' Jane took a sip of coffee. 'I think it's rather sad though – if he was telling the truth. Okay, he's facing up to his responsibilities and not abandoning her but if he didn't love her enough to marry her before, I don't see how that's going to change because she's pregnant – and that's not a good way to start married life is it? It's rather old fashioned too. I mean, in this day and age, you don't need to marry someone just because you're having a child together.'

Lizzie's brows creased. 'No. That's true. But maybe when he heard about the accident – and the baby – he decided he did still love her or maybe, he'll fall back in love with her once the baby's born.'

'Hmm. You've been reading too many romance novels whilst you were at Max's. I'm not sure that sort of thing happens in real life.'

Lizzie shrugged. 'Perhaps not. Or maybe he's just a lying, cheating shit who doesn't give a damn about anyone but himself. Anyway, I hope they'll both be very happy.' She banged her coffee mug on the table. 'My biggest regret is the part I played in it all. If only I hadn't slept with him – but it's water under the bridge now and I'll never see him again so there's really no point in thinking about it, is there? He's probably forgotten it already.'

Jack, as it happened, was thinking about very little else. He and Phil had talked about it more times than either of them wanted to acknowledge and today was no different.

They were drinking coffee at Jack's apartment, waiting for Ross to arrive and remove Kim's belongings. She didn't have that much at Jack's; she'd only moved in just after Christmas and she'd sub-let her small apartment furnished – so it was really only clothes, make-up and personal items – but it would still need the three of them to carry the bags, cases and boxes to Ross's car.

'The thing I still don't get, no matter how many times I go over it, is how Lizzie could spend the night with me to get revenge on her husband and Kim and the next day be back in her husband's arms all lovey-dovey. She just didn't seem that cold hearted. And ... she was so convincing. I really thought she had feelings for me.'

'Yeah, I agree. Plus, I still think it's an odd thing to do. She told us they were separated – and okay, that may have been part of the plan to lead you on but ... how could she be so sure you'd fall for her? Yeah, I know,' Phil said as Jack was about to interrupt, 'she's pretty stunning but even so, she'd have to be very manipulative to scheme like that – and I just don't believe it. Anyway, what I was going to say was, if she and Max were getting back together, why would she risk sleeping with you? I can't see any man accepting the "you did it so I did it too" line and certainly not someone like Max.'

'Perhaps she hasn't told him. Maybe it's one of those secret revenge things; it's enough to know you've got your own back without anyone else knowing about it.'

Phil snorted. 'Come on Jack. You said it yourself, she isn't that cold hearted.'

'I said she didn't seem that cold hearted. Maybe she is. Let's face it, we were only with her for two days, hardly enough time to get to know someone is it?'

'I guess not. I still can't see it though.'

'You didn't see her in the pub. She was pretty sodding cold then I can tell you. I can still see the look on her face. And another thing, we were supposed to be in Scotland for the whole weekend so that means she must have decided to come down after we left. Why would she do that? Unless she was worried that her husband might find out she'd spent the night with me. Maybe she thought you'd say something, once she realised you knew him.'

Phil sipped his coffee and considered this. He shook his head. 'Still don't believe it. That would mean she'd told him herself and as I said, I can't see Max just accepting that.' Phil thought for a moment. 'Although, Max did say something about it giving them a push to sort things out or something, remember? I told you about the conversation we had in his office.'

Jack sighed. 'How could I forget?'

The doorbell rang and Jack sprang to his feet to answer it, knowing it would be Ross.

'Come in Ross. D'you want some coffee?'

Ross smiled sheepishly. 'Yes please.' He still felt awkward with Jack and Phil even though he'd seen them a few times since the day of his confession three weeks ago.

Jack had been to visit Kim in hospital a few days after, partly to see how she was but mainly, to show there were no hard feelings on his part, and Ross had been there. A week later, Phil and Jack were in The Mucky Duck when Ross had popped in and Jack, like the true friend he was, had bought Ross a pint. And of course, Ross had joined them all for dinner on Emma's eighteenth birthday. There was still a frisson of tension between the three men but none of them dwelt on it.

They'd also met up a couple of times in the pub with Pete, Jeff and Steve, who'd all been totally stunned when Ross and Jack had apprised them of all the developments. It was on one of those evenings that Jack had suggested to

Ross it was time he moved Kim's things out of his apartment and they had arranged it for Saturday.

'Everything's packed and ready to go,' Jack said. 'Are you taking it to your place?'

'Oh! Um. I guess so. Kim's staying with her mum for the time being so she's got someone with her all day, you know, whilst I'm at work, but now the wedding's rearranged I suppose she'll be moving in with me after that.'

Phil raised his eyebrows. 'You suppose?'

Ross stuck out his bottom lip and thought about it. 'Yeah. I mean, of course she'll be moving in with me.'

'You could move into her mum's,' Jack said, grinning.

Ross's eyes shot to Jack's face. 'Yeah right!' he said, grinning back. 'I'll pay someone to come and look after her if she still needs care during the day. There's no way on this earth I'm starting married life living at my mother-in-law's!'

Jack laughed. 'I'd put that in a pre-nuptial agreement, if I were you.'

Phil nodded. 'Me too! I'd also add that the mother-in-law couldn't move in to the spare room – and I'd get moving on turning it into a nursery.'

Ross became serious. 'A nursery! God, I don't think it's really sunk in yet. You know, the whole, I'm going to be a father bit.' He dropped on to the sofa.

Jack handed him a mug of coffee. 'It took me a few days to come to terms with the fact that I wasn't going to be.'

Ross glanced up at him. 'I'm really sorry Jack.'

'Hey no! Don't be sorry. I didn't mean it like that mate. It wasn't a dig at you. I was glad the kid's not mine. Honestly Ross, I do mean that but still ... it was a weird feeling. One minute I thought I was going to be a father, the next, I wasn't, and even though I'm pleased, it was all kind of surreal, that's all. I expect it'll take a long time for you to get used to it'.

Ross shook his head. 'I don't think I'll really believe it's happening until I hold it in my arms. I hope it's a boy.'

Jack smiled. 'I hope so too but as long as it's healthy, that's the main thing. I still can't believe you'll be a married man in a few weeks' time, let alone a father.'

Phil put his empty mug on the coffee table. 'I can't believe Kim's agreed to get married with her leg in plaster! I know it's a registry office but even so.'

Ross smirked. 'Yeah, that kind of threw me too. I thought we were going to wait but Kim and her mum had it all arranged within a week after I proposed. I just had to take Kim along so that we could both give notice and they did the rest. I think she just wants to be married now – what with the baby and everything.'

Jack and Phil exchanged knowing glances.

'So what's the plan then?' Phil asked. 'I know you said the wedding's on April 4th but are you going away or anything? Bit difficult with her leg in plaster, I suppose.'

'Actually, we're not going anywhere. Not just because of her leg but also because of the baby. I know the doctor said she's okay and the baby's fine but it was a lucky escape and I just want to be on the safe side. Kim says we can go somewhere exotic when the baby's a few months old, so maybe next year we'll do something. I'm not that fussed to be honest.'

Jack smiled. 'Well, at least you've got the wedding day sorted. Must admit, I was a little surprised to get an invite even though you'd told me in the pub.'

'You ... you're okay with it aren't you? I mean we're not having anyone at the registry office other than family but I ... we ... both wanted you to be at the lunch afterwards. It's not too weird is it?'

Jack grinned. 'It's weird, but it's okay. To tell you the truth, it would feel more weird to not be there. Just don't ask me to do any speeches!'

'I won't. Thanks Jack.'

'For what?'

'For everything, but mainly, for being such a good

friend.'

'Oh God,' Phil said jumping to his feet. 'Don't start getting all mushy. Let's get Kim's things in your car and over to your place and then, let's go to the pub. I could murder a pint.'

'Really Max, I'll be fine,' Lizzie said, 'I can't expect you to stay here any longer. You've been marvellous and I really appreciate everything you've done but I need to stand on my own two feet. Literally! Although no pun was intended.'

They were driving from the registry office in Aviemore, on Jane and Iain's wedding day, to The Drovers Rest in Kirkedenbright Falls, where a small reception was being held to which all the village was invited.

Max smirked. 'Very funny. But how will you cope while Jane and Iain are away? They'll be gone for four days. Why don't I stay on till they get back? I really don't like the thought of you here on your own.'

Lizzie sighed. The truth was she would kill for a few days on your own. Max had been wonderful and she wouldn't have been able to cope very well without him she had to admit, but being in his company for so many weeks now was starting to make both of them feel a little too comfortable.

'Well I'm not suggesting you leave today Max or even tomorrow, but maybe the next day. Then Jane and Iain will be back a couple of days after that and besides, I won't be entirely on my own.'

Max glanced at Lizzie. 'Oh? And what does that mean. I hope you're not suggesting Alastair will look after you. He's a dog Lizzie.'

Lizzie grinned. 'Of course not, although, he can load the washing machine and ... no, I'm not suggesting him. Fraser's new girlfriend Annie has offered to help out while Jane's away and I thought I might take her up on it. She's interested in the hospitality sector so learning a bit about how a B&B runs is a start, sort of. I don't need carrying up and down the stairs anymore and if I need anything heavy lifted or moved, I'll ask Fraser.'

Max seemed to be concentrating on the road. He didn't answer and Lizzie wondered if she had upset him in some way. She was about to ask when he pulled the Land Rover over to the side of the road, switched off the ignition and turned in his seat to face her.

'Okay,' he said looking her directly in the eye. 'I know we've talked about this and I know we've started divorce proceedings but being with you these last few weeks has been like old times. No.' He held up his hand, palm towards her like a stop sign, 'please just let me say this. I know you said you'll never get over the affair and I understand that, really I do but Lizzie, we are good together. Don't tell me you haven't enjoyed the past few weeks, even with a sprained ankle. Couldn't ... couldn't we carry on as we are and see if it takes us somewhere.'

Lizzie's lower lip trembled and she struggled to hold back the tears she'd been fighting with since Jane and Iain's wedding ceremony. She shook her head sadly and fiddled with the strap of her handbag, not wanting to look at Max's face.

'I ... I have enjoyed being with you Max, of course I have. I always do and ... you've been absolutely wonderful but that's not the problem is it? The problem is I don't want to spend the rest of my life wondering if you might do it again. I know you say you won't – and I believe you mean it, I really do but something may happen, someone may come along and wham, it could happen again.'

'Lizzie it won't. I swear!'

'No Max! Please don't. I ... I didn't want to bring this up and please don't get cross but ... well, I don't love you like that anymore.' She cast her eyes to his face. 'I do still love you and I think part of me always will but ... I just don't love you enough. Not enough to take that sort of risk and get my heart broken again.'

Max studied her face. 'You've changed Lizzie,' he said with a hint of sadness. 'I realised it when you came down that first weekend, that's why I agreed to start the divorce proceedings.' He smirked and took her right hand in his, his thumb stroking the wedding and engagement rings she wore there. 'I suppose I knew it the moment I saw you'd moved the rings. You'd never have done that unless it was really over in your mind. Funny, for the last two years I think I took it for granted that you'd come back to me, was sure you would and I suppose ... I took you for granted too. I'm so sorry.'

Their eyes met and Lizzie smiled sadly. 'So am I Max. For the last two years you've been able to twist me around your little finger without even trying and I'm not even sure you always realised you were doing it but ... well, you can't do that anymore.'

'You don't blame me for one last try do you?' The corner of his mouth curved up.

Lizzie shook her head. 'No. But I think it's time you went back to London.'

He leant across and kissed her on the head. 'We've got Jane and Iain's reception to go to first,' he said turning on the ignition. 'May I just ask you something – and don't you get cross either, but, is this because of that stag weekend?'

Lizzie's guard came up and she tensed her shoulders visibly. 'What ... what do you mean?'

Max's right arm rested across the steering wheel and he cocked his head to one side. He tried to sound casual. 'Just that I know something happened with one of the guys – you admitted as much – but I didn't think it was serious. You said it was a mistake and I assumed you meant it didn't mean anything but, did it? Is that what you really meant? It was a mistake because it meant too much? Lizzie ... did you sleep with Kim's fiancé?'

Her eyes shot to his and he noted the horrified expression on her face.

'Wh ...' Words deserted her.

'My God! So that's it.' Max shook his head in disbelief and stared through the windscreen. 'Did you know? No, of course you didn't. Did he? I mean,' he looked back at Lizzie, 'did he know you were my wife and ... and about the affair?'

Lizzie gasped. 'No!' she turned startled eyes to his perplexed ones. 'He knew nothing about it until I told him that morning.'

'You told him! Why?'

Lizzie shook her head. 'Oh God Max. I don't know! That ... that whole morning was just mad. He said he was going to break off the engagement, then he got the phone call and I thought ... well it doesn't matter what I thought, then Phil told me about Kim and I realised and, well, like you, I put two and two together and made five and then everything got even more crazy and we said things and ... well, anyway... he didn't know until I told him.'

'Wait a minute. Go back a bit. He said he was going to break off the engagement?'

'Oh God! Me and my big mouth. Forget I said that Max. It ... it doesn't matter now anyway.'

'I think it would matter to Kim! And, quite frankly, it seems to have mattered to you too!'

'Oh Max, please. They're having a baby. What use is there in talking about this?'

'I just want to know, that's all. You really care about him don't you? Does he feel the same?'

'Max!' Lizzie shrieked. 'Let it go! It's over. It was just one night for heaven's sake.'

'One night that seems to have changed your life, Lizzie. One night you can't seem to forget!'

'Okay Max! Yes I care about him. I care about him so bloody much that it hurts even now, four weeks later. I care about him so much that I want to go to London and shout it from the Bank of bloody England. Don't marry her, I want to yell. Leave her and the baby. Come back to me! But I don't and it wouldn't do any good if I did. He couldn't give

214

a damn about me – and he's going to marry her and there's not a bloody thing I can do about it! Okay? Happy now?'

Chapter Seventeen

'There you are! We were starting to get worried,' Jane said when Lizzie and Max arrived at The Drovers Rest half an hour later. 'Is everything okay? You look ... like you've been crying.'

'I always cry at weddings, you know that,' Lizzie said hugging Jane. 'We ... had a problem and had to pull over for a while. Nothing serious. All okay now. So, how are you ... Mrs. Hamilton?' Lizzie held hands with Jane and stood back a step. 'You're looking pretty radiant.'

Jane laughed blissfully. 'I'm feeling pretty radiant! I can't get enough of being called Mrs. Hamilton. Come and have some champagne. Oh, by the way, thanks for that Max. It was really kind of you to pay for six cases of it! I'm not sure I'm going to be very sober on my wedding night.'

'My pleasure,' Max said kissing Jane on the cheek. 'And congratulations. Iain's a very lucky man.'

Jane shook her head. 'I'm the lucky one Max believe me. Come on. Let's get this celebration well and truly started.'

Lizzie and Max followed Jane to where Iain was standing, beside the three tier wedding cake Lizzie and Jane had made. He was in deep conversation with his son Fraser but his eyes lit up with love when Jane approached.

'I was wondering where you'd got to,' he said, pulling Jane into his arms and kissing her on the lips, 'thought you'd had second thoughts and run off with someone else.'

Jane laughed. 'You won't get rid of me that easily. I went to see if I could see Lizzie but she walked in just as I got to the door. I was getting worried.'

Iain leant forward and kissed Lizzie on the cheek. 'What happened to you? You left the same time we did.'

'Slight problem,' Lizzie said, 'all sorted now. When do you leave for your honeymoon? Jane says it's all a big secret.'

Iain nodded. 'Aye it is. Just waiting for a fair wind.' He winked at her.

Max grinned knowingly.

'You know something don't you?' Jane said seeing Max's grin.

Max gave her his most disarming look. 'Not a thing,' he said as Iain handed him a glass of champagne.

'Somehow,' Lizzie said, 'I don't think I believe you.'

Max's eyes met hers. 'Story of our lives,' he said, 'Excuse me.' He brushed past her and beckoned Iain and Fraser to the bar.

'Is everything okay?' Jane whispered. 'Max seems a bit ... distant.'

'Everything's fine,' Lizzie said, then glancing around the bar area and into the dining room, 'Looks like everyone's turned up.'

'Yep! It's been a fabulous day so far. Thanks for all the help with the food. That seems to be going down a treat too.'

'Good thing Dougall's so easy going. We've brought all the food and Max brought all the champagne, doesn't leave much for him to make a profit on.'

'Auch no – oh my God, I sounded just like Iain then – anyway, I don't think Dougall cares about profit where his friends and neighbours are concerned.'

Lizzie laughed. 'No. I suspect he makes enough out of the tourists.'

'He said he made a fortune out of Jack and – oh sorry Lizzie, didn't mean to mention his name.'

Lizzie put her arm around Jane. 'Don't worry about it. When are you going to cut the cake?'

'Fairly soon I think. Iain says we'll be leaving sometime around four. How's your foot holding up?'

'Not bad actually. I keep balancing on the other one when I can just to give it a rest but, so far so good. Don't think I'll be dancing any time soon though. In fact, if you don't mind, I'm going to grab a seat now and have something to eat. I'm starving.'

'Me too! Mind you, we haven't had anything since you came over after breakfast to help me get ready so I suppose we would be.'

'Unless champagne is a food group.'

At three thirty Iain and Jane cut the cake and Fraser made a short speech.

'I just want to wish my dad and my new mum all the happiness in the world. They are two of the nicest people I know and anyone can see they belong together. Mind you, I didn't think dad would ever get around to asking Jane out – and come to think of it – I'm not sure he ever did but I'll spare their blushes and simply say that they finally realised they are crazy about one another. So please, raise your glasses in a toast to the happy couple. Mr. and Mrs. Hamilton. Iain and Jane.'

Everyone cheered and toasted them then Iain said. 'I'm a man of few words as you all know and I won't change that now but I just want to say that when Jane Munroe agreed to become my wife I felt as though I'd caught the moon in my hands. Well, I cannae take her to the stars but I can, hopefully, take her closer to heaven – and not in the way you're all thinking – well, not until later anyway.'

Loud cheers and laughter reverberated around the pub then a whooshing sound from outside broke in on the jollity.

Iain took Jane's hand and kissed her on the lips. 'You carriage awaits,' he said and led her outside.

'Oh my God Iain!' Jane screamed, laughing and crying at the same time.

In the field opposite the pub stood a hot air balloon, its basket covered in ribbons and bows, a few tin cans and a "Just Married" banner. Iain swept Jane up in his arms and strode to the basket where he gently deposited her inside, before climbing in himself.

Fraser handed his dad a bottle of champagne and three glasses. 'Don't drink yours until you've safely landed,' he said to the balloon pilot, laughing. 'Have a great flight dad – and you ... mum. See you in a few days.'

'Don't worry sweetheart,' Iain said 'we're not spending our honeymoon in this. A car will pick us up wherever we land and take us to the airport.'

'Airport! I thought we were just having a few days in an hotel.'

'So we are – an hotel in Florence.'

Jane gasped in delight. 'Iain Hamilton, I love you more than anything on earth.'

'Even chocolate?'

Jane leant into him and kissed him softly, as the balloon slowly lifted off from the ground and the balloon company staff, released the restraining ropes.

'Even chocolate,' she said.

Lizzie waved them off, tears streaming down her cheeks.

Max came and gently put his arm around her as the rest of the wedding guests cheered and waved to the newlyweds.

'Lizzie!' Jane suddenly shouted from several feet above the ground and she threw her bouquet into the crowd.

Instinctively Lizzie reached out and, as Jane had aimed it directly at her, she caught it with both hands.

Max returned to London two days after the wedding as Lizzie had suggested. Neither of them mentioned the conversation they'd had on the way to the reception but there was a definite cooling off on Max's part. It was as if he'd put a barrier up and no one would be able to knock it down, least of all Lizzie.

She was glad in a way and when Max said goodbye at the front door of Laurellei Farm, she felt as if they'd moved into an entirely new relationship, one of friendship and nothing else and she felt oddly relieved.

Fraser's girlfriend Annie had come over the day after the

wedding to learn how to feed the animals, as Lizzie still wasn't really up to being barged by the pigs, Peter and Penelope or playfully pecked at by the chickens and Annie had taken over from Max with no effort at all.

Just like Fraser, Annie seemed very sensible, which was why Lizzie got such a shock when Annie told her about a booking she'd taken, the day that Jane and Iain were returning from their honeymoon.

'Lizzie I'm really sorry but I think I've screwed up a booking.'

Lizzie had just come downstairs after taking her shower and Annie was in the kitchen. She'd made a pot of coffee and some toast for Lizzie. She had the bookings print out for Easter weekend on the table in front of her.

Lizzie sat down and poured herself a mug of coffee. Spreading butter on her toast she said, 'I'm sure it's nothing we can't sort out. What seems to be the problem?' She bit into her toast and glanced at Annie.

'Well, you know that a couple cancelled for Easter weekend, I mean next weekend, so there's a room free.' Annie took a swig of her own coffee and licked her lips nervously.

Lizzie reached out a hand to her and brushed her fingers. 'I don't bite Annie. Don't look so worried. And next weekend is Easter weekend.'

Annie forced a weak smile. 'Yes, that's what I meant. I mean it's next weekend and Easter. Oh Gosh. I wanted to do everything right and be a help to you and now I've ruined it.'

Lizzie's brows shot up. It wasn't like Annie to be a drama queen – that was more her own domain, Lizzie thought ruefully. 'You have been a great help Annie and believe me, there's nothing you could have done that can't be sorted. What is it?'

'Someone phoned while you were in the shower and asked if by any chance we had a double room over Easter. I said they were really lucky because we had just had a cancellation yesterday due to ill health so he said he'd like to book the room and he and his wife would arrive on Good Friday.'

Lizzie waited but Annie fiddled with her coffee mug. 'That's not a problem Annie. That just means we're full again over Easter – and that's great.'

'Yes but ... my mobile rang and ... well I forgot to take any details. I just said that was great and we'd see them on Good Friday, then I answered the mobile and it was Fraser to say that Jane and Iain have landed and will be home soon and ... well, it wasn't until then that I realised I hadn't taken a deposit or a contact number or anything. I'm so sorry Lizzie. Really I am –'

'Calm down Annie! It's not the end of the world. Did you get a name?'

Annie shook her head. 'I don't know what came over me, I –'

'Annie it's okay. Really. I've done it myself. Don't worry about it. Just see who the last caller was and call the number and explain. They won't mind.' Lizzie poured herself more coffee and held up the pot to offer Annie some. Annie nodded and Lizzie refilled her mug.

Annie dialled the last number on the calls list and held the phone to her ear. 'It's gone to answer phone,' she said a worried expression on her young face.

'Just say it's Laurellei Farm about the booking and could someone please get back to us – and leave the number,' Lizzie added hastily.

Annie left the message and hung up the phone, beaming at Lizzie. 'Well at least I have their name now, it gave it on the machine,' she said, writing it on the booking sheet. 'It said the Drake residence so I suppose that's Mr. & Mrs. Drake.'

Lizzie spat her coffee all over the table in shock.

'Well Jane, I've got some news for you,' Lizzie said when she and Jane were in the sitting room later that afternoon, and Jane had told her all about the hot air balloon flight, the honeymoon and Florence.

Iain had brought Jane over whilst he caught up with Fraser on the farm as he knew Jane would want to see Lizzie within hours of getting home. He was right of course and after having a cup of tea with them, he left them to chat saying he'd be back for his wife in an hour.

'What? Please don't tell me you're getting back with Max,' Jane said teasingly.

Lizzie snorted. 'No. It's worse than that. Annie took a booking today and forgot to take any details. When she called the number she got an answering machine so she left a message but – guess whose it was?'

Jane shook her head. 'No idea. One of the guys from the stag weekend?'

'Yes but guess which one. I'll give you a clue. He's bringing his wife!'

'His wife ... um ...Bloody hell! You're kidding! Not Jack!'

'Yes. Bloody Jack Drake! Of all the nerve!'

'Well ... Actually, I don't know what to say! Are you sure it's him? Have you spoken to him? Did he call back?'

Lizzie gave her head a quick shake. 'Hold on! One question at a time. I'm having trouble thinking clearly at the moment as you can imagine. I'm pretty certain it's him because otherwise it would be an incredible coincidence. Jack's the only person I know with that surname. No I haven't spoken to him and no, he hasn't rung back. I'm sort of hoping that he's had second thoughts and won't turn up. Surely he must realise how unbelievably awkward it would be for everyone?'

'Awkward! It's just downright cruel. Have you called again?'

Lizzie nodded. 'I got Annie to actually. I told her to lie and say we'd made a mistake and that I had already confirmed another booking so we didn't have anything available but she just got the answering machine again.'

'Well, did she leave the message? If so, he wouldn't need to call back would he?'

Lizzie shook her head. 'No. I told her not to. He might turn up anyway and say he never got the message. I'd rather we, well she, actually spoke to him so that we know he's got it.'

'Are you going to call again then?'

'We have, five times. Still the bloody machine. We'll keep trying but we've only got two days.'

'Two days? Why?'

'The booking's for Easter weekend.'

'No!'

'Yep! Perhaps he's decided to have his honeymoon here as well as his bloody stag party.'

'When did they get married then? Have you heard something?'

'No. I'm just assuming. You know me. Why wait for facts when you can jump to conclusions?'

Jane giggled. 'Yeah. I never did think that was a very good mind-frame for a solicitor.'

Lizzie smirked. 'Perhaps that's why I gave up the Law so easily. Not really cut out for it.'

'Nonsense. You were a good lawyer. Mind you, you are better at making cakes ...'

'I've missed you Jane,' Lizzie said hugging her friend. 'It's so good to have you home.'

'It's good to be home and, of course, I'll be spending my first night in my new home tonight. Talking of which, I think I can hear Iain's Land Rover.' Jane stood up and peered out of the window. 'Yep. It's my husband. Ooh, I just love saying that. I'd better go. Will you be okay?'

'Of course I will. Stop worrying about me and go and make mad passionate love to your husband.'

Jane's smile went all the way up to her emerald green eyes. 'Oh I intend to – several times in fact. Iain's paying for Fraser and Annie to go out for dinner and Fraser's staying at Annie's I believe, so we'll have the house to ourselves. I'll see you tomorrow. Not sure when. Depends how much sleep I get.'

Lizzie walked to the door arm in arm with Jane. 'See you tomorrow evening then,' she joked.

Jane waved at Iain and started towards the Land Rover then she stopped and turned back to Lizzie. 'Keep trying that number, Lizzie. I still can't believe Jack would do this though. He seemed so nice.'

'They all do at first – but we know different now. Oh, with the exception of Iain, of course, he really is nice.'

'And my new son too,' Jane said, laughing as she headed towards her husband. 'See you tomorrow.'

'I've tried that number again but it still goes to the answering machine,' Annie said from behind Lizzie.

Lizzie turned to her. 'Okay thanks. You get off now Annie. I hear you're going out to dinner tonight.'

Annie gave her a shy smile and grabbed her things. 'Thanks Lizzie. We're going to a restaurant in Aviemore apparently. Iain and Jane booked it for us as a treat.'

She reached the door and stood beside Lizzie. Iain and Jane were waving and just pulling away and Annie waved to them.

'I really am sorry about the booking Lizzie I –'

'Annie please. Don't worry about it. We'll sort it out.'

'But ... you seemed really shocked when I told you their name.'

Lizzie rubbed Annie's arm. 'Just a surprise that's all. I ... thought it might be someone I knew. Forget it and go and have a great evening. Fraser's a lovely young man.'

Annie blushed and lowered her eyes. 'I know. I'm very lucky. My last boyfriend was a real sh... I mean, he wasn't very nice.'

'I know exactly what you mean Annie. Now go.' Lizzie hugged her. 'Say hello to Fraser for me. See you tomorrow but don't rush in early. I can feed the animals for one day. You make the most of your evening and spend the morning with Fraser if you want.'

Annie laughed. 'No chance of that unless I learn to drive a tractor. He'll be back at the farm straight after breakfast and that'll be at six if I know him. See you tomorrow.'

Lizzie waited until Annie had driven off then she took a deep breath and dialled the number Annie had written down. Annie had made all the previous attempts to get hold of the Drakes so Lizzie hadn't looked at the number until now and she realised it wasn't a London number. She didn't recognise the area code and it suddenly hit her that she had no idea where Jack lived – not that there was any reason why she should.

'Hello, this is the Drake residence,' a woman's voice said, 'we're probably out spending our son's inheritance so leave your name and number and we'll get back to you.'

Their son's inheritance! Oh my God, did they already know Kim was having a boy? Lizzie slammed the phone down. She grabbed for the hall table to steady herself as a wave of dizziness and nausea swept over her. She took several deep breaths and when the wave had passed she went into the kitchen and opened a bottle of wine. She really needed a drink.

Two gulped down glasses later a thought struggled to the front of her brain. The woman on the machine was very well spoken and sounded older than Kim would be. She couldn't be sure of course, a voice can be deceptive, but there was something about it, an intonation, and the more Lizzie thought about it the more she was convinced. She grabbed the phone, hit the redial button and waited.

'Hello,' a woman's voice said.

Lizzie waited to hear the rest of the message.

'Hello,' the voice said again.

It wasn't the machine.

'I think it's one of those computer calls,' the woman was saying to someone else, 'it's all quiet but I can hear breathing.'

'Computers don't breathe,' a man's voice said from close by, 'maybe it's one of those heavy breathers Maisie across the road keeps saying she gets. Just hang up.'

Lizzie had to act. 'H ... hello!' she said, flustered. 'Sorry I was expecting the answering machine. It's ... it's Lizzie Marshall from Laurellei Farm. You ... you made a booking for Easter weekend today.'

'Oh! Hello. Yes. Yes we did.'

This was definitely not Kim. The voice sounded older and very friendly. Funny, why didn't Lizzie think Kim would sound friendly.

'Hello-o,'

'Sorry,' Lizzie said. 'It's been one of those days today. Um, we called you back because we ... ' if this wasn't Kim, then the booking wasn't Jack so she needn't try to cancel it need she? 'Um ... because we didn't take a name or any details and ...and we always do that in case of emergencies or something.' Lizzie was babbling. She sounded like an idiot, she thought.

'Oh of course. It was all so last minute. We didn't think you'd have a vacancy but we called on the off chance and it must have been fate because you'd just had a cancellation. I suspect my husband was so surprised he just hung up. He does that.'

'Oh. Um, no. I think it was us actually. As I said, one of those days I'm afraid. It's Drake though isn't it? I heard the name on the answering machine message when I tried earlier.'

Mrs. Drake giggled like a naughty schoolgirl. 'Oh the message! Was it the one about spending our son's inheritance? It was wasn't it? I meant to change that but I forgot. Oh dear, how embarrassing. You must think I'm very silly. It was a joke you see. Our son was due to call us and I left the message for him, as a tease, you know, to make him laugh. No, of course you don't know. I'm rambling. Sorry. Yes. The name is Drake, Jack and Evelyn Drake.'

Lizzie almost dropped the phone. 'J ... Jack?' she stammered.

226

'Yes, that's right. You know our son I believe, also Jack. Yes I know, it's a family tradition. The first born males are always called Jack. Bizarre but it goes back generations. I called him JJ when he was little so that it wasn't so confusing but he doesn't really like it. He stayed with you last month for his stag weekend. Well, that was a disaster wasn't it? Oh! Not his stay with you – that was wonderful, he can't stop singing your praises. No, I meant the accident and then everything that followed. Oh dear, Jack's shaking his head. My husband not my son; you see what I mean about confusing. Anyway, my husband obviously thinks I'm talking too much. I always do. I do apologise. Where were we?'

Mrs. Drake wasn't the only one in the family who talked too much, Lizzie remembered, as something sharp and painful poked at her heart.

'Um. You were giving me your names.'

'Oh yes, of course I was. We're really looking forward to our stay with you. Jack, my husband, loves photography and Jack, our son said the scenery is stunning, although most of it was covered in snow when he was with you. That was unbelievable too wasn't it ... Oh dear, my husband is sighing. I'm doing it again.' Mrs. Drake burst out laughing. 'Just can't seem to stop myself. Sorry, Lizzie. You don't mind if I call you Lizzie do you? Jack said you were very friendly. My son that is. Oh dear, off again. Was there anything else you need from us? Would you like a deposit?'

Lizzie's head was spinning. 'No. No it's fine. I've got everything I need. I'll ... I'll see you on Good Friday then. Are you flying up or coming by train?'

'We're driving actually. We're leaving early tomorrow so you only just caught us. We're stopping off to visit a friend on the way and ... sorry, just tell me to stop dear. Jack does, my son that is. He says "Mother stop waffling" and then he gives me one of his grins, even when he says it on the phone I can tell he's grinning, although lately ...'

Lizzie didn't want her to stop now. 'Lately?' she coaxed.

'Oh. Nothing dear. We'll see you on Good Friday. Should be arriving mid afternoon if that's okay.'

'Yes that's perfect. See you then. I'm ... looking forward to meeting you.'

'And we're looking forward to meeting you. Jack has said ... No, I won't start again.' She giggled. 'See you soon. Goodbye.'

Lizzie wanted to scream, 'Jack said what?' but she didn't. She merely said 'Goodbye.'

Chapter Eighteen

'Hi Lizzie. How are you? Jane and Iain back safely?' Max leant back in his office chair and put his feet up on the desk.

'Hi Max. I'm fine thanks and yes, they got back safely. They had a wonderful time and the weather was superb apparently. How're things with you? Bet you're glad you don't have to clean out the animals anymore.'

Max smirked. 'Oddly enough, I am. I still don't know how you can prefer living up there to being here in London. Don't you ever miss it?'

'The City you mean? Sometimes but not for long. I love it here Max. It's where I belong. Just as you belong in London.'

'I agree with that. It does feel good to be back behind my desk I have to admit – and not to have to walk miles to get to a pub. Speaking of which, that's one of the reasons I called.' He studied his Armani tie and fiddled with the tips of it.

'About a pub?'

'Well, not about the pub, just what I heard when I was in it last night. Thought you might be interested – or not, actually, after our conversation on Jane's wedding day I'm not sure how you'll react but I thought you ought to know.'

Lizzie felt every muscle in her body tense as her veins began to pump adrenaline. 'Tell me what?' she said trying to remain calm.

'Kim got married yesterday.'

Lizzie dropped on to a kitchen chair as if she'd received a punch to her chest – which in fact, she had – that was where her heart was, after all.

'Lizzie? Did you hear me? I said –'

'I heard you!'

'You sound annoyed. Are you ... are you really upset?'

She wanted to shout, 'Of course I bloody well am!' but

she didn't. 'Why should I be? I knew it was coming. I hope they'll both be very happy.' She gripped the edge of the table and closed her eyes in an effort to hold the nausea at bay.

'I don't think there's much chance of that. I'm not sure anything would make Kim very happy.' Max took a deep breath. 'There's something else Lizzie – and I don't want you to get angry. I didn't do it on purpose.'

Lizzie sat bolt upright. 'Do what on purpose?'

Max hesitated. 'Well, Kim's fiancé – this was the day I came back to work so they weren't married then – came to the office to collect Kim's things and the wedding present the rest of the secretaries had bought her and ... it just so happened that we got in the lift together when he was leaving.'

'Oh my God Max! What did you do? You didn't hit him or something did you?'

'What? Of course not! Did you think I beat him to a pulp or something? Give me some credit Lizzie.'

'Okay ... so, what happened then?'

'He introduced himself and said he knew I was Max, your husband and he just wanted to say how great he thought you were and that he'd heard we'd got back together and he hoped things would work out this time. And that he knew what it felt like to nearly lose someone you really loved. Actually, come to think of it, I should have beaten him to a pulp. Arrogant little shit.'

Lizzie found herself agreeing with Max. Of all the nerve! Then a thought struck her. 'Got back together? What made him think we'd got back together?'

'What? God knows. Nothing I've said I can promise you that and I put him straight on that score – and that's the bit I don't want you to get mad about, well one of them.'

'What did you say Max?'

'I hadn't intended to say anything but the lift stopped at my floor and he was grinning like a Cheshire cat and before I knew it I'd said something like, "We're getting divorced actually. Mutual decision although, you screwing her had quite a lot to do with it." I know. I'm sorry. I shouldn't have said it.'

'No Max! You shouldn't! Wh ... what did he say?'

'Nothing. He looked rather surprised but he didn't say a word. Shall I tell you the rest?'

'There's more?' Lizzie hung her head and rubbed her forehead with her hand. 'Tell me. What more could you possibly have said to him.'

'Nothing to him. The lift door closed and he was gone. It was a few minutes after. I bumped into Phil and we started talking about a deal he's doing, then, out of the blue, he asks how you are. I said something along the lines of "why don't you call her and ask," I wasn't in a good mood; it had been a really shitty day and Ross had already pissed me off. Anyway, he says sorry but he was only asking because he'd heard you'd hurt your ankle and I'd taken you back to Scotland and would I give you his best wishes.'

Lizzie heard paper rustling and assumed Max had finished. 'That's not so bad – but it's Jack.'

'What? Oh sorry, I hadn't finished. My secretary just came in to get some urgent papers.'

'Oh.'

'Well, anyway, I said he seemed to be under the same impression as Ross and that, for the purposes of clarity, I would tell Phil what I had told Ross, that we were getting divorced and it was partly because my wife had fallen head over heels in love with my ex-lover's fiancé!'

'What? Max how could you? Oh my God! How embarrassing! And it's Jack! Why do you keep calling him Ross?'

'Because it is Ross and it's true – you have fallen head over heels in love.'

'It isn't!' Lizzie jumped to her feet and paced the room, ignoring the slight twinge in her ankle.

'It is Lizzie! That was quite obvious on Jane's wedding day. You may be trying to deny it but we both know you're in love with the guy. You've got to get over it though. He's married now with a kid on the way.'

'Thank you for pointing out the obvious Max! Is this giving you some sort of perverse pleasure? I wouldn't take you back so you're rubbing salt into my wounds now. Is that why you called to tell me he's married?'

'What? No! If you think I get pleasure out of hurting you, you are very much mistaken. Even now, I still love you. Even when I know you're in love with another man. But that's irrelevant. You've made it quite clear that we're over and I accept that. I told you because I thought you should know, that's all and because I promised you I'd never lie to you again.'

Lizzie slumped on to the window-seat and stared out of the window.

'Lizzie?' Max's voice was gentle again. 'Are you okay? I'm sorry perhaps I shouldn't have told you after all.'

Lizzie sighed. 'No Max. It's better that I know. And you're right – about all of it. I'm sorry I lost my temper with you.'

'That's okay, sweetheart. Are you going to be all right?'

'I'll be fine. It's Good Friday tomorrow and we're full over Easter so I'll be busy. You going anywhere?'

'No plans but I may just get in the car and drive. See where I end up.'

Lizzie gave a short laugh. 'We used to love doing that.'

'We used to love doing a lot of things Lizzie. Anyway, you look after yourself and have a great Easter. And Lizzie ... if you need me, I'll always be just a phone call away. You know that don't you?'

'Yeah. I know that Max. Have a good time. Bye.' Lizzie hung up and burst into tears.

The phone hadn't stopped ringing for over an hour and Lizzie was close to throwing all of them out of the window. No matter where she was in the house one of the hands free phones seemed to be harassing her. First it had been Max and it had taken her twenty minutes to pull herself together after that call. Then it was the butcher to tell her the delivery would be an hour late. Then Annie had called to say her car wouldn't start and she was waiting for Duncan from the garage to come and take a look at it.

When the phone rang again a few minutes later, Lizzie was close to breaking point.

'Laurellei Farm!' she snapped.

There was a pause before a male voice said, 'Hello Lizzie, it's Jack Drake.'

Lizzie almost fell down the stairs she was standing at the top of; her bundle of towels did. Then she realised it was Mr. Drake, Jack's father who would be arriving tomorrow. The relief was almost audible even though having Jack's parents staying so soon after Jack's wedding wasn't going to be easy.

'Hello Mr. Drake. How are you and what can I do for you?'

Another pause. 'Um I'm fine thanks. Um can I come up and see you?'

Lizzie's brows shot together and a warning bell started ringing somewhere within her. 'I ... I don't understand Mr. Drake. You are coming up tomorrow ... aren't you?'

A third pause. 'No I ... oh, you mean my dad. He and mum are coming to stay.'

'J ... Jack?'

'Yes. I know it's confusing isn't it, us both having the same name. Stupid idea. If I ever have a son there is no way he'll be called Jack. Three of us is just too ridiculous.'

Lizzie stiffened at the mention of the baby. 'What do you want Jack?'

'Well, I ... I heard something and I thought we could discuss it. I can come up anytime, just say when and –'

'What did you hear?'

'Oh! Um, well, it's not really the sort of thing I'd like to talk about over the phone. I ... I thought it would be better in person –'

'No. It's better over the phone. What did you hear Jack?'

'Um. Well. I heard that you may have feelings for me and ... and I wanted to know if that's true because I have feelings for you Lizzie. God. I've thought about nothing else but you since we met. Can I come up? Please? I just want to take you in my arms and –'

'You bastard! How could you? You're worse than Max. At least he waited for a few years. How dare you! Phil told you that Max said I was head over heels in love with you didn't he? So you thought you could pop up here and I'd fall into bed with you. You utter shit! My God. I can't believe that I thought you were special. How wrong could I be? Well, I won't. D'you hear me Jack. If you think you can just come here and screw me you're very much mistaken. Now sod off and don't ever call me again.'

Lizzie pressed the off button and threw the phone down the stairs.

To say Jack was stunned would be a gross understatement. He sat on the sofa for a full half an hour with the phone still in his hands going over and over the conversation. What had he said? Why was she so upset? Was Max lying?

Phil arrived and Jack let him in.

'You okay Jack? You look ... troubled.'

Jack snorted. 'That's a bloody understatement. I feel like I've been hit by a truck and then another one and then they've both reversed over me, for good measure. Either I'm going mad – or she is.'

Phil headed to the fridge. 'I take it we're talking about Lizzie. Can I grab a beer?'

Jack nodded. 'Yeah and get me one please, I need it.'

'I think I will too,' Phil said. 'So come on, what's happened now.'

'Well, after you and Ross both told me what Max had said I thought about it and I, well I just called her. I thought we could talk, you know. I mean, I'm free and so is she apparently, so there's nothing in our way, or so I thought.

But when I suggested going up to see her she went ape and ranted about me thinking I could just screw her or something and she called me a bastard and a lot more besides. Then she told me to sod off and never to call her again, and then she hung up. If that's someone who's head over heels in love with me I'd hate to meet the woman who dislikes me.'

'Shit! What on earth did you say to her?'

'Nothing. Honestly. I just asked if we could talk and that I'd heard she had feelings for me and how I felt about her and ... well, I did say I'd like to take her in my arms but ... well I didn't mean like that.'

'And she went ape?'

'Bloody King Kong ape!'

'Wasn't King Kong a gorilla?'

Jack cast Phil a withering look. 'Does it matter?'

Phil shrugged 'Probably would to King Kong but no, sorry, being facetious.'

Phil gulped his beer and Jack followed suit.

'Listen Jack, as nice as she is, I think I'd lick my wounds and walk away. It's been nothing but trouble since you met her. Maybe some things just aren't meant to be.'

Jack shook his head and looked wistful. 'I just can't get her out of my head mate and believe me, I've tried. I ... I love her.'

Phil eyed his friend warily. 'Jesus Jack! You sure?'

'Pretty sure yeah. I've never felt like this about anyone. Not even Kim. You said it yourself, I've always been so easy going. Seriously, I've just gone along with the flow and if it felt okay then that was fine but with Lizzie, it's never felt okay. From the moment I laid eyes on her I've felt as if something's crawled inside me and is taking me over. Everything was Lizzie – is Lizzie. I think, breathe and feel her every waking hour and I dream about her every night.'

'Shit Jack. I think you need an exorcist! If that's what being in love feels like you can keep it!'

'But that's the weird thing, it feels great, well most of the time it feels as if my heart's being ripped out but when I was with her it felt, I don't know, like I was experiencing creation, seeing things and feeling things like I've never seen them or felt them before. It felt ... feels as if I'm really alive for the first time ever. I'm not just going with the flow anymore – I'm fighting against the tide.'

Phil was looking worried. 'Okay mate, now I'm really worried. You sound as if you've lost it. Have you had any of these before I got here?' He held up his beer bottle.

Jack shook his head and smirked. 'I know it sounds crazy but maybe that's what love is. I mean real love, passionate, all consuming love. Maybe that's where the expression being crazy about someone came from.'

Phil nodded and pursed his lips, 'And being madly in love, I guess.'

'Yeah! And I think that's what I am, madly in love, only I've never been madly in love before so I'm not absolutely sure. All I know is that I need to be with her like I need to drink to stay alive – and I don't mean alcohol.'

'I know what you mean mate. Never felt like that about anyone myself so couldn't tell you either way – and I'm sorry to put a lid on all this Shakespearean tragedy stuff but isn't there just one problem? Hasn't she just told you to fuck off?'

Jack dropped on to the sofa beside Phil. 'Sod off actually – and to never call her again.'

'Well mate. I think you're stuffed. I need more beer.' Phil got to his feet.

'Do you really ... think I'm stuffed I mean? Do you think I should give up and crawl away?'

'I would. But then, I've never been madly in love. The other option is to get on a plane and go up there and have the door slammed in your face – but that was a bloody heavy door mate. Your choice. I can only tell you what Max said. He could have been lying but I really don't see why. What does he have to gain from that?'

'And he definitely said she was head over heels in love with me?'

'Yeah. Well ...'

'Well?'

'Sorry. Something just occurred to me but it is so bizarre that ...'

'What?'

'Well, you know I overheard Max's phone call and told you Lizzie and he were getting back together and that the weekend had given them the push they needed and now we all realise that they're not and he meant the push they needed to get the divorce started?'

'Yeeeees.'

'Well, the last thing Lizzie knew was that you were going to see Kim in hospital because she'd had an accident and – from what you said – that you were going to marry her because of the baby, only Lizzie didn't know about the baby, just that you were going to marry Kim, right?'

'Yeah.'

'Think about it Jack. She still thinks you're marrying Kim! She doesn't know about the baby or Ross or that they got married the other day or ... well, any of it. How could she? Unless Max knows – but how would he know about Ross? And, bearing in mind her husband cheated on her, maybe Lizzie thinks that you're married to Kim and you're trying to have an affair with her on the side. That would explain a lot – if it makes any sense.'

It was as if Jack had seen the light. 'That's it! It's got to be. It explains everything. I'll call her and explain.' He reached for the phone.

Phil stretched out his hand and stopped him. 'Not a good idea. Didn't she say never to call her again?'

'Yes but once I explain ... No. You're right. I can't do this over the phone. I'll go up there and tell her in person.'

'And risk the door?'

Jack grinned. 'She's worth the risk – even though, it is a very heavy door.'

'Well, let's just hope she doesn't slam it.'

'Hi mum, it's Jack.'

'Darling how are you?'

'I'm fine thanks. You?'

'Wonderful darling. We're at Bessie's tonight and we're heading over the border first thing tomorrow. Should be at Laurellei by mid afternoon. Well, that's the plan anyway. Oh sorry, the reception on my mobile's not good here, can you hear me?'

'Yes mum. Listen, I need you to do me a favour. Mum ... mum are you there?' The line went dead.

Seconds later Jack's landline rang.

'I don't know, we can send a man to the moon but can we get good mobile phone reception? I'm calling from Bessie's landline. We're going out to dinner shortly so you've just caught us. There's a new Ghurkha restaurant just opened down the road and you know how much your father loves Nepalese food. It is Nepalese isn't it? Oh your father's shaking his head at me. What darling it isn't Nepalese but I ... oh, he's saying I'm waffling. Sorry darling, what were you saying, you need a favour?'

Jack grinned. 'I need a favour, but first, let me just say I love you mum, even though you waffle.'

'And I love you Jack and so does your father of course and ... sorry darling. Your favour.'

'I told you about Lizzie and the stag weekend but what I didn't tell you was ... well, something happened between Lizzie and me.'

'Good heavens Jack! How? You were engaged! Mind you, who can blame you after what that woman did to you – but you didn't know about that then so ... are you saying you cheated on your fiancée?'

'Yes mother, I am, but it wasn't like that. I had already decided to call off the engagement so as far as I was concerned, it wasn't really cheating and besides, I ... well, I just couldn't help myself.'

'Oh, I know what that's like darling believe me. Did I tell you about when your father and I ... oh, sorry, best not get into that now, Bessie's here, but anyway, you don't have to explain anything to me. I told your father something had happened between you and Lizzie. I could tell. It was the way you looked when you spoke about her. That and the fact that you spoke about her quite a lot, much more than one would expect in the circumstances. Anyway, sorry, the favour.'

'It's all very complicated and I won't go into details now but I think Lizzie still thinks I'm engaged to Kim. Well, actually I think she thinks I'm married to Kim now, so I just wanted you to see if you can casually mention that I'm not.'

'Oh! Is that all? Well of course I can but ... why does she think that and why don't you just tell her yourself?'

'I've tried but it's a little awkward at the moment. I'm trying to get a flight up but it's Easter weekend and everything is booked solid. I may have to get the train or drive so that won't be until sometime tomorrow or the next day. It would just help if she knew I wasn't with Kim anymore before I arrive. It's an oak front door.'

'What's the front door got to do with it?'

'She may well slam it in my face.'

'Good heavens! Why on earth would she do that?'

'Doesn't matter mum, as I said, it's complicated. Will you do it?'

'Of course I will darling and I'll tell her just how lucky she is to have you –'

'No mum. Please don't do that. Just let her know, casually, if you can, that it was Ross who married Kim – oh and that it's Ross's baby and not mine. Although, I don't know if she knows about the baby so that may just complicate things even more.'

'Well, I'm certainly confused; but leave it with me darling. I'll do whatever I can. I don't think she's got any vacancies though. If you're coming up I mean. Your father and I were lucky because someone had just cancelled but I think she's full so you may have to find somewhere else to stay. I suppose you could stay in our room for one night and ... oh, your father is doing his Queen Victoria impression, clearly not amused. Anyway we'll sort it out. I'm sure she'll find somewhere for you to sleep and ... oh, I suppose ... No. I won't say another word. Call us on the mobile and let us know when you'll be there. Assuming we can get a signal in Scotland. Do you want me to say you're coming or do you want that to be a surprise?'

'A surprise. And Scotland's not the moon mum, it has mobile phone towers. You'll get a signal. See you soon.'

'So does Northumberland darling, but I've had to call you back on the landline. Oh your father's clearly starving to death, he's tapping his watch, oh and he's saying hello – to you I think. See you soon, Jack.'

'You must be the only man on earth who tells his mum everything and isn't a wimp.' Phil said when Jack had hung up.

'I've just got a great mum, that's all. And I don't tell her everything just the bits I don't mind her knowing. Besides, you tell her things too. You always have.'

'That's true but then, she's not my mum. You're right though, she is great. Anyway, I think we should leave things as they are for now and adjourn to the pub. Emma's going to pop in with some of her mates and Pete's going to be there with his new girlfriend.' Phil got up and stretched.

'Pete's got a girlfriend? When did this happen?' Jack stood up and headed towards the door.

Phil shook his head benignly. 'Last Friday night in The Mucky Duck. Her friend was all over you like a rash.'

'Really? I don't remember that.'

'You wouldn't. You were madly in love with an ape from Scotland. You didn't notice anything.'

Jack slapped Phil's arm. 'Watch it. That's my future girlfriend you're talking about.'

'Yeah. If your mum can get her to play with you that is.'

240

Chapter Nineteen

'Hello, you must be Lizzie. I'm Evelyn Drake and this is my husband Jack,' Evelyn Drake said holding out her hand on the doorstep of Laurellei Farm.

'Hello. Yes I am. Pleased to meet you and welcome to Laurellei.' Lizzie shook hands with Evelyn and Jack. 'Please, come in. I'll show you to your room and then if you'd like to come down to the sitting room once you've settled in, I'll make some tea. There'll be cakes and scones too so please help yourselves to those.'

'Oh thank you Lizzie. We've not long had lunch actually but a cup of tea would be lovely.'

Lizzie showed them to their room. She'd given them the toile de jouy room, which had meant some rearranging. The vacant room had been the one Jack had occupied. The one they'd made love in, but that was too weird. She couldn't put his parents in the same bed, no matter how many times the sheets had been washed since.

Evelyn chatted on the way. She said how lovely the house was, how spectacular the scenery was, how pleasant the drive up was and finally, when Lizzie handed her the key to their room, how lovely Lizzie was – just as Jack had told them she would be.

Evelyn then swept into the room leaving Lizzie feeling a mixture of pleasure and anger.

She stormed downstairs and shoved the kitchen door open almost hitting Annie in the face.

'Sorry Annie,' she said, as she stomped over to the table and plopped on to the chair she was sitting on prior to the Drakes arrival. 'You'll never believe it, his mum just said that Jack had told her how lovely I was! I could cheerfully wring that man's neck.'

Annie pulled a face. 'Shall I make you some tea?' she asked, glancing towards Jane who so far, had said nothing.

'I'll do it,' Lizzie said. 'I need to keep myself occupied or I may just break something.' She jumped up from her chair and went to put the kettle on.

Annie got the cups.

'Thanks Annie.' Lizzie glanced at Jane who seemed to be intent on reading the paper. 'You haven't said anything since they arrived. Cat got your tongue?'

'No, but you might. Doesn't really seem any point in saying anything. You've been like a bear with a sore head ever since he called and you won't listen to anyone when you're like this. You were the same when you discovered Max's affair.'

'What? That's not true. I listen to you all the time and ... oh, okay, you're right. I have just been snapping at you all haven't I? Sorry.'

'That's okay. I would be furious too, if he'd done that to me, but you can't let it fester like this. I mean, when you said you'd stay out of his parents way all weekend and leave them to Annie and me, that really was the limit.'

'But you wouldn't let me! And I didn't appreciate being dragged to the front door.'

'If you behave like a child, I'll treat you like one,' Jane said, her grin belying her comment.

'God. You've really jumped into the step mother role haven't you?'

'Yes. And I feel I'm rather good at it.'

They both laughed as Jane arrogantly flicked her hair behind her shoulder.

'Okay mum,' Lizzie said, 'tell me next time I do it and I'll try to stop but please come in the sitting room with me when they come down. I can't face them on my own and the other guests may not be back by then.'

'We'll both come in with you so don't panic. Strength in numbers. Now make the tea will you. I'm gasping. Being a mother is hard work.'

Half an hour later, as Annie was taking the tea service into the sitting room, she popped her head back into the kitchen. 'They're coming down,' she said, 'and four of the other guests are walking up the drive.'

Lizzie and Jane got to their feet. Lizzie made tea and Jane made coffee. They put the pots, milk jugs and sugar bowls on trays, and Annie and Jane ferried them into the sitting room. Although Lizzie's foot had healed, she still couldn't walk without a slight limp so carrying trays was out of the question.

Lizzie performed all the introductions between the various guests and then they all settled down to tea, coffee and cakes.

'There are brochures and leaflets on the hall table,' Lizzie said to the Drakes and the other four guests, 'giving details of all the nearby attractions, including restaurants, pubs and the like. Aviemore is about fifteen minutes away by car and there's quite a lot to do there. Inverness, just over half an hour or so in the other direction. There are lots of villages in both directions and there are walking trails, cycling and riding paths, whisky distillery tours, fishing, canoeing, climbing, you name it, you can do it within a few miles of here. If there's anything you're particularly interested in that you can't find details of, just ask one of us. We'll be around and about so just yell.'

'It is really lovely here. We've just been for a walk to the village and everyone is so friendly, especially in the local pub, The Drovers Rest is it?' Mrs. Bartlett from Surrey said.

'Yes, it is but we just call it Dougall's. He's the owner, I expect he introduced himself.'

'Yes he did. Lovely man.'

'Good food too. Not Gastro pub but good hearty meals, mainly from fresh, local ingredients. His wife Isabel does all the cooking. And her puddings are to die for. Anyway, breakfast is from seven till nine thirty and if you want we can arrange a picnic basket for you, just let us know the night before. I think that's everything but feel free to ask, as I said, one of us will always be around here somewhere.'

Jack senior caught Lizzie's eye. 'My son tells me you've got a dog Lizzie, Alastair is it?'

Lizzie was surprised. 'Yes. He's in the kitchen. He's very friendly. Is ... is that a problem? Do you not like dogs?'

'Oh! Quite the opposite. I love dogs. We all do. Ours passed away six months ago and we haven't been able to bring ourselves to get another yet, have we dear?'

Evelyn shook her head. 'No. Jack gave us JJ as an anniversary present fifteen years ago. He was a rescue puppy. Something awful had happened to him. Jack wouldn't tell me but he told his father. He was absolutely adorable. That's why I called him JJ. I think I told you I used to call Jack that, my son, but he didn't really like it. It seemed so appropriate to call the puppy JJ as he was a gift from Jack – and Jack is adorable too.'

'Very appropriate,' Lizzie said, thinking it should have been a snake not a puppy, 'excuse me I can see some of the other guests coming back. I'll just go and make some more tea.'

'Could we be really cheeky and come and meet Alastair?' Evelyn asked.

'Um. Yes, of course. I'll bring him into the hall. He's due for a walk now anyway.'

Jane followed Lizzie into the kitchen. 'Don't you think it's odd that they haven't mentioned their adorable son has just got married?'

Lizzie switched on the kettle to make more tea then grabbed Alastair's lead from the coat rack. 'I suppose so. I'm glad they haven't though, I really don't want to hear details of that.'

'No but it's odd. Most parents would be full of it, especially as they are going to be grandparents.'

'Thanks for reminding me.'

'Sorry but I can't help wondering whether something's

wrong. Maybe they don't like Kim or maybe they're embarrassed because she was pregnant before the wedding. No. I can't see that bothering anyone these days so I just don't get it. I'm going to ask.'

'Don't you dare!'

'Why not? He had his stag do here so it's not as if we didn't know there was going to be a wedding and why shouldn't we ask how it all went? We don't have to say we know about the baby or anything.'

'No Jane. Please don't. I ... I get the strangest feeling that Jack has said something to them – about me I mean. Obviously he wouldn't have told them what happened but, well, they keep looking at me, as if they know something I don't, or like they're summing me up or something, especially his mum.'

'Well she did say Jack had talked about you and how lovely you are, so maybe she thinks something did happen and wanted to get a look at you for herself. I mean, it is curious that they suddenly phone to make a booking the same week as their son gets married and that they want to come up a few days later. No. The more I think about it the more odd it seems.'

Lizzie made the tea and considered Jane's words. 'It is odd, I agree but quite frankly Jane everything to do with that stag weekend and Jack has been bloody odd, so nothing would surprise me anymore.'

'That's true. When you think of everything that's happened in just over one month, you're getting divorced and I'm married with a grown up son!'

Lizzie giggled. 'Will you take this tea in whilst I get Alastair ready for inspection?'

Jane took the tea through to the sitting room and found the Drakes waiting in the hall with their outdoor jackets on. Realising that they might be planning to join Lizzie and Alastair on the walk, she got Annie's attention away from the guests who had just come in.

'Annie would you do Lizzie and me a huge favour and

take Alastair for his walk. I think the Drakes are thinking of joining her and we both know she couldn't face that.'

'Oh, yes of course.' She dashed past the Drakes and into the kitchen just as Lizzie was about to come out. 'Lizzie! The Drakes are in the hall and Jane thinks they might want to join you and Alastair. Would you rather I take him? Jane said you would.'

Lizzie's mouth fell open. 'Good God! Yes please, if you don't mind.'

'Not a problem.'

Annie, Lizzie and Alastair strode into the hall.

'Here he is,' Lizzie said and Alastair wagged his tail and barked hello.

'Oh he is gorgeous!' Evelyn stroked Alastair behind the ears. 'Yes you are aren't you?'

'I'm taking him for his walk,' Annie said smiling warmly at Evelyn. 'Are you going out? Would you like to join us?'

Evelyn's eyes darted to Lizzie who was smiling innocently. 'Yes, if you don't mind, that would be lovely,' Evelyn said just as her mobile phone rang. She pulled it from its pocket in her handbag and answered it. 'Hello.' Her eyes shot back to Lizzie. 'Yes dear. ... Oh! That's nice. ... No, not yet, haven't had a chance. ... Are you sure? ... But you're right darling; it is a very heavy door. ...Okay, see you soon. ... Safe journey.' She hung up and beamed at Lizzie then smiled at Annie. 'Well then, shall we go?'

Lizzie got the feeling something very strange was going on as she watched Annie, Alastair and the Drakes head off in the direction of the village.

'That was a close shave,' Jane said, coming into the hall from the sitting room.

'Evelyn just had the strangest phone call,' Lizzie said still watching the Drakes from the doorway.

'Strange? In what way?'

'I'm not sure. Couldn't really make sense of it but it sounds as if they're meeting someone about a door.'

'A door? How odd. Oh well. All the guests in the sitting room are going to the village tonight. Dougall and Isabel are having their Good Friday Hot Cross Bunnies night. I'd totally forgotten about it. D'you fancy going? I expect Iain will want to.'

'Oh yes of course. I forgot it too what with everything that's been happening. I remember seeing the poster in the pub at your wedding reception though. They do realise the main dish is rabbit stew don't they?'

'No idea and I don't plan to tell them, it might put some of them off. Isabel always has other things on the menu if they don't like rabbit so it's really not an issue. You coming? It'll do you good to have some fun.' Jane headed into the kitchen.

Lizzie closed the front door and followed Jane. 'I remember the last time you said that on Jack's stag weekend and look where that got me.'

Lizzie told the Drakes about Dougall and Isabel's Hot Cross Bunnies night soon after they returned from their walk, and said that Iain would be picking her and Jane up at seven thirty.

Evelyn checked her watch and seemed to be calculating something. 'Oh that should work out perfectly.'

'There's room in the Land Rover if –'

A crash from the kitchen cut Lizzie short and she dashed off to see what had happened.

Alastair was sprawled across the floor, his tongue hanging out, his fur soaking wet, surrounded by a smashed teapot, other crockery and scones.

'Alastair!' Lizzie screamed and ran to him, dropping down on her knees beside him. His eyes were closed and he wasn't moving. Her eyes shot to his rib cage and she could see it was rising and falling so at least he was breathing.

Jane and Annie, who had been in the sitting room with the other guests, came rushing in followed by the Drakes, who stayed by the door until they saw the dog on the floor, then Mr. Drake rushed forward. He dropped to the floor beside Lizzie and took a quick look at Alastair.

'Jane!' Lizzie shrieked, 'call Hamish. Ask if he'll come right away.'

Jane was already dialling.

Lizzie turned her attention back to Alastair and gently stroked his head. There was lumpy, sticky blood on her hand and she let out a strangled scream. 'He's bleeding!'

'Hamish says he'll be here in five minutes. He's at Heatherdown with Iain,' Jane said, trying to sound calm after hanging up the phone.

Jack senior dabbed at the blood and his brows knit together. He put a finger in it and put his finger to his lips then he let out a sigh. 'It's raspberry jam.' His eyes met Lizzie's and he smiled. 'I think he was after the cream and jam scones, and the tray must have tipped up. He's probably just stunned. Looks like the teapot might have hit him on the head.'

Alastair opened his eyes, lifted his head an inch off the floor, whimpered and dropped it back down again.

'I think you're right,' Lizzie said, tenderly stroking Alastair's side.

'It was my fault Lizzie. I left the tray on the table instead of putting it on the worktop. I'm so sorry.' Jane came and knelt down beside Lizzie.

Lizzie shook her head. 'Don't worry Jane. I think he'll be okay. Mr. Drake's right I'm sure.' She cast tearful eyes to Jane and forced a weak smile. 'He does love cream and jam scones doesn't he?'

Jane nodded. 'We'll let him have one as a treat when he's recovered.'

She got up and put the kettle on to make some tea and shortly after, Hamish arrived with Iain.

'Where's the patient?' Hamish asked stepping between the broken crockery.

'We think a teapot hit him,' Lizzie said, moving aside to let Hamish examine Alastair.

'Well that wasn't a very nice thing for a teapot to do was it?' He rubbed the red icky goo with his thumb and licked it just as Mr. Drake had done. 'Raspberry,' he said. He pulled up Alastair's eyelids and shone a light in his eyes, then he lifted Alastair's head and flexed it. He ran his hands all over Alastair's body and the dog's tail started wagging, albeit limply.

'Is he okay?' Lizzie asked.

'Aye, he's fine, just a bit dazed. Nothing's broken – other than the crockery – but he'll have a headache and a lump if I'm not mistaken. Just keep an eye on him for the next twenty four hours and call me if he seems worse but I think he'll perk up in the next hour or so.' He stroked Alastair behind the ears.

'Thanks Hamish,' Lizzie said. 'And for getting here so quickly.'

'Auch, no problem Lizzie. Now you take care young man,' he said to Alastair.

'I'm just making tea Hamish, would you like a cup?'

'Aye, I would please. I'll just clean this jam off the laddie and get him in his basket.'

'Thanks Hamish and thank you Mr. Drake,' Lizzie said smiling at him. 'I don't handle this sort of thing very well I'm afraid. I always panic.'

Jack senior smiled back. 'I'm glad he's okay. He's a lovely chap. Is there anything we can do?'

'No thanks. We'll just get this cleared up and have some tea. Would you and Mrs. Drake like some?'

'No thanks I've –'

'That would be lovely,' Evelyn interrupted, 'if you're sure we won't be in the way. And please Lizzie, call us Jack and Evelyn. May I help you Jane?'

Jane glanced at Lizzie who gave a little shrug. 'You could get the milk from the fridge if you don't mind.'

Iain got clean cups whilst Annie and Lizzie cleared up the broken crockery, tea and the remains of the scones. Evelyn put the milk on the table and pulled out a chair and

Hamish gently lifted Alastair and put him in his basket.

'You should sit down Lizzie,' Evelyn said, 'you've had a nasty shock.'

'I'm fine thanks. I'm just glad he's okay.' She stood up and walked to the bin with a dustpan full of broken china. A car pulling up outside attracted her attention. 'I really thought ... Oh my God! What the hell is he doing here?'

All eyes turned to the window where Jack Drake junior had just got out of a taxi and was walking towards Laurellei Farm.

'Ah,' Evelyn said, sitting down on the chair she'd pulled out for Lizzie and all eyes turned to her.

The room fell silent and the scrunch of gravel beneath Jack's feet as he marched towards the kitchen was amplified in the quiet. No one seemed to move during the few seconds it took him to reach the door and everyone waited, their focus now firmly fixed on either Lizzie or the open kitchen door.

'Hello,' Jack said, his eyes scanning the room and taking in Jane and Iain, his mum and dad, a girl he didn't know and a man he vaguely recognised stroking Alastair, before coming to rest on Lizzie. 'Is everything okay? Has something happened?'

Alastair was the first to respond. He lifted his head a fraction and let out a half bark, wagging his tail.

'Well,' Hamish said getting to his feet, 'at least Alastair's pleased to see you. How are you Jack? I'm Hamish, we met at the pub and Iain's ceilidh.'

Jack dragged his eyes from Lizzie's stunned face. 'Oh hello Hamish. Yes I remember. I'm fine thanks, you?'

Hamish let out a deep, gruff laugh. 'Good thanks but from the look on our Lizzie's face, you may be needing more than a vet.'

Jack's sapphire eyes shot back to Lizzie and he could see her initial shock was rapidly turning to fury. 'Just let me explain,' he said. 'I think you –'

'You've got a bloody nerve! I told you I never wanted to

250

see you again.' She turned away from him.

'Actually, you told me never to call you again – and I haven't.'

Six pairs of eyes – seven including Alastair's – darted back and forth between Jack and Lizzie as if they were spectators at a tennis match.

Lizzie spun back to face him, her lips pursed, her eyes shooting arrows of fire. 'Don't be sarcastic, this isn't funny.' She spat the words at him.

'I'm not. I'm just stating a fact,' he said, a little too calmly.

'Well! Let me state a fact,' she hissed. 'You're an arrogant, cheating, deceitful bastard and you're no more welcome here than the plague.' She turned and stormed towards the door to the hall.

Jack senior stood in her way and Lizzie stopped sharply as if someone had her on a restraining lead. She blinked several times and blushed furiously as she realised that she'd totally forgotten Jack's parents were in the room. 'I'm sorry,' she mumbled, 'excuse me please.'

Jack senior shook his head. 'I don't know what's happened between you two and it's probably none of my business but –'

'Dad.' Jack shook his head and smiled affectionately at his father. 'I can fight my own battles.'

Lizzie spun round. 'Oh, so I'm a battle now am I? Is that it? Just what do you think you've got to gain by coming here? Do you think I'm completely stupid?'

'I don't think you're stupid at all. I think you're wonderful.'

Lizzie's mouth fell open and her eyes drifted from Jack to his father and then his mother as if they had pressed a slow motion button.

'Doesn't this bother you?' she said to Evelyn in astonishment.

Iain stepped forward. 'I think maybe you should leave Jack,' he said gently but firmly.

'I can't believe this,' Jane said at the same time.

'What's going on?' Annie asked simultaneously.

'If you'll just give me five minutes,' Jack was saying.

Everyone was talking at once and even Alastair started making gruff, throaty barks.

Evelyn Drake banged her fist on the kitchen table and all the crockery danced. Silence descended and everyone stared at her, even her husband.

'Jack is not married to Kim, Lizzie, Ross is, and the baby isn't Jack's it's Ross's. Ross and Kim got married this week. My son is single and, I can assure you, he is neither deceitful nor a bastard but he can be arrogant and he does cheat at Monopoly. There. Is there any chance of a glass of wine Jane dear? I really feel in need of a drink.'

Evelyn smiled sweetly at Jane, whose mouth, like Lizzie's had fallen so wide open that a toy train could have used it as a tunnel.

Jane and Lizzie stared at one another in disbelief then Lizzie slowly turned her eyes towards Jack.

'I ... is that true?' she said, clearly stunned.

Jack's mouth curved slightly at one corner. 'Which part? That I cheat at Monopoly or that I'm single?' The curve turned into his devilish grin.

'But ... but how? Why didn't you tell me?'

Jack gave a little cough. 'I have been trying to.'

'God!' Jane said, 'Kim and Ross? When did that happen?'

Everyone looked at Jane.

'Sorry,' she said. 'It's just sunk in. I'll get the wine.' She turned, grabbed three bottles from the wine rack and handed them to Iain to open. Annie got glasses.

Jack and Lizzie were staring at one another. 'Apparently, Ross has been in love with Kim since before I knew her and when I was in Hong Kong on a business trip a few weeks before we came here, it seems Kim realised she felt the same way about him. They just forgot to mention it to me.'

Lizzie's eyes softened. 'And ... the baby. How...?'

252

'How do I know it's Ross's?'

Lizzie nodded.

'Pure mathematics. I won't go into details – Phil said it was too much information – but because Kim was five weeks pregnant at the time of the accident, it couldn't possibly be mine.'

Hamish let out a raucous laugh. 'I cannae believe this,' he said, taking the glass of wine Jane was offering him. 'This is better than any soap opera.'

'When did you find out about Ross then?' Iain asked, taking Jack a glass.

Jack was still holding Lizzie's eyes with his. 'The morning after we went back. I did the maths and when Ross came round later, it all came out. He proposed to Kim, she accepted and they got married on Wednesday. I was at the reception and there are photos to prove it.'

Hamish sniggered.

'So why has it taken you so long to come and tell us this?' Jane asked.

Jack briefly glanced at Jane then back to Lizzie. 'I hadn't planned to tell *you*! I'd planned to tell Lizzie. I thought you had gone back to Max. I saw you together on that Saturday night, after we got back from here.'

'What? Where?' Lizzie said.

'Outside a restaurant, you were arm in arm and you were balancing on one foot. I now know you'd hurt your ankle but then I thought ... well. How is it by the way? Your ankle?'

'Better thanks. But why did you think we were together? Because we were arm in arm you mean?'

'Yes, but also because later, Phil overheard part of a conversation Max was having with you, and Max then said you were staying with him and that the weekend had given you both the push you needed to sort things out. Phil and I thought that meant you were giving it another try. I only heard this week that you were getting divorced.'

'And ... that's why you called me and asked to come and

see me? I thought ...'

The devilish grin spread across his face. 'I think I know what you thought.'

Their eyes locked.

'What about the woman in the pub?' Jane asked, still filling wine glasses and failing to realise that this wasn't the time to ask.

Jack's brows furrowed. 'Which woman? What pub?' His eyes darted from Lizzie to Jane and back to Lizzie again.

Lizzie looked as if she had just remembered. 'Yes, Jack. What about her? The stunning nineteen year old with the black, curly hair. The one you couldn't take your eyes – or your hands off in The Black Swan that day we ... met by chance. Who is she? And don't tell me she's just a friend because any fool could see she's much more than that.'

He was clearly perplexed.

'That sounds like Emma, darling,' Evelyn Drake said, her wine glass hovering just below her lips. 'But she's eighteen. You went to her birthday dinner a few weeks ago didn't you?'

Jack's expression lifted, as if everything had suddenly become clear to him. A huge smile spread across his face and his eyes sparkled with delight. 'Ah! Now I understand. So that's why you were so ... unpleasant to me that day. You were jealous! You thought ... Oh Lizzie. That was Emma – Phil's baby sister! It was her eighteenth birthday and I've known her since the day she was born so yes, ... she means a lot to me – but not in that way. I could never –'

'Phil's baby sister?' Lizzie interrupted.

'Phil's baby sister! Of course!' Jane said as if it should have been obvious.

'Did you know Phil had a sister?' Lizzie asked her, astonished. 'I didn't.'

Jane shook her head. 'Nor did I. But they always are aren't they? In romances I mean. The mystery woman always turns out to be the sister.' She offered Lizzie a glass of wine and everyone nodded in agreement.

Jack sighed good-naturedly. 'Look Lizzie. As much as I enjoy discussing my love life in front of an audience, including my parents, and as much as I appreciate Jane's input, I somehow think this might work better if it were just the two of us. Perhaps we could discuss this in private.'

'What? Oh yes.' Lizzie let out a little squeal. 'How embarrassing.' She shot Jane a telling look.

Hamish gave a brief clap. 'Well, I enjoyed it anyway – but you're right Jack. Some things a man needs a bit of privacy for. I must be off. Going to Dougall and Isabel's Hot Cross Bunnies night.'

'Ooh, us too!' Jane said. 'We'll dash off as well then. Come along darling.' She grabbed Iain's hand.

Lizzie's eyes were transfixed by something she could see in Jack's. Without looking at Jane she said, 'I'll be staying with Alastair, so don't worry about me.'

'Okay,' Jane said, 'call if you need me.' She glanced between Jack and Lizzie. 'Not that I think you will. Annie, you come with us. Bye you two. Evelyn, would you and your husband like a lift to the pub? There's room.'

Jack glanced at his mum and then his dad. 'I think I can take it from here.'

'Right son. We'll head off to the Hot Cross Bunnies thing then. Come along love,' he said to his wife.

'God!' Lizzie said, as Evelyn got to her feet and walked towards her son. 'I'm really sorry about the things I said. You must think I'm dreadful!'

Evelyn kissed her son on the cheek then hurried towards Lizzie and to Lizzie's astonishment, did the same to her.

'No dear. I just think you're a woman in love. Don't wait up for us Jack, your father and I are going to make a night of it.'

Jack's father patted Lizzie on the arm. 'Have a good evening and I hope Alastair's up and about before long. See you later son.'

'Thanks Mr. Drake.' Lizzie smiled at him, then turned back to Jack.

Neither of them spoke until they heard the front door close then Jack took one slow step towards Lizzie. 'What's wrong with Alastair?' he asked, his eyes fixed firmly on her face.

'Too much cream tea,' Lizzie said taking a step towards him. 'He should be fine in a few hours but I've got to keep an eye on him.'

'We can do that together – if I'm now more welcome than the plague,' he grinned.

Lizzie looked forlorn. 'I'm sorry about everything I said Jack.' She took another step forward.

'You can make up for it later.' He matched her step for step until they were just inches apart. 'I love you,' he said, 'you do know that don't you?'

'I do now. And I think I've loved you from the moment I saw you with that stupid inflatable doll.'

The devilish grin spread across his handsome face. 'Don't be mean about one of my ex-girlfriends,' he joked, his sapphire eyes dark with passion.

'That relationship was just hot air, this one's for real.'

'I think this one's forever,' he said, kissing her before she could respond, his arms encircling her, pulling her to him.

Several minutes later, Lizzie raised loving blue eyes to his. 'I thought you wanted to talk.'

Jack smiled. 'Talk is highly overrated.' Then he pulled away slightly and gave her his most serious look. 'Besides, someone once told me I talk too much.'

The grin Lizzie loved, reappeared.

'Shut up and kiss me,' she said, grinning back at him.

Jack didn't need to be told twice.

***

RELEASED IN AUTUMN 2012

"Lizzie Marshall's Wedding"

Becky Cooper has "let herself go" – at least, that's what her friends say. But as a thirty-two year old widow, Becky hasn't got time to worry about the way she looks. Her husband wasn't the man she thought he was and she's struggling to pay off his debts, raise their five year old daughter and come to terms with the past. Make-up and new clothes are way down on her list of "must-haves" and as for romance – forget about it. A man is the last thing she needs.

Her friends think she's wrong, and when the undeniably gorgeous, divorcee, Max Bedford, arrives in the village, they decide he would be perfect for her. His mum's just moved into Beckleston Hall and he's staying for a while. But Becky's already met him, and feels he's far from perfect; he's rude, arrogant and annoying. Besides, if the gossip is true, he can have his pick of women, so he wouldn't be interested in her.

That's just one of the things Max and Becky disagree on. For some reason that he can't quite fathom, Max is very interested in the feisty woman he's just rescued, and whilst the last thing he's looking for is a serious relationship, dating her could be a lot of fun.

When Becky is employed to organise Lizzie Marshall's Wedding, introducing her to Max's ex-wife and a group of people whose lives seem even more complicated and confusing than her own, she begins to discover she's not the only one with "baggage".

Can love set her free? Or will Max Bedford break her heart?

Printed in Great Britain
by Amazon.co.uk, Ltd.,
Marston Gate.